WORKS OF DARKNESS

A Matt Foldy/Sara Bradford Novel

Book One

V. B. TENERY

DEDICATION

To my Savior Jesus Christ.
May all I do honor You.

And

To my beloved sister Mary McFadden.
I still miss you, Sis. The poem inside
is dedicated to you. Someday, we'll walk
those streets of gold together and
you can show me around.

WORKS OF DARKNESS
A Matt Foley/Sara Bradford Novel
COPYRIGHT © 2013 by V. B. TENERY
Published by CBC Press
Printed in the United States of America

Cover Art by Nathan R. Adams
Editor: Deborah K. Anderson

Scripture quotations, unless otherwise indicated are taken from the King James translation, public domain.

Publishing History: First Electronic Edition, 2014
Paperback Edition 2015

ISBN:13-9780692512937
ISBN:10-0692512934

A Matt Foley/Sara Bradford novel

WORKS
OF DARKNESS

CRIME SCENE DO NOT C

V. B.
TENERY

"The night is far spent; the day is at hand, let us therefore *cast off the works of darkness.*"

—Romans 13:12

CHAPTER 1

Bay Harbor Development

Construction foreman Jason Watts stood by his truck and gazed across the job site. Heavy equipment cleared the prime lakefront property of stumps and rubble as machinery shifted sand from one place to another. The smell of damp earth permeated the air around him. An early morning chill crept under his coat collar making him shiver.

Across the way, his backhoe operator scooped up a load of sand, lowered the bucket, and stopped the machine. Isaac Hummingbird, the Native American operator, stepped off the front-end loader and tossed something to the ground.

"Hey, Jason, you'd better come take a look at this." Hummingbird stood next to what looked like a large, white trash bag.

Jason shoved his clipboard onto the truck's bench seat and trotted across the field, the dirt still sticky from the recent storms. He noted the heavy, dark clouds hovering overhead as he crossed the field. Fierce October rain that pummeled the area had thrown him behind schedule, forcing him to play catch-up. Big time. The moneymen who financed the project were popping Xanax by the handful.

Those clouds would dump any minute, and he'd have to send the crew home. Again. And lose another day's work. "Whatcha got, Hummingbird?"

The machine operator didn't reply. He stepped back and pointed at the open bag, the side folded back. It was the tattered remnants of a sleeping bag. Cold sweat broke out on Jason's brow, and a tight knot clutched at his gut, his breath shallow as he gazed into the opening. Inside, were the skeletal remains of a child, the bones white and clean.

Pink overalls hung on the shoulder bones of the wasted frame. Tennis shoes had slipped from the feet. A small birthstone ring hung loosely on the right ring finger.

Jason rubbed his hand over his face and drew in a lung full of moist air. He removed a cell phone from his jacket pocket. "I'll call it in."

Home of Police Chief Matt Foley

After finishing an eighteen-hour shift Wednesday, Matt Foley hadn't made it to bed until after two o'clock. He'd finished a full day at the station and then spent the evening at a political dinner with his boss.

Matt's Yorkie awakened him at six o'clock before the alarm went off. Rowdy's whines predicted storms better than *The Weather Channel* and he stuck to Matt's side like a burr under a saddle until the sky cleared.

The dog shivered and tried to nose his way under the covers. Matt lifted the blanket and allowed the frightened animal to snuggle close. Otherwise, he would keep whining and neither of them would sleep. With luck, they'd both catch a few winks before it was time to get up.

Half-awake, Matt reached over to touch Mary, to hold her close. But the sheet was cold and empty, her pillow undisturbed. He closed his eyes and turned over, refusing to revisit the dark memories.

In his state between drowsiness and slumber, the phone rang.

He waited. The caller might give up and the message go to voicemail. Didn't happen.

Whoever it was kept redialing.

Fumbling for the bedside lamp switch, he snatched up the phone, and pressed it to his ear. "Foley."

Static filled the line before Sheriff Joe Wilson's voice came through, strong and clear. He chuckled. "It's me, Matt. Did I wake you?"

His friend was persistent, if nothing else. "No, I always let the phone ring fifteen times before I answer. I'm awake now. What's up?"

The cell phone connection faded for a second before it came back. "Construction workers turned up the remains of a child at Bay Harbor. It's about a mile past the bridge on the reservoir road. You know the place?"

Matt tossed the cover back and slid his feet into slippers beside the bed. "What are you doing out there?"

Lightning filled the bedroom with flashbulb brightness, followed by a bass roll of thunder. Rowdy whimpered and moved closer.

"The foreman called me, but this one's your baby. It's within the city limits."

"Yeah, I know." Matt tossed the cover back and headed towards the shower. "I'll find it. Anything else?"

Joe paused for a second. "I spoke to the desk sergeant at the station. Your people are already rolling on it. Since it's a kid, I thought you might want to get involved."

7

"Thanks, Joe. I'm on my way."

"Wear your rain gear. It's coming down out here."

Matt rubbed his eyes and yawned. "Don't remind me."

"I'll keep the scene clear of tourists and media until you get your lazy behind out here."

In twenty minutes, Matt had showered, dressed, and headed downstairs, the Yorkie whimpering at his heels. Matt picked Rowdy up. "I hate to leave you here alone in a storm, buddy, but I can't take you with me."

Rowdy still in his arms, Matt snatched a Benadryl tablet from the medicine cabinet. He stopped in the kitchen, wrapped the pill in a hunk of bologna, and fed it to the dog. That would calm him until Stella came in at ten.

He didn't have time for a pet. Keeping Rowdy wasn't good for either of them. But Matt had never been able to consider finding the dog another home. They both missed Mary. The Yorkie was the only reason he came home at night.

Home had become an insidious adversary he didn't want to face. Everywhere he looked, there were reminders of his wife. Even Rowdy had been her dog.

Mary hadn't been a morning person, but she had insisted on seeing him off each morning. A cup of coffee in her hand, eyes half-closed, she'd leaned into him for a lingering goodbye kiss, saying, "Something to remind you to come home."

He recalled the first time he'd kissed her. They'd met at a political fund raiser and afterward he'd walked her to her car. She'd opened the door then turned to thank him. He'd leaned down and placed a light touch on her lips. A nice-meeting-you acknowledgement of his attraction to her. When he turned to walk away, she'd said, "Call me, Matt."

His job and his friend Joe had saved him. Kept him from

falling into the abyss of grief. He couldn't think of his own sorrow while helping others with theirs.

Perhaps he should sell the house, find the dog a good home. But that was a decision for another time and another day.

He strapped on his nylon holster, stuffed the 9mm Glock in the pocket, then retrieved his slicker and rain boots from the closet. With the galoshes securely snapped over his shoes, he strode through the kitchen to the garage and climbed into his Expedition. He backed out of the driveway and headed towards the city. Coffee would have to wait until the Starbucks drive-through.

Bay Harbor Development

An ocean of gray mist greeted Matt's turn onto the aqueduct roadway. The downpour had stopped, but a steady drizzle persisted. In the distance, a flock of geese honked their way farther south for the winter. The fresh smell of wet pine needles drifted through the SUV's window.

Ahead, blue-and-white strobe bars of two sheriff's cruisers pierced the gloom. The vehicles formed a roadblock just before the bridge. Uniformed deputies, in canary-yellow ponchos, stood in the road and turned back a press van and onlookers. The grim set of the officers' jaws spoke volumes.

One of the deputies recognized Matt and waved him through the maze.

Matt made a right turn after the bridge. A mile down the gravel road, he swung his SUV in beside the sheriff's vehicle. The mire clung to his rubber boots as he trudged up the muddy incline. At the top of the knoll, the land leveled out for fifty yards where construction trucks, sheriff's patrol cars, black and whites, and a coroner's van formed a half-moon around a muddy, yellow backhoe. The worksite lay about a hundred yards off the lake's beachfront.

Matt's detectives had beaten him to the crime scene. Lead detective, Miles Davis, waited near the mud-splattered machine. He stood six-feet tall, with a tight, muscular frame. No ordinary slicker for Miles. In his belted London Fog coat and Denzel Washington good looks, he appeared more at home on the cover of a men's fashion magazine than at a grubby crime scene.

Within the cordoned-off area, Davis motioned for the Crime Scene Unit Chief, Dale McCulloch, to join him. Dale's people set up two portable lights to dispel the morning gloom while he recorded video and pointed his assistant to locations where he wanted still shots. Camera flashes added sporadic brilliance to the gray morning.

To the untutored eye, a murder scene looked chaotic as people moved in different directions. But to a cop, the investigation progressed like a synchronized ballet, a symphony of precise motion. The company missed nothing. Cataloged everything.

Matt stood out of the way as the detective squatted like a catcher behind home plate beside the remains of a sleeping bag. Davis pulled the flaps aside and exposed the contents. He straightened and called the photographer to move in for close-ups.

Sheriff Joe Wilson caught Matt's eye and lifted a coffee cup in a salute. Joe's fullback physique and chiseled features lent authority to his slicker-covered uniform. At six-foot-three, he could never meld into the background, and the Stetson he wore negated Matt's one-inch height advantage.

Joe saluted Matt with the foam cup in his hand. "It's about time you showed up, Foley. I'm tired of standing in the rain, babysitting your crime scene."

"And a good morning to you, too," Matt said and reached to shake hands.

Joe scowled at him.

County medical examiner, Lisa Martinez's petite frame looked smaller than usual standing next to the sheriff's bulk. The ever-present cigarette between her fingers was missing. Probably difficult to smoke in the rain. Her thick, dark hair was pulled into a ponytail under a navy blue cap—strikingly beautiful, despite the miserable weather.

"Hi, Lisa," Matt said. "Is he always this grumpy in the morning?"

She laughed. "Only when he misses his fiber."

Matt inclined his head towards the taped-off area. "Who found the body?"

Joe pointed to a group of men near the backhoe with his coffee cup. "One of the workers uncovered it before the rain started. He unzipped the bag—found the skeleton. I haven't talked to him. Detective Hunter is doing that now."

Matt followed his gaze to the crowd of construction workers. Detective Chris Hunter stood in their midst, notebook and pen in hand.

A hole yawned in front of the machine. Dale had stretched a tarp over the grave, but it hadn't stopped the storm's runoff from seeping into the hole.

Lisa left to join the CSU team, and Joe put his hand on Matt's shoulder. "So, how are you doing?"

Matt shrugged. They'd been friends too long for him to lie.

"That doesn't tell me much." Joe released the grip,

giving Matt some space.

"I don't know what you're looking for, Joe. Why do you ask?"

"Because I've seen you in the valley, my friend."

Matt knew Joe cared. Really cared. But his questions brought back emotions Matt didn't want to deal with. Not here. Not now.

Matt hesitated. He needed to change the subject. "Lisa been out here long enough to reach any conclusions?"

"She arrived shortly after I did." Joe nodded towards the group headed their way. "You can ask her."

Lisa, Miles, and Dale caught up with them.

"Anything so far, Lisa?"

She gave a slight shrug. "The articles we found, as well as the skeletal remains, are those of a child. Can't be sure, but the age appears to be about six or seven. Two front teeth are missing, which is consistent with a child that age. I'll have to have DNA tests done, but based on the clothing, it's a girl."

"Any idea how long ago?" Matt asked.

She turned and scanned the gravesite. "A very long time. My best guess is twenty years or more. The skeleton is intact. The depth of the grave and the sleeping bag kept animals from scattering bones across the countryside."

Davis handed Matt a plastic bag that contained a small piece of red plaid fabric "We found this still inside the bag with the manufacturer's label attached. The plastic liner is intact. Lucky for us, vinyl doesn't decompose quickly. One reason landfills keep piling up."

"Any thoughts on cause of death?" Matt asked.

Lisa shook her head. "Too soon to make a prediction. I'll let you know more after I get back to the morgue."

"Anything to help with identification?"

"Relatives, if and when we find them, should be able to make a positive ID of the clothing and a birthstone ring that were inside the bag."

A construction worker near the backhoe skirted around the crime scene tape and stopped in front of Davis. He held out his hand. "Jason Watts, job foreman. We're packing up. How long you guys gonna hold on to the worksite?"

The detective turned to the grim-faced supervisor. "As long as it takes, but just this area. You guys can work the other sections, weather permitting." He shoved his rain hat off his brow. "Look, it's a moot point. You can't work today in this mess anyhow. We'll have to sift through every shovelful of dirt inside that hole before I can let you guys back in."

Watts punched his hands into his pockets. "The developer will not be happy. We're working on a tight schedule."

"I understand," Davis said. "Nevertheless, I have to secure the scene, big and messy as it is. Homicide 101."

The man shook his head and turned to leave.

Matt stopped him. "Those buildings over there, are they part of the Bay Harbor project?"

Watts turned back and faced Matt. "Yeah, they'll come down though. The plan is to clear the lakefront property first. That's where we'll start putting up homes as soon as it's ready."

"Are they safe for us to go inside?"

"They're structurally sound," Watts said. "But they're a mess. A bunch of drunks and druggies have used them as crash pads."

"We'd like to take a look. Is that a problem?" Matt asked.

"Knock yourself out." He waved as if to say 'They don't pay me enough to do this job," and walked back to his crew.

Davis shook his head. "He thinks he has problems. Years of weather, people, and animals have erased any evidence there might have been here. You want to check out those buildings now?"

"Yeah. It shouldn't take long."

They trekked fifty yards uphill to the two structures. Davis moved up beside Matt as they stepped around the mud puddles that dotted the path. "What were they used for?"

"For more than fifty years, twenty acres of this property belonged to the Twin Falls First Baptist Church. They sold it when the developer bought all the land around them. These buildings were a retreat. The two-story structure was a housing complex for guests, and the one-story was used as a fellowship hall for meetings and meals."

Davis raised an eyebrow. "What's a retreat?"

Matt's gaze swept the property. The grass came up to his knees, most of the windows were broken, and a tree had fallen against the roof. "It was a place for people to get away from telephones and televisions, to reconnect with each other and God. As a kid, I used to come here for summer camp. It looked a lot different then."

The apartment's outer door clung to its upright position by a single loose hinge. Matt shoved the door open and kicked trash out of the way. Inside, a wide hallway ended at the stairs that led to the second floor. There were eight bedrooms on each side of the corridor, all with built-in bunk beds. The same upstairs, six bunks per room.

He and Davis checked the downstairs. The foreman was right. Empty wine bottles and drug paraphernalia were scattered on the bare wood floors.

Deep down, it squeezed Matt's gut to see the place in

such disrepair. He'd spent some of the happiest times of his childhood here. At the last upstairs bedroom on the west side, he stepped to the window and stopped. "Davis, come look at this."

The detective's footsteps sounded in the hallway. "You find something, Chief?"

"Take a look."

Davis entered and stepped to the window. "What?"

Matt moved aside so Davis could get a closer look. "That's a perfect view of the burial site from here. Have Mac get some pictures. When we find out who our victim was, someone may have seen something. It's worth a shot."

After a baleful glance at the debris on the floor, Davis rubbed both hands down his face. "McCulloch will have to bag and catalog all this stuff just in case we get a suspect."

Matt grinned. "It's a long shot, but if it was easy..."

"I know, I know...anybody could do it."

Matt slapped his shoulder. "You're learning."

The CSU Chief met them as they came back down the hill. "We're outta here. The weather forecast looks better tomorrow, and it'll give this place some time to dry out. I'll bring some extra help from the lab, maybe some college kids I know, and we'll do a grid search. We'll be here by first light." He glanced at Davis. "You gonna leave people to guard the site until we return in the morning?"

"Yeah. Probably not necessary but I'd rather be safe. Mac, before you leave, I have a job you're gonna love." He led Mac towards the retreat.

Joe Wilson came forward as Matt reached the crime scene. The sheriff stopped, removed his hat, and smacked it against his leg before replacing it. "I'm heading out. I'll give you a hand with the authorities in surrounding areas. Ask them to check old files for missing children."

15

"Thanks. That'll save us some time."

"Tell that housekeeper of yours to throw an extra potato in the pot, and I'll come to dinner one night." He took two steps then turned back. "Even better, you can buy me a steak at Ruth's Chris."

Joe crunched a foam cup in his big fist and handed the trash to Hunter who had just joined them. "Here, hold this."

Hunter took it then stood there, glanced at the crumpled cup in his hand, and shook his head.

Matt grinned. "I'll give you a ring."

The lab techs began to pack away their gear, and Matt plodded back to his vehicle.

When he reached the truck, Lisa leaned against the door. She backed away with slow, easy grace. "I didn't expect to see you today, Matt. You haven't been around much lately."

"I've been busy. How's Paul?"

"He's fine." Her tone held a slight edge. "He asks about you often. The other kids were impressed the police chief came to watch his games."

Matt attended a few of Paul's little league games in the summer, but stopped when Lisa's attraction to him became apparent. Divorced from Paul's father only a few months, she was vulnerable. Not a situation he could handle right now. Besides, involvement with someone he worked with was asking for trouble.

His hand closed around the door handle. "Tell Paul I'll try to catch a game soon."

Davis shouted Lisa's name. She gave him a wave of acknowledgment and called back to Matt as she departed, "Better hurry. There's only one left on the fall schedule."

He started the ignition and watched Lisa walk away.

Joe came into view as Matt backed out. The sheriff stood beside his cruiser. His gaze followed Lisa Martinez with an expression Matt hadn't noticed before. Joe and Lisa? Funny, he'd never have put those two together. Joe, laid back and easy going. Lisa, volatile as a firecracker. Another reason to avoid the woman. He didn't want to get in his old friend's way.

Matt pushed the hood of his slicker back and stared at the horizon. The deaths of children haunted his dreams long after the cases ended—ghosts that took up permanent residence.

Mist swallowed the scene behind him as he drove back across the aqueduct. The last sound that drifted through the open vent was a chorus of katydids—singing a requiem for a fallen child.

CHAPTER 2

Twin Falls Police Station

At ten o'clock, Matt turned onto the county road that passed the site from which the city had taken its name. The falls had lain dormant for fifty years after an upstream dam diverted the tributary that fed them. Embarrassed by the poor condition of the town's namesake, city leaders took action six months ago, starting a water re-circulation project now hidden behind a white construction fence. Friday, water would once again flow freely over the historic site. The unveiling would take place tomorrow, with a full-scale celebration banquet at the country club Saturday.

Matt merged with the traffic on I-75, the expressway that separated the haves from the have-nots in his town. The courthouse and police station sat in the older, less-affluent side of the city.

Traffic around the square brought him to a standstill. The somber scene at Bay Harbor claimed his thoughts, triggering a memory. When his life spiraled out of control two years ago, he'd spent many nights at the station unable to be alone at home with the memories. He'd brought Rowdy's bed to the office to keep him company. The job kept him focused—gave him a reason to keep going. Despair had led him to the cold case files.

Not many murders in his town. Domestic violence accounted for the four or five annual homicides. The old files had turned up two unsolved cases.

The most recent, Joshua Bradford. Killed four years ago in a hit-and-run accident. That happened on his watch.

His only contribution to the cold case files. The second, a six-year-old girl who'd disappeared twenty-five years ago, long before he'd become chief.

He'd spent a lot of time playing "what if" with those cases, especially the Bradford accident. It wouldn't be ignored, like a fever blister he kept running his tongue over.

Matt hated loose ends. Even more, he hated that a killer still walked the streets.

He parked behind the station at his private entrance. Still early, the station looked almost empty. Administrative help had arrived but the day watch officers had already hit the streets.

In route to his office he stopped for a cup of coffee, and got lucky. Someone had brought in a box of donuts. He tossed a five dollar bill in the kitty and took two, one cake, one glazed.

Seated at his desk, he ran a finger under his shirt collar, wiggled his tie loose, and sipped coffee while he waited for the computer to accept his password. After a moment, the unsolved case files flashed on the screen. He found the Pryor file in the database then strode down the corridor to pick up the casebook.

It took twenty minutes to find the notebook on a dusty, bottom shelf. He wiped the cover with his handkerchief and returned to his office. He put the book down on his desk, then checked his voicemail for messages. He was clear.

Matt flipped through the familiar pages. The book held all the notes from the original investigation, complete with the child's grade-school photo and a list of the witnesses interviewed the night she'd vanished. The timeframe was right. And the age and sex were consistent with the evidence from the gravesite. Including descriptions of the clothing she wore. Looked like their victim was Penny Pryor, but the dental records could confirm or dismiss it.

Thumbing through the witness list, two names caught his attention. Brandt Michael Ferrell, Texas' newly elected governor, and Sara Taylor, widow of Joshua Bradford. Taylor was Sara's maiden name.

Sara Taylor was six at the time the girl vanished, and now the primary suspect in the hit-and-run death of her husband. Matt just hadn't been able to prove it.

Book in hand, he carried it upstairs to the Detective Bureau on the second floor. The room was large, furnished with desks for the four investigators, three males and one female.

Even though most crimes happened at night, detectives worked days, and rotated for night call-outs. They worked days as support branches, such as the coroner, technicians, and labs were on eight to five schedules.

He found Miles Davis and Chris Hunter at their desks, and handed the book to Davis. Matt tapped the cover. "Looks like this is our victim."

Davis's eyebrows rose almost to his hairline. "How'd you find it so fast?"

"The crime scene rang a bell and I know the cold case files like the back of my hand. When do you want to speak to the parents?"

"Hunter and I can handle it, Chief, unless you just want to be there."

"I need to be involved in this one, Miles. Penny was the niece of Brandt Ferrell, our esteemed governor."

Home of Sam and Lily Pryor

Matt dreaded next-of-kin notifications. It was the most

difficult part of being a cop. No matter how many times he'd tackled them, they never got easier. And those involving children were the worst of the worst.

He and Davis parked on the street in front of the Pryor's two-story brick home in an older, but still exclusive, part of town. Tall pointed cedars formed privacy walls on both sides of the property. Thick Bermuda grass lay across the lawn like a soft green carpet.

Matt glanced at his watch. Past six in the evening. They had waited to give Sam Pryor time to get home so his wife wouldn't be alone to get the bad news.

They got out of the car, Davis carrying his briefcase with the items for identification. When they reached the door, Matt rang the bell. The photo image of Penny's pert face flashed before him. A pretty little girl with red hair and a sprinkle of freckles across her nose—an innocent upward tilt of her lips revealed a gap-toothed smile. The face of a future unfulfilled.

What had it been like for Sam and Lily Pryor to lose this child, have her disappear for a quarter century? To always wonder what happened, hoping she was alive somewhere? To wonder what kind of woman she might have become? He couldn't imagine the pain that must have caused.

He started to ring the bell again when the door opened. The woman in the entryway was too thin, but attractive in a fragile kind of way, with curly red hair and blue eyes. Eyes the same color as Penny's.

"Mrs. Pryor?"

"Yes. May I help you?"

"Mrs. Pryor, I'm Chief of Police Matthew Foley, and this is Detective Miles Davis. We'd like to speak to you and your husband for a moment. May we come in?"

He held out his badge wallet.

She stood in the doorway, not moving, eyes wide and unfocused. She stepped back and gripped the door handle, her voice almost a whisper. "You've found Penny."

The view through the door revealed an open floor plan of the kitchen, dining room, and living room. A slender man with glasses and receding dark hair stepped away from the kitchen sink and came towards them. "Lily, what's wrong?"

"Sam—"

Sam Pryor quick-stepped to the door, and Matt reintroduced himself and Davis. "May we come in, sir? It would be better if we discuss the purpose of our visit inside."

She moved farther back into the entrance and cast an imploring glance at her husband. "Sam...it's about Penny."

Sam Pryor moved closer to his wife and put his arm around her. "Please, come in. My wife seems to be in shock. Is it true? Have you found Penny?"

He led his wife to the sofa and offered them a seat with a wave of his hand. "Is she... alive?"

Lily's eyes welled with tears, her face flush with emotion. Her shaken husband embraced her and tried to maintain a brave face for his wife. "We haven't heard from the police in years...it might not be Penny."

"I'm sorry. We think the remains found this morning may be your daughter." Davis opened the attaché lid and brought out the three color photograph of the victims clothing and ring. "I know this is difficult, but can you identify these items? Did they belong to your daughter?"

Sam took the photo of the ring. He stood and walked to the window. He cleared his throat, his voice husky, but didn't turn around when he spoke. "This is her ring. We bought it for her sixth birthday."

Lily had taken the other shots. She clutched them to her

22

chest and rocked back and forth, tears rolling down her cheeks.

As gently as possible, Matt asked, "Are those Penny's?" She nodded.

Sam seemed to realize he'd left Lily alone. He came back to her side and lifted his gaze. "Where—"

"The Bay Harbor construction site," Davis said. "You know where that is?"

"Yes. It used to be a church retreat." Sam pulled his wife close. "I'd heard they sold the property."

Davis collected the photographs and placed them back in the briefcase. "We'll return the ring to you as soon as we can, but for the present, it's evidence. This is the home you lived in when your daughter disappeared?"

Lily wrapped thin fingers around her husband's arm and spoke in a near whisper. "We decided not to sell. Afraid Penny would return someday...and be unable to find us."

"We have just a few more things to cover before we're finished," Matt said. "Can you get us the name of Penny's dentist, and the names of any neighbors who lived here when your daughter disappeared? You can email it to Detective Davis when you have the information."

Davis handed Sam his business card.

He took the card, glanced at Davis, then back at Matt. "When can we claim the...her?"

"As soon as the coroner is finished." Matt shook his hand. "I'll give you a call."

He and Davis stood. Matt reached in his jacket pocket and handed Sam his business card. "I'm sorry for your loss. This is my personal cell phone number. Please call me if there's anything we can do to help."

Sam nodded and placed the cards on the coffee table.

"We'll let ourselves out."

Penny's parents sat huddled together on the sofa, as Matt closed the door softly behind him. Lily's soft sobs followed them out.

He and Davis drove back to the station in silence.

CHAPTER 3

Global Optics

Cloaked by the downpour, the man sat in the car and sipped his black Starbuck's Pike Place. While he watched Sara Bradford enter the building, people went in and out of the Global lobby.

Discovery of the child's body yesterday had forced him into a decision he'd hoped never to make. Sara held his future in her hands though she wasn't aware of the knowledge tucked inside her head. Too bad. Really. He'd grown fond of her. She had matured into an intelligent, beautiful woman.

Safe for so long, he'd been lulled into believing no one would ever know—the secret would go to the grave with him. But the gods of fate decided otherwise.

He rotated his neck to ease the tight muscles, stiff from his painstaking work last night, and the job he'd assigned himself today. Taking a human life was never easy, but it wouldn't be his first time. He'd do what must be done to protect the life he'd built.

Lightning flashed across the dark sky, illuminating the interior of the car. In the brief glare, he caught sight of his reflection in the rearview mirror and realized he no longer knew the stone, gray face that stared back at him.

CHAPTER 4

Global, Optics

Sara Bradford shook her head. Some days you get roses, some days you get thorns. No roses today.

Traffic routed around the wreck on the rain-slicked freeway made her twenty minutes late to work. She hated being tardy. Punctuality was encoded into her genes at birth. A gift from her father.

She hurried through the lobby and into the skywalk separating the distribution center from the home office complex. Rain misted the walkway's windows but didn't conceal the threatening sky that hovered outside.

Inside the warehouse, the corridor split. One way led to the production area, the other to management offices. A waist-high counter ran across a reception area for greeting salesmen and visitors. Her secretary, Jane Haskell, whose desk was just outside Sara's office, glanced at her watch when Sara entered. "Better grab a fast cup of coffee. Things are happening. There's a veep meeting in the boardroom in ten minutes. I thought you weren't going to make it. Want me to get your coffee?"

"No, thanks. I'll get a cup upstairs." Sara unlocked the door, placed her handbag and briefcase inside, and grabbed a leather legal pad holder from the desk drawer.

On her way out, she stopped at Jane's desk. "Any idea what the meeting's about?"

Jane's ebony eyes crinkled with mirth and the corners of her mouth tilted upward. "Who, me? No, no. I just work here."

Arms crossed, Sara grinned. Her secretary had the inside track on the company grapevine. "Don't kid a kidder. You know more about what goes on here than the CEO. So give it up."

White teeth flashed in Jane's pretty, dark face. "Well, if I were to guess, I'd say it's about the buyout rumor that's circulated all week."

Jane had nailed it. Sara expected an official announcement from the front office before the end of the day. "I guess we'll know after the meeting."

She hurried back through the skywalk. Time was short, so she took the elevator to the fourth floor rather than her usual route via the stairs. Corporate life offered few chances for physical activity, and she took advantage of the stairway whenever possible. At thirty-two, she attributed her healthy glow to a commitment to avoid the easy path.

The elevator's one glass wall offered a rain-splattered view of tall oaks and a rippling pond in the park next to Global's property. A ding announced the top floor, and the silver doors slid open.

The welcome aroma of roasting coffee beans exuded from a high-tech coffee maker in the butler's pantry adjacent to the executive boardroom. Sara ducked inside, filled a foam cup and stepped next door.

Orange oil mixed with the scent of leather, greeted her as she entered. An impressive mahogany conference table flanked by fourteen plush leather chairs held center stage. Original oil paintings, highlighted by hidden ceiling lights, adorned the fabric-covered walls.

She scanned the table's occupants, recognizing the faces of her counterparts on the executive staff. With a good morning nod, she eased into the closest vacant chair.

Senior Vice-President Charles Edwards entered and sat beside her. He checked the time on his Rolex and leaned close. "It must be something important. Roger called in the big guns."

Hiding a smile behind the cup in her hand, she glanced at him. In his early to mid-fifties, Charles was tall, well tanned, with short-cropped gray hair. He wore an immaculate dark-blue suit, always elegant and touchingly gallant. Jane called him *GQ* Man. He could be a bit arrogant, but Sara liked him. Perhaps because he reminded her of her father.

Before she could comment, Global's CEO Roger Reynolds strode into the room and stood behind his chair. The first thing she noticed when she'd first met Roger was his charisma, packaged in a thin frame with perfect teeth and short blond hair. The second impression had been to stay on her toes. His reputation for ruthlessness preceded him. And in short order she understood why.

He placed a well-manicured hand on the back of his chair and scanned the faces around the room. His gaze stopped at Sara for a fraction of a second, then moved on. "People, this will be a short meeting. I'm aware rumors have been floating around about a Global buyout. The rumors are true. Yesterday, Millennium Ventures, a large investment firm, acquired Global Optics. The public announcement will hit newspapers this morning."

Fragmented conversations erupted, filling the room with an audible buzz.

Roger held up his hand. "Two weeks from Monday, the new owners will arrive here at nine o'clock to meet with department heads and to tour the facility."

Charles Edwards sat back in his chair, a furrowed frown on his face, clicking his Mont Blanc pen. He asked the question on everyone's mind. "Will they bring in their own management team?"

Roger shrugged. "You know as much about that as I do, Charles. However, it's always a possibility. I think we can expect some changes. A word of caution. Make sure your departments are spotless when the management team arrives for the tour." He glanced around the table. "Any other questions?" Signaling that the meeting was over.

Sara remained in her seat for a moment.

Amazing. No rallying encouragement for the troops. Roger left them with the impression some or all of them could lose their jobs. Not a model of good leadership.

She retrieved her folder from the table and fell in behind the solemn group exiting the conference room. As she stepped into the corridor, Roger touched her elbow and guided her away from the crowd. "Come back to my office. We need to talk."

A summons to Reynolds' realm was a rare occurrence for her. Although one of Global's eight vice presidents, she'd never been part of Roger's inner circle. He liked yes-men, and she didn't fit that mold.

She eased into step beside him. They moved without speaking into the executive suite. As they entered, Roger's phone rang. He waved her to a seat and stepped behind his desk to take the call.

Sara sat on one of the earth-toned sofas grouped near the windows. Her gaze roamed to Roger's massive desk clear of everything, except a pen set, computer, and telephone. No family pictures, nothing personal.

She studied the bookshelves above his credenza. Books said more about a man than his clothes or bearing. For a moment, her father's study flashed into her mind. The classics found a home there, as well as his light reading collections by Zane Grey and Louis L'Amour. The King James Bible held a prominent spot within easy reach.

Roger's books consisted of business management best sellers. Nothing to give insight into the man. Perhaps that in itself, said something. She mentally shook herself—being too critical. After all, this wasn't his home library.

The call ended, and Roger crossed the room. He sat on the sofa across from her and sucked in a deep breath. "I need you to clean out your office. Pack your files and personal items. Leave the cartons there until further notice."

Shock must have registered on her face. Heat warmed her cheeks, an event always followed by red splotches on her neck. A curse she'd lived with through every emotional crisis in her life. "I...don't understand. Are you letting me go?"

He laid one arm across the sofa back, his face void of expression. "That's not what I said."

"Then what...?"

"The new owner hasn't given any specifics, except to say you would be leaving your current position. There were no instructions to let you go." He winced as though trying to show compassion. "I assume these people have other plans for you. Details have been vague, to say the least."

She didn't buy his lack of knowledge. How much input Roger had in the decision to move her out, she didn't know. However, she felt certain he hadn't gone to bat for her. Whatever happened when the new firm took over, she couldn't expect any support from Roger.

No point in pursuing it now. Difficult as it was, she had to keep it together. Stay professional.

Roger asked, "Do you understand what I need from you?"

Of course, she understood. "The part about cleaning out my office came through crystal clear."

He leaned back and crossed his legs. "Take the rest of the day off, if you like."

She shook her head. "I'd rather pack after the warehouse staff leaves at noon. I've scheduled two weeks of vacation to start Monday."

Roger nodded. "That's probably best. The time off will do you good. I'm confident you'll be offered another position, either here or in one of their other divisions."

He stood and walked her to the door. "You will, of course, need to be here for the meeting Monday after your vacation. You should get answers to any concerns you have then."

She released the breath she'd been holding and lifted her chin. Roger wouldn't get the satisfaction of seeing her angst. She felt his gaze linger until she disappeared around the corner.

~*~

The rest of the morning passed in a blur. Warehouse personnel left at noon on Friday, so she had the place to herself. She sorted through the desk drawers, packed the files in cartons, and labeled them.

Jane would be curious when she saw the boxes. If she asked, Sara would have to tell her the truth.

Leaning back in her chair, Sara stretched tense muscles in her neck and shoulders. She'd packed, everything except a picture of Josh she'd kept in the desk drawer after his death. Misty eyed, she lifted the silver-framed photograph and ran a finger over the glass, smoothing back the lock of hair that always fell across her husband's brow. A motion performed so many times in private before the relationship took a left turn.

The marriage had been anything but ideal, but she missed his dry sense of humor and his gentleness. She hadn't had a chance to say goodbye, to say she was sorry she'd failed him—to say she loved him. He'd left for work that morning and never returned. She blinked back the moisture that stung her eyelids, and slipped the picture into her handbag.

Financially, she would be okay if she lost her job. At least for a while. She still had most of Josh's insurance money. Aunt Maddie also insisted on contributing to the household expenses. But in a job market flooded with laid-off executives, finding another position that paid as well as Global could take a long time.

From the doorway, her gaze roamed over the office that had been hers for five years. Her chest tightened and she inhaled a deep breath. This might be her last walk-through inspection.

~*~

Security guard Don Tompkins, glanced at the monitor as Sara Bradford left her office. His gaze shifted to the next screen as the warehouse camera clicked on, activated by motion sensors. Cameras followed her progress. With shoulder-length dark hair and olive complexion, she stood out in a crowd. In a quiet way. Large hazel eyes and a generous mouth took her looks to the next level, from just pretty to beautiful.

She stopped before a bank of high-rise forklifts plugged into battery chargers. A lone machine sat apart, unconnected.

Unusual.

Don leaned in for a closer look.

Warehouse supervisors routinely connected the machines before leaving at the end of a shift. Dead batteries meant lost productivity the next day.

Sara stopped and glanced around, then dropped her handbag on the lift platform.

A bright flash filled the monitor. The floor quaked, and a loud *boom* sounded from the distribution center.

The video screen went dark. Emergency lights immediately snapped on, casting an eerie glow over the scene.

Don dashed towards the skywalk and shouted at the young guard behind the counter. "Call 911. There's been an explosion in the warehouse. Sound the fire alarm and evacuate this building. Now!"

A rush of adrenaline made the blood pound in his ears as he broke into a full run. In the dim lighting, the camera showed the forklift, mangled and enveloped in flames.

CHAPTER 5

Global Optics

A deafening thunderclap blasted in Sara's ears. The air around her burst, and heat pushed against her skin. Shockwaves hurled her through space like a rag doll thrown by a petulant child. She landed on flat cardboard boxes, and skidded across the dock into rolls of shrink-wrap, where she lay gasping for air. Fireworks exploded before her eyes as she sucked oxygen back into her lungs. After a shake of her head, the pinwheels dissolved.

The silence made her pulse race.

Through a haze of smoke, flames consumed the forklift. Why didn't the rain put out the fire? She blinked to clear the fog and realized the shower came from overhead sprinklers that had snapped on when heat from the explosion reached the sensors.

Great gushes of oily water spewed, coming in waves with each rotation of the sprinkler heads, soaking her clothes and pasting wet strings of hair to her face.

A form appeared in the dim lighting and moved towards her.

The security guard, Don Tompkins.

She pushed against the wet boxes and struggled to a sitting position.

Don knelt beside her, his face white and strained in the faint glow. He'd spoken but she couldn't comprehend his words. Some of her hearing returned but not all. "Sorry...my ears."

He nodded he understood and slowly mouthed, "Are you

all right?"

That time she understood him. "I'm not sure...still taking inventory, but nothing seems to be broken."

"What in thunder happened?"

She shook her head and leaned against the slick, wet plastic. "I don't know, but if I lie here much longer, I may be the first person ever to drown in a warehouse."

"I'll see if I can shut off the sprinklers. They did their job—the fire's out."

Don disappeared for a few minutes, and the water trickled to a stop. Moments later, he returned to her side.

She raised a hand and wiped her face. "Why is the water oily?"

"They coat the inside of the pipes to keep them from rusting. It flushes out when the lines are flooded." He squatted beside her. "Sara, I need to get you out of here before the emergency response folks arrive. The firefighters won't let anyone inside until they make sure there are no more bombs. You'd have to stay here until they clear the building. The fire department will have to get a bomb squad from Dallas or Fort Hood. That could take hours. Do you think you can walk?"

She tried to process what he had said. "It was a bomb?"

He nodded. "Only two options. A bomb or battery explosion. I've seen both. I'd be surprised if it turns out to be the battery."

Don rose to his feet and put his hands on his hips. "I'll carry you out, and we can load you right into an ambulance. Do you think you're up for that?"

Sara wiggled her toes and nodded. "Y-Yes, I don't want to stay here for hours while they search for more bombs or whatever. Let me lean on you, and I think I can walk."

His brow wrinkled. "Moving you goes against everything

I've been taught. Your injuries could be more serious than you realize, and movement could make them worse. If Human Resources terminates me for this, you'll have to find me a job."

She squeezed his arm. "I'll do better than that. I'll see you don't get fired."

They had just reached the exit when police, fire trucks, and an ambulance converged on the parking lot. Firefighters swarmed from the truck, grabbing hoses and equipment.

A police officer reached them first. "Anyone else inside?"

"Not in the warehouse, and we've evacuated the home office building." Don pointed to the fire truck. "They won't need the water hoses. The sprinklers doused the fire."

"What happened?" the officer asked.

"Looked like a bomb to me." Don turned to Sara and patted her arm. "I'll need to answer some questions for these guys. The EMTs will take over from here."

A paramedic appeared and handed Don a blanket to wrap around his wet shoulders. Another EMT secured Sara to a backboard, positioned a brace on her neck, strapped her on the gurney, and covered her in blankets.

Sara closed her eyes and gave in to the warmth. Gurney wheels bumped over the rough parking lot, and EMTs lifted her into the ambulance.

Before the doors closed, a face came into focus among those in the crowd. A face that awakened old wounds—Police Chief, Matthew Foley.

~*~

Matt stood on the curb as the ambulance pulled away, and scanned the crowd for the fire marshal's thin frame.

He found Blake Dennis, in a corner of the parking lot, with two firemen and a police officer. Blake glanced up and waved Matt over.

The sharp stench of smoke still hung in the air, and the dank smell of wet cardboard grew stronger as he neared the warehouse dock.

"Anything of interest so far?" Matt asked.

"Explosions are always interesting." Blake rocked back on his heels and readjusted his cap. "We'll know more when the bomb squad arrives. They're on their way from Fort Hood, ETA twenty minutes."

Blake removed his sunglasses and placed them over the brim of his cap. "From what the security guard told us, there was a blast in the distribution center. The experts will want to run tests for explosive residue. Pretty straightforward stuff. According to the guard's description, it appears someone planted a bomb in the product mover."

"Want to make an early prediction?"

"You know me better than that." Blake scratched the stubble on his chin. "But my guess would have to lean towards the battery. Not many people planting bombs in warehouses these days just to blow up a high-rise forklift."

Matt jerked his head towards the receiving bay, where the ambulance had just pulled away. "Who was injured?"

Blake flipped the notepad in his hand. "Sara Bradford. She was in the warehouse when the blast occurred."

"Serious?"

The fire marshal shrugged. "A doctor I'm not. You'll need to check that out at the hospital."

"How come you're always so helpful?" Why could he never get a straight answer from the man?

Blake grinned. "It's part of our indoctrination."

Focusing on the details that mattered, Matt asked,

"Your folks collected the warehouse security tapes?"

An edge entered Blake's voice. "We tried. One of my men went to the guard station. Seems the tapes are gone."

Matt fell silent for a moment, realizing the implications. The explosion wasn't an accident. "Did the guard know when the security tapes were removed? Or why?"

"Nope. Too busy evacuating the building. He thought we took'em."

Blake could be obtuse. Tunnel vision made him miss the whole picture. The fire marshal was dead wrong on this one. If the battery exploded, there would be no reason for someone to take the security discs.

Twin Falls Memorial Hospital

Sara was cognizant, except for the swarm of bees that buzzed in her ears. She closed her eyes, shutting out the piercing rays of light as the paramedics lifted her onto the concrete dock.

Emergency room doors hissed open, and the overhead florescent lights blurred into one as she moved quickly along the corridor. Green curtains rolled back and the gurney stopped. A nurse followed the two paramedics into the cubicle. "She's the only victim, right?"

A heavyset medic flipped the chart open and nodded. "Yep, just one." He handed the nurse a copy of their report, and they left.

ER personnel rushed into the small space. The nurse glanced down with friendly, blue eyes. "My name is Gaye. I'll be taking care of you." She fastened a bar-coded band on Sara's left wrist and a yellow "Fall Risk" band next to it. "Don't let the tag scare you. We put one on everyone from eight to eighty."

Gaye nodded her head towards a Hispanic woman, standing just inside the cubicle with a clipboard. "Feel like answering a few questions for the admittance office?"

Sara nodded. "I don't have my insurance card with me, though."

Gaye stepped aside as the admittance clerk moved to Sara's bedside. "No problem. We'll get it later."

While the clerk took down the personal information, Gaye strapped a blood-pressure cuff to Sara's arm and stuck a thermometer in her ear. The nurse punched information into a hand-held computer. "I'll bring you a gown and some blankets, then we'll get some x-rays."

The change into dry clothes and warm covers stopped Sara's chills. Soon after, the technician came and she rolled her down to the x-ray department.

Later, back in the cubicle, Sara had almost fallen asleep when the ER doctor entered and pulled a stool beside the bed. He patted her hand. "You're a very lucky young lady. The x-rays are clean, no major complications from the accident. There will be some soreness and a few aches, but otherwise, you should be fine. You can go home, but take it easy for a while. I'll give you a prescription for pain."

The doctor left, and Sara shifted to a comfortable position on the narrow bed and wondered how she would get home.

While she waited to be released, her thoughts drifted back to Matt Foley. She'd only seen him from a distance at church after Mary's death. Even though she and Mary had been best friends, Sara never got to know Matt. His cold indifference the evening Josh died felt like a betrayal when she most needed a friend.

He'd been all cop that night.

The nurse interrupted her musings when she entered

with the prescription and another hospital gown. "Put this one on backwards, it will prevent a draft and keep from exposing your backside to the world. I'm not supposed to let patients leave with our fashionable garments, but I'm not sending you home in wet clothes. You could catch pneumonia. Bring them back next time you come this way."

She helped Sara into the gown, then handed her the prescription and paperwork. "You have friends waiting to see you."

From behind the curtain, Don Tompkins called, "Knock. Knock."

Sara straightened the blankets and smoothed a hand over her damp hair. Oh well, nothing she could do about her bedraggled appearance now. Besides, he'd already seen her at her worst. "Come on in. I'm decent. Almost, anyway."

Don pushed aside the drapes and stepped in, concern in his brown eyes. Charles Edwards followed.

Don's gaze searched her face. "How're you doing, kid?"

She lifted both thumbs.

Charles walked over to her bedside and reached into his coat pocket. "I found your car keys in the warehouse, and followed Don in your car. There wasn't much left of your handbag. Didn't see your cell phone. I thought I could drive you home, if they released you. Don will tag along and take me back to Global."

"My cell was in my pocket and somehow survived the water and the blast." The mention of home brought Maddie to mind. "You didn't call my house, did you?"

The two men exchanged glances. Charles said, "I didn't."

Don shook his head.

Sara touched Don's hand. "I really appreciate you guys

bringing my car. That was so thoughtful, but I can drive myself. I'm fine."

Charles hesitated. "Are you sure? It's really no bother. We'd be glad to take you, and it might not be a good idea for you to get behind the wheel right now."

Gaye chimed in. "I'm sorry, Mrs. Bradford. We can't allow you to drive home. What you do when you turn the corner is out of my control, but our policy doesn't permit trauma patients to drive themselves from the hospital." She grinned. "Call us control freaks, if you like, we'll only take that as a compliment."

Sara held up both hands. "Okay, I know when I've lost a battle." She smiled at the two men. "I'd love to have you escort me home."

Charles reached and took back her keys. "Good girl. Your car's parked at the emergency entrance. I'll drive around front and pick you up. I insist you take my coat. You can return it later."

Emotions welled inside her and the lump in her throat felt like a boulder. She swallowed hard. His kindness brought tears to her eyes, and she turned her head away.

Gaye settled Sara into a wheelchair and turned her over to an attendant who pushed the chair out to the curb. Charles helped her into the passenger side and closed the door.

On the way home, Sara punched in her home number. "I was detained at work for a while. I'm on my way home." Stretching the truth a bit, but she didn't want Maddie to worry.

A sigh of relief filled the phone line. "I'm glad you called. I tried to reach you earlier, but the calls went to voice mail. I have some unsettling news. Lily Pryor called. The police found Penny's body yesterday."

CHAPTER 6

Sara Bradford's Home

Charles parked Sara's car under the portico, and Don pulled in behind them. He got out and opened the car door for her.

Muscles knotted when she stepped from the vehicle. In many ways, she was thankful for the bruises. They reminded her how blessed she'd been.

Charles joined them and passed her the car keys. She removed the cashmere coat he'd loaned her and handed it to him. She grinned. "You should both be happy now." The words caught in her throat. "I...thanks guys. Your kindness is appreciated more than I can tell you."

Don patted her shoulder. "Glad to do it, kid. Do you need help getting inside?"

She shook her head. "I've got it."

"Nice pad. Looks like the governor's mansion." Don grinned and gave her a slight wave.

The two men got into Don's car and drove away.

She trudged through the entryway, headed for the seclusion of her bedroom. The aroma of spices and lemons drifted from the kitchen. She passed the library door, and an audio book sounded from the CD player. "Maddie, I'm home."

The disc stopped with a click, and her legally blind aunt called her name. Sara turned back and stepped into the doorway.

Maddie sat in an overstuffed leather chair near the

fireplace. "I took two messages for you, one from Matthew Foley, and one from Lily. They both asked that you return their call."

The library had been Josh's domain, and Sara changed nothing after his death. Honey-toned panels covered the interior walls and bookcases, giving the feel of an Old World gentlemen's club. Smooth leather-bound books gleamed, their rich earth tones adding warmth to the room. A large mahogany desk sat in one corner, an antique left to Josh by his grandfather.

Sara leaned against the doorframe, afraid if she came closer, her aunt would notice the hospital gown and smell the smoke that clung to her hair.

"Thanks for taking the messages. How did Lily handle the news?"

"About as well as you might expect. The detectives brought articles from the grave for her and Sam to identify."

"Poor Lily. How terrible for them both. I'll call her later, after I've had a bath."

As Sara left the library, the CD player snapped back on.

The grandfather clock struck six as she left the library. Sara's stomach growled a reminder she'd missed lunch. She grabbed an apple from the kitchen and made her way upstairs to the bedroom.

She dropped the wet clothing and hospital gowns down the laundry chute. When the tub filled, she lowered her abused body into the warm water. A large bruise had already formed on her right hip and thigh. Soon, heat from the tub's power jets relaxed the tension and soreness from strained muscles. It took two shampoos to remove the oily water and smoke from her hair.

The revelation about Penny pushed her own discomfort

aside and crowded her thoughts. Her friend vanished more than twenty years ago. A loss branded into Sara's mind since childhood. While she soaked, she visualized Penny's face as she'd last seen the little girl. Buried memories, too painful to recall.

Sara slipped down into the tub, water up to her chin. Her heart squeezed into a knot for Penny's family. After their only child's disappearance, they'd stayed close to Sara. What could she possibly say to help ease their pain?

With a white terrycloth robe tied around her waist, she picked up the phone and dialed Lily's number. No answer. Next, she punched in the number for the police station and asked for Matt. The desk sergeant said the chief had gone for the day.

O-kay.

The calls could wait.

Matt Foley's call piqued her curiosity. She gazed out the window into the darkness and bit her lip. He probably just wanted to grill her about the Global incident—something she knew nothing about.

Global Optics

After leaving Global, Matt drove to the city manager's office, hoping to catch Doug Anderson before he left for the day. Matt had wanted to bring his boss up to date, but missed him. He left Doug a detailed voicemail on the morning's activities, instead.

Doug had no background in law enforcement, and he never interfered in police business. But he didn't like surprises. Matt made it a point to keep him in the loop.

A call to a friend in the hospital ER assured Matt that Sara Bradford had received only minor injuries and they'd released her.

By the time he returned to Global, the bomb squad had cleared the buildings. A lone fire truck, two city vehicles, and a police cruiser remained in the parking lot. Matt pulled in behind the black and whites. All the warehouse doors and receiving bays hung open in an attempt to clear the air of the stench from the fire and wet boxes. Matt waved one of the uniformed officers over. "Have you seen Blake?"

He tilted his head towards the back of the warehouse. "Blake's in the office with Lucy, Cole, and the security guard."

Lucy Turner and Cole Allen were his other detective team, both new to the Twin Falls investigative bureau—both young and smart. He'd lured Lucy away from Oklahoma City's

Detective Bureau, and Cole from the Dallas Cold Case Section.

At thirty, Lucy was attractive with beautiful hazel eyes and glossy auburn hair, if a little too full-bodied for her five-feet-four inch height to be fashionable. She was angry, argumentative, and wore a chip on her shoulder, but she was a talented investigator and worth the effort to smooth out her rough edges. Cole, two years her junior was cocky, afraid of nothing, and gave Lucy the misnomer of "Sweet Thang."

The police captain in Oklahoma had warned him Lucy Turner was a great detective but she wasn't a team player. Matt got the impression the captain had a crush on her. He'd seemed reluctant to let her go, but gave his blessings, alluding to personal reasons she needed to leave the state. The man had been right on both counts. She had great investigative skills and she didn't play well with others.

Before heading back to the office area, Matt toured the warehouse. Narrow rows of shelving rose to the twenty-foot-high ceiling, filled with cartons of eyeglass frames and sunglasses. If the flames had reached that section it would have been an inferno.

He moved on to the charred wreckage of the forklift that sat apart. How the woman escaped death or serious injury had been a miracle.

In the office complex, his two detectives, Blake, and a man in uniform Matt assumed to be the security guard, stood in a circle in the middle of the room.

"Hey, Matt," Blake said. "Tompkins made coffee. Come join us."

The security guard stepped forward and stuck out his hand. "That would be me, Don Tompkins." In his early sixties, Tompkins was a large, broad-shouldered man whose posture and neat, short hair suggested a military background. His firm-jawed face exuded the quiet confidence of someone accustomed to command.

Matt gripped his hand but declined the coffee. He didn't like to get too comfortable at a crime scene. "Have you been here since the explosion?"

Tompkins shook his head. "I went to the hospital to check on Sara. Charles Edwards and I took her home, and I had to bring him back here to get his car."

"What do we know so far?" Matt asked.

Blake picked up his clipboard and tapped it against his leg. "The Fort Hood people confirmed it was a bomb. They found explosive residue on the lift. So it's your case, Matt. I'm outta here. I can still get home in time for dinner."

As Blake left, Matt caught Lucy's gaze. She was lead detective on this one. "Are you up to speed on what happened?"

"Hardly," she said, and set her coffee cup on the waist-high counter nearby with a pugnacious gesture. "We arrived five minutes before you did."

Not for the first time, Matt wondered if he could live with her behavior until she realized he wasn't the enemy. "It was a question, Detective, not an accusation."

He turned his attention back to Tompkins. "Why don't you run down what happened?"

"There's a conference room around the corner. Let's go have a seat. I've been on my feet most of the day." He led the way down the hall and opened the door to a rectangular room with a six-foot conference table and eight chairs. Nothing fancy but functional with a wet-bar near the entrance. Probably served as a break room. The pictures on the wall were advertising flats from Global's TV commercials. When everyone was seated, Tompkins started at the top.

Lucy gave Cole an I'm-lead-I-don't-take-notes glare. He dutifully removed his notebook from his jacket as Tompkins spoke.

"I've told this story about ten times today." He leaned back in the chair and ran through seeing the explosion on the monitors, and finding Sara in the warehouse. "I spent twenty years on the bomb squad in the city. It looked like a bomb to me."

"Did you mention this to anyone when the police interviewed you?" Matt asked.

"Yeah, but fire marshals and police officers are not always receptive to suggestions from security personnel. I spoke to one of the Fort Hood techs I knew. He said they found bomb residue inside the control panel. The perp wired a pressure-sensitive button under the platform. Rigged to explode whenever someone stepped aboard.

Luckily, Sara tossed her handbag on the platform. That saved her life."

"Next question," Matt said. "Sara Bradford is management. What was she doing near a forklift?"

The security guard leaned forward and adopted the pose of instructor. "She always does a walk-through the warehouse before she leaves. She calls it 'management by walking about.' Says you can spot bottlenecks and problems when everything stops moving."

"Is this walkabout common knowledge?" Matt asked.

Tompkins rose and went to the wet bar to fill a cup with coffee. He held up the pot to see if anyone else wanted another cup. They declined. "I can't speak for everyone, but it's certainly no secret."

"Tell me about the security-camera discs. Where are they stored? How could someone walk in and take them without being noticed?"

Tompkins drained his cup and stood. "Why don't we go over to the lobby next door? I'll show you the procedure."

On the way across the skywalk, Matt couldn't help wondering why anyone would want Sara Bradford dead. Could it be connected to her husband's murder? A jealous lover with access to Global? All possibilities.

Tompkins led the small group into the home office complex, then to an impressive lobby. A wide expanse of marble floors led to a bank of elevators on the right and a large water feature in the center of the foyer. Exotic oriental rugs defined the seating areas. Above it all hung an enormous crystal chandelier, like something from Versailles.

The guards' station sat near the entrance surrounded by a marble-topped counter. Tompkins moved past the desk to a small office.

The room measured about twelve by twelve, no outside window. A large one-way mirror looked out over the entrance and lobby. A Xerox machine and two files cabinets set in one corner. Someone's empty lunch sack sat on the desk. Tompkins squeezed the sack into a ball, tossed it in the trashcan, and took a seat at the desk.

Matt leaned against the doorframe. "With all the surveillance cameras you have, can you explain how someone might get inside the distribution center to plant a bomb?"

"It wouldn't be difficult for anyone who worked here. Security personnel only work the day shift. Management can enter any time, day or night. They have keys and a security code to enter the building after hours. The system tracks all entries after the alarms are set."

Tompkins hesitated, as though deciding whether to divulge additional information. "The entry list would be of little help to you right now. Since the announcement of the buyout, management has been coming and going at all hours. I pull the report off the computer every day and file it chronologically. I can give you copies, if you like."

"We'll need those," Matt said. "Is your code reflected on the report?"

"Mine and my partner's."

Lucy took one of the chairs along the wall. "Could anyone other than management have planted the explosives?"

"It would have been pretty easy for hourly personnel working in that area doing maintenance on the machine. It isn't slack security. We don't expect anyone to bomb the place. We look for people who try to steal things. If someone who doesn't work in the area fooled around near the forklifts during work hours, we would have noticed.

"However, if the regular operators or a member of management messed with the lift, we wouldn't have paid much attention.

"My partner and I monitor the cameras during the work day. After the building closes, the motion-detection cameras kick in. We file the discs for three months, then we recycle them. My thoughts are that the bomb was probably planted after the crew left for the day. Those machines are in constant motion most of the time."

Tompkins' brows drew together in a frown. "It would only take a few minutes to plant the bomb. A little longer to wire the platform."

"Did the bomb techs identify the kind of explosive used?" Lucy asked.

Rubbing his chin for a moment, the guard shook his head. "They suspect a plastique explosive, but they'll test it to make sure. Something small, designed to kill, maim, or frighten, not to destroy the building. Unless, of course, you have some nutcase who made it off Internet data and got it wrong."

Matt and Lucy exchanged a glance, and he said, "Let's get back to the missing security data. How could that happen?"

A flicker of hardness, almost bitter humor crossed, Tompkins' face. "I know the discs are important." He shook his head. "They apparently disappeared in all the excitement after the explosion. Only the Thursday and Friday discs are missing. They're kept here in the office." Tompkins pointed to the metal file cabinet in the corner. "This office is locked, but the cabinets aren't."

Matt gazed at him for a long moment. "Convenient for someone. How many people have keys?"

"My partner and I, the maintenance supervisor, as well

as almost everyone on the executive staff. Management is anyone at the director level or above. They have master keys that open most doors, including this office."

A red flush crept up Tompkins' face, probably embarrassed about the lax security. He pulled the after-hour entry list from the file, made copies, and handed one to Matt and one to Lucy.

One name stood out. "Does Sam Pryor work here?"

Tompkins nodded. "He's in charge of MIS, management information systems."

"Anything else we should know about the list?" Matt asked.

"Some of the names on there no longer work here."

"Does that mean ex-employees can enter the building after hours?"

"As far as I know, the codes are active until they're removed from the system. Terminated employees turn in their keycard when they leave, and we would know if an ex-employee entered. His or her code would show up on the report."

"Do you review the overnight information every day?" Matt asked.

"Either me or Ben. My boss in Human Resources also receives a copy. I went over the printout today. No unauthorized personnel codes on Thursday or Friday."

"What is Ben's last name?" Lucy asked.

"Miller, Ben Miller," Tompkins replied.

"How old is he," Lucy asked.

"Twenty-three. Birthdays in March." Tompkins knew what they were after.

Cole wrote the information in his notebook. He would run a background check on both guards.

Matt gave Tompkins a look that said what he thought of

their security system. "It's just a suggestion. But you might tell your boss security measures around here could use some tightening before somebody gets killed."

CHAPTER 7

Twin Falls Police Station

Lucy Turner left Global and followed Matt Foley to the station. She felt drained, upset, angry and friendless.

She'd been out of line with Matt. How will you feel, Luc, when he busts you to patrol duty, she asked herself. It was her own fault, but sometimes she couldn't hide her hostility. The Lord knew she couldn't afford a demotion. Her salary barely covered living expenses now.

The part-time security job she'd started in June, to buy school clothes for her two boys, left her on edge and tired. The long hours sapped her energy and left no time to spend with Charlie and Mack. She shook her head and heaved a long breath. Christmas was coming and she would still need the extra money.

Stopped at a red light, she read the bumper sticker on the car in front her. *Honk if you know someone who is alive only because you can't afford a hit man.* She thought of her ex-husband and gave the horn a long blast.

Cole shot her a dirty look.

Her animosity towards Matt Foley was irrational, she knew, but she resented him for his charmed life, his wealth, his good looks, and his intelligence. Just the sound of his voice grated like an unspoken reprimand.

It wasn't his fault she'd married an abusive heel like Hank Turner and made a mess of her life. But Matt's presence reminded her of the bad choices she'd made.

Leaving Oklahoma had been her chance for a new beginning, but she hadn't anticipated the financial strains and the desperate loneliness of living away from her family.

Whenever Matt asked her a question, it was as if he challenged her competence. Would he have asked if she were a man? Fighting chauvinism had been part of the job since she'd decided to become a cop.

Suck it up, Luc, if you want to keep this position, she told herself. Keep your mouth shut. Do the job.

At the station, she stomped back to her desk and slammed her purse into the bottom drawer, then picked up the phone and called the bomb tech at Fort Hood.

~*~

Matt headed down the hall to the break room. Detective Miles Davis stood at the bulletin board, coffee in hand. Matt tapped his shoulder. "When you finish here, find Hunter, then meet me upstairs in the conference room."

"He's calling the church office to check on their old records," Davis said. "I'll get him. We'll join you in five."

The conference room lay just off the homicide bureau. Matt took the first chair by the entrance and waited. He rubbed the tense muscles at the back of his neck. He'd leave the Global explosion with Lucy and Cole. For now, he had to focus on the Bay Harbor case.

He hated opaque cases. No viable crime scene, no evidence, and few clues. Finding a killer after almost three decades added a dimension he didn't even want to consider. And this one had huge political overtones.

Thanks in part, to Dale McCulloch, and the state-of-the-art CSU facility, Twin Falls solved-cases stats ran over ninety percent. He'd lobbied hard for the crime lab but despite the fact that Twin Falls was an affluent town, the budget office turned him down. When Mary had offered to foot the bill for the extra space and equipment, the city council rolled over.

With an in-house CSU facility, tests took a matter of hours or days instead of weeks or months.

What one of his professors in college had told him proved to be true. Old-fashioned legwork solved crimes, but forensics got the convictions.

This case was different. Past success would mean nothing if they didn't solve this one.

At least the timing on the Pryor case would be good for him. The diversion would absorb his attention. Something to keep him away from home. The emptiness there still closed in on him. Wouldn't be the first night he'd spent on his office sofa, and Rowdy wouldn't mind a change of scenery.

He rose to fill a mug from the conference room coffee bar when Chris Hunter entered. The detective carried Archie, the station mascot, a yellow tabby trying for the *Guinness World Records* book for most obese cat. Hunter, not to be outdone by Archie, stood five-six with a paunch that hung over his belt.

Hunter set the cat on the floor, then pulled out a chair. "You wanted to see us, Chief?" He nodded towards the door. "Miles is behind me. Had to make a pit stop. Probably needed to comb his hair."

Davis strode through the doorway and gave his partner a pointed look as he smoothed his perfectly trimmed hair with both hands. "I heard that."

The two made a good team, despite their different personalities. Laid back and easygoing, Hunter was the opposite of his partner, who was high energy, introspective, and often moody. Somehow, the conflicting personas blended into a cohesive team of investigators.

Matt placed a yellow pad on the table. "Anything new turn up at the crime scene after I left?"

Davis shook his head. "No, but I'm not surprised."

It didn't surprise Matt, either, not with a crime scene that old. "The fact the body was Governor Ferrell's niece hasn't hit the news yet, but it won't be long."

"Don't I know it. We'll be knee deep in reporters." Davis' face scrunched into a frown. "I can't wait."

Hordes of reporters blinding them with flashbulbs and sticking microphones in their faces made a difficult job harder. Matt brought the conversation back to the job at hand. "You guys know your business, but I wouldn't wait for forensics. Check out the old neighborhood, see if anyone remembers anything new about that night. All the reports from the first investigation are in the casebook." He shrugged. "Which I guess is now the murder book. Did you get anything yet from Sam Pryor?"

Davis shook his head. "Overtime on this, Chief?"

"Whatever you need," Matt said. "McCulloch is trying to track down the sleeping bag, but it's probably too early to expect answers." Matt picked up the casebook and stood. "I'll return this later. We'll meet here for a daily update at 0930. The mayor, city council, and my boss will be breathing down my neck until this case is closed."

Back in his office, Matt called the morgue. Lisa Martinez answered.

"Just FYI, Hunter and Davis will be there for the Pryor autopsy when it's scheduled. It has taken on some political importance. Anything yet?"

"No. I do have other cases ahead of that one. Tell Davis I'll schedule the exam for tomorrow morning at eight. Don't let them show up early. All I need are those two underfoot, pressuring me."

"Lisa, they won't come by until you begin the autopsy. You control that. Just let them know when you're ready. I only called to give you a heads-up. The case is going to get a lot of media attention, so you might want to rearrange your priorities."

"Don't tell me how to run my department. I'll call you when I have answers. But not today."

The line went dead.

He stared at the phone in his hand. Unbelievable. He must have said something to set her off. After replaying their conversation in his head, he still couldn't see it. Perhaps he should tell Davis to take her a new broom when he went for the autopsy.

County Morgue

Lisa Martinez slammed the receiver back on the hook. The man made her crazy. Dense was the only word to describe Matt Foley.

Why did she have so much trouble with relationships? First Paul's father, now Matt Foley?

Matt found her attractive. She hadn't imagined the appreciation in his eyes. Too many men had cast that look her way for her to miss it. But for some reason, he avoided her attempts to get close to him. His wife had been dead for two years. He should be over that by now.

Why couldn't she fall for a nice, solid guy like Joe Wilson? He would be a good husband and a great father for Paul.

She shook her head. Who could explain the laws of physical attraction? Maybe it was time to listen to her head. Following her heart hadn't worked out too well. Anyway, it was too soon to be shopping for a husband.

All this introspection made her crave a cigarette. She didn't have time for a smoke break outside. Stupid rules. The people she worked with could hardly complain about secondhand smoke. But there was always the possibility she could set off an inferno with all the lab chemicals.

Lisa pushed through the double metal doors into the autopsy lab. Removing a clipboard from a hook, she scanned the log sheet—a busy week. They had six bodies, besides the one from Bay Harbor. Four from an accident, two from local nursing homes, and Joe Wilson had just called to say another body was on its way.

Tired, she pulled on a Tyvek apron and sleeves over her scrubs, added a hair cover, facemask, protective eyewear, and latex gloves. She gave the gloves an angry snap and made her way to the steel exam table.

Microphone in place, she stated the victim's name and started the cut on one of the women from the nursing home, recording her findings as the autopsy progressed. Most senior care patients died from loneliness and a broken heart, but she couldn't put that on a death certificate. This one suffered from malnutrition. Common in nursing home deaths. Not always because they were mistreated. Mostly, the patients just gave up and stopped eating.

As she finished with the woman, Joe Wilson's big hulk pushed through the swinging doors. She placed her hands on her hips. "You personally delivering bodies these days, Joe?"

His face flushed a dusty pink under his tan. "No. Things are just a little slow, so I decided to come along. You're here kinda late."

"Paul's with his dad." She waved at the chart on the wall. "Good thing I came in."

Joe turned to assist the ambulance driver with the gurney.

"Who is it?" Lisa asked.

Joe handed a copy of his report to a nearby tech. "Robert Cook. All the information is here. He lived out on FM10. Apparently, died of natural causes, but that'll be your call. A neighbor found him."

Joe slid his hands into his pockets with a wistful grin. "You have time for coffee?"

Lisa switched off the microphone and turned away from her table "Sure, Joe, I have time. Give me a minute to wash up."

At the sink, she removed her lab gear and added a generous dollop of anti-bacterial soap, working it over her hands and arms. Joe's profile reflected in the mirror above the sink. She studied his face. Handsome, yes, but he didn't have the animal magnetism of Matt Foley.

Lisa dried her hands and joined him at the morgue entrance.

Joe crossed the break room to the coffee maker in the corner. "We're in luck," Joe called over his shoulder. "Someone made a fresh pot."

He pulled two foam cups from the plastic sleeve. "You still take it with one cream and two sugars?"

She joined him at the counter. "Yeah. It's sweet that you remembered."

He grinned down at her. "I'm a sweet guy."

"And modest, too." She laughed, then lit a cigarette as she took a seat in the booth.

He slid in across from her. "How's Paul doing?"

Lisa smiled. Paul was her favorite subject. "He's good. He's a bright kid, but he likes fishing and baseball way better than school."

"That makes him normal. He's a fisherman?"

"Oh yeah. My dad takes him when he feels like going. Dad has emphysema, so he's not up to fishing very often."

Joe pointed at her cigarette. "Think those could have anything to do with your dad's illness?"

Her brow knitted into a scowl. "Don't you start on me. I get enough of that from Paul."

He held up both hands. "Subject closed. You like to fish?"

Fishing expeditions with her father flashed information from the past. The tranquility of the water, the quiet, cool mornings, eating breakfast burritos filled with sausage, eggs, potatoes, and hot sauce. Good times. "I haven't been since I was a kid, but I loved it."

"I go every weekend I'm off duty." He took the last sip of coffee in the cup. "You and Paul want to join me next time?"

She lowered her gaze and looked up at him through her eyelashes. Then flashed a flirty smile. "Give me a call. I'll bring the burritos." She glanced at her watch. "I need to get back to work."

In the morgue, she picked up the phone and dialed Miles Davis's number. "If you and Hunter can get here in thirty minutes, I'll do the Pryor exam tonight."

"We're on our way," he said.

If Matt wanted a fast turnaround, he could pay his detectives overtime.

By the time she finished setting up, Davis and Hunter were climbing into the paper smocks, booties and masks. They joined her at the table that held the small skeleton. A lab tech had x-rayed the remains earlier. The films hung on a clip above the table.

She switched on the microphone and began. The date

Penny disappeared wasn't necessarily the date she died. Lisa accepted she might never be able to nail that down, but a hands-on examination could help determine the cause of death.

With efficient fingers, she inspected the neck's fragile bones, speaking into the mic as she progressed. The vertebrae leading to the skull's right side were shattered. Most likely the cause of death. The x-rays showed massive head and neck injuries. She detailed her findings into the recording—careful to note the heavy equipment at the gravesite may have caused some of the fractures, though she didn't buy it. With heavy equipment, the damage would have been more extensive and not isolated to one area.

Matt had emailed her a copy of the missing persons report on the Pryor girl and the parents identified the personal effects. Could she rely on their memory after such a span of time? Probably. She would remember every detail if something happened to Paul.

Lisa laid the small skull back in place. A vision of her son's dimpled smile nudged its way into her mind. She missed him already. She couldn't bear the thought of something like this happening to Paul. His mental image reminded her that this little girl had also been cherished by her parents.

Lisa shivered. At times like these, she wished she'd chosen another field. Pediatrics maybe. Healing had to be more rewarding than this.

She turned to the two detectives. "You guys have what you need?"

Davis still had his notebook out. "Any idea what caused the blow to the head?"

She shrugged. "Something big."

"How big?" he asked.

She leaned back against the table. "Hard to say without the tissue. Smaller than a tree, bigger than a fist."

Hunter shook his head. "Or as it's known in our profession, the unidentified blunt object."

"Great," Davis said. "That narrows it down to a few million possibilities."

City Manager's Office

Douglas Anderson sat at his desk, scanning the file labeled *Matthew Foley*. City Councilman Terrance Randall Hall was on his way to discuss a case under investigation.

The pompous little man made Doug's blood boil, but Hall had political connections, so Doug had to tread softly. But then, Matt Foley also had a few political heavyweights in his corner.

He flicked the file open to review the sheets that comprised Foley's personnel file. Already familiar with most of it, he wanted to refresh his memory in case Hall tried to con him.

The top sheet reflected Matt's military career. Six years in the U.S. Army 75th Brigade, a Ranger special mission unit sharpshooter. He spent his last two years of service in Afghanistan in the second Gulf War. After leaving the Army, he attended Texas A&M at Kileen, graduating in the top ten percent with a degree in Criminal Justice. Pursued by large police departments across the country, Matt applied for the Twin Falls position when the old chief retired. Doug snapped him up. One of his better personnel decisions.

Doug closed the file, then tapped it with his index finger. There was more to Matt Foley than his file reflected. Most of Doug's information came from trusted sources, stories repeated often enough to have the ring of truth.

Matt lost both parents when he was nine years old, after a drug dealer picked the wrong house. Raised by an abusive, alcoholic uncle, he'd joined the Army as soon as he turned eighteen.

After college, he met the daughter of the richest man in Texas at a political rally. They married a year later. Rumor had it Matt could become the next U.S. Senator. All he had to do was say the word.

Unlike Hall, who would chew his right arm off for a shot at the Senate, Matt didn't want it. He was a good cop. No, better than good. Matt Foley was a great cop. It was his passion.

The irony reminded him of a quote from Scottish author George MacDonald. "It is not in the nature of politics that the best men should be elected. The best men do not want to govern their fellow men."

The office door opened and his secretary stepped in. "Councilman Hall is here, Doug."

"Show him in, please."

Terrence Hall strode into the room and sat in a chair in front of Doug's desk. At five feet four, Hall wore his Napoleon complex like a badge of honor. Dark brown hair reached his collar, blow-dried with every strand in place. His expensive suit, navy with a tiny gray stripe, finished the look of a man with an eye on the mayor's office.

Hall settled himself into the chair for what Doug hoped would be a short visit.

"You heard about the governor's niece?" Hall asked.

Doug's expression didn't change. "Matt keeps me informed."

The city councilman's left brow lifted, probably a looked

he practiced before a mirror. "Do you think he can handle such a high-profile case?"

Doug smiled, but not because he thought it was funny. "He's never given me any reason to think otherwise, Terry. His ratio of solved cases is higher than any police department in the state."

"Like I said, he's never handled anything like this."

"Neither have you, Terry."

Hall stood and walked to the door like an actor delivering his exit line. "Just don't say I didn't warn you, Doug. You put too much faith in Foley."

CHAPTER 8

Sara Bradford's Home

Sara awoke to the clock's buzzer a little after daylight and shut it off on the second try. She lay back against the pillows and tugged the comforter up under her chin. Through half-drawn drapes, dawn's slim pink fingers reached into the slate-gray sky as day gently pushed back the night.

With a groan, she gave the pillow a punch, then pulled the cover over her head. "Arrrrrgh."

As the doctor predicted, she suffered no serious after effects from the accident. A few bruises and some sore muscles. But that didn't stop the mental horrors of yesterday from coming alive. She still refused to accept the reality of the explosion, the terror as the detonation sent her sailing. By God's mercy, she'd hit the plastic sheeting rather than the cement-block wall.

It seemed so senseless. Who would plant a bomb? And more important, why?

No time or inclination for a pity party now. Life had never been fair. Why should it start with her?

Giving the pillow another punch, she heaved a deep breath, flung the covers aside, and shuffled her stiff muscles across the thick carpet to the bathroom. She stood in the shower, letting the hot spray pulse against her face. The pounding water couldn't erase the humiliation in Roger's office yesterday. He'd brushed aside her years of service like flicking lint from his jacket.

It wasn't just the uncertainty of her job, the explosion,

or even that after four years the police still considered her a suspect in Josh's death. Her life had taken a downward spiral she couldn't control. She didn't believe in luck, good or bad. But there was no denying a dark cloud had taken residence over her head. The urge to kick something overwhelmed her. Almost as soon as the thought occurred, she dismissed it. That wouldn't help. She grabbed a towel from the rack and dried off with more vigor than the task required.

Roger would probably find some way to blame her for what happened at Global. She could see the headline DISGRUNTLED EMPLOYEE BOMBS WAREHOUSE.

She grinned at the irony. At least he couldn't fire her. He'd already taken away her job.

A wisp of hair fell across her eyes and she pushed it away. From the closet, she selected a sweater and tartan slacks, appropriate for ministry visits. Saturday morning's ritual began by joining bus workers headed out to the poorer parts of town, knocking on doors to see if the children wanted to come to church on Sunday morning. The rewards were many, but the best part was that many of these youngsters became Christians because of the church's outreach.

After she finished dressing, she made up her bed. A ritual instilled by her mother. She could still hear her voice. "No matter how bad you feel, you need to maintain order in your life. It helps you stay grounded."

The aroma of fresh-baked bread wafted up the stairwell, teasing her nose and stirring her appetite. She followed the smell downstairs and out the door that led onto the deck. Aunt Maddie greeted her with a smile. Breakfast outside had become a ritual whenever the weather permitted.

"This looks wonderful." Sara waved a hand at the table

display of crusty loaves of apricot bread and cream cheese.

"I waited for you." Maddie filled her cup from the teapot. "Come help me do justice to all these calories."

Maddie Jamison's petite figure appeared fragile, but fragile she wasn't. As the star pitcher on her college softball team, she had a cabinet filled with trophies to prove it.

Sara dropped into a chair across from her aunt. "I'm not sure this is representative of the five major food groups, but two out of five isn't bad."

Maddie laughed. "Beatrice has been on a baking spree. I'm certainly not complaining." Beatrice and her husband, Pete, took care of the house and grounds.

"Nor am I." Sara leaned back in the chair gazing out over the garden. Autumn hadn't yet dimmed its color. Dew-kissed roses of brilliant red and gold, filled the morning air with their sweetness. Her reverie broke when Maddie asked, "Are you going out? It's a little early for the bus meeting, isn't it?"

"I want to get an early start. I'd like to visit Lily and Sam when I'm finished, see if there's anything I can do for them."

"I'm glad you're going. They always love to see you. I'm sure they'll appreciate it, especially now."

She reached across the table to touch Maddie's hand. "What are your plans today?"

"Don't worry about me. I have some textbooks to look over for the school board. That'll keep me busy most of the morning. Speaking of which, I'd better get started if I'm to return the books by Monday."

Sara's thoughts flashed back to her job status. After she'd cooled down, she realized Roger hadn't terminated her. At least not yet. If he'd fired her, security would have followed her to her desk, then escorted her out of the building. She'd have to tell Maddie soon. But not until she had more information.

With a last sip of tea, Sara followed her aunt inside. Maddie turned into the library and sat at her electronic reader, a first cousin to the microfiche scanner technology that made even the smallest print easy for her to read.

"See you later," Sara called, then hurried to her car.

~*~

Church visitations failed to lift her spirits as they usually did. Mixed emotions about Penny had heightened her concern for two of her favorite bus children. Danny and Poppy Morgan had missed church last Sunday, and they weren't at home when she stopped by today. The trailer-park manager said the family had moved without leaving a forwarding address.

That in itself wasn't unusual. Bus kids were often transient, but that didn't stop her from worrying. Perhaps they'd moved to another mobile home park. She kept her eyes open, hoping to see them, but no luck. News of Penny's death had spooked her. Predators lurked everywhere.

No child was safe in today's crazy world.

At five o'clock, she arrived home after a short visit with the Pryors. Only time could heal their wounds but she'd offered what consolation she could. At least they now had closure.

"You'd better hurry, dear. Dinner starts at seven o'clock," Maddie called as Sara entered the foyer.

No! That couldn't be tonight. With all that happened, she'd forgotten about the banquet, the gala honoring the town's restoration. "I'm headed to the shower right now."

"Did you see Sam and Lily?"

"Yes, I just left there."

"How are they doing?"

Sara stopped at the bottom step. "They're coping, but it's hard. I'm sure it's almost as bad as when Penny first vanished. I think they'd held out hope she was alive somewhere."

Sara hurried upstairs, wanting nothing more than to fall into bed, but that wouldn't happen. If she begged off, Maddie would ask questions. They'd bought tickets months ago, and invited guests.

After her shower, Sara hurried to her closet to consider her dress choices for the evening. She soon realized the dinner's black and white theme left her only two options. After a moment, she selected a black crepe evening dress with a Grecian neckline that would be comfortable. When finished with her hair and makeup, she slipped into the dress and went downstairs to see if Maddie needed help.

Maddie smiled when Sara entered her room. "Well, am I sufficiently coordinated? Shoes matched, no lipstick smears or mascara smudges?"

"Everything's fine. You look lovely."

Weeks ago, Sara offered Don Tompkins a ticket to the banquet and he accepted. It wasn't exactly a blind date for Maddie. But she might like him. Her aunt was still an attractive woman. Heaven knew after a disastrous marriage, Maddie deserved a break. Neither Sara nor her aunt had made stellar choices for husbands.

"Is Jeffery Hayden your escort tonight?" Maddie's question brought Sara back into the moment.

Sara laughed. "Yes, he invited himself a month ago while we were having lunch."

Maddie turned to face her. "Well, he's certainly one of the most attractive young men I've seen. Do you see this relationship going anywhere?"

"Handsome, yes, but he's about as deep as a salad plate." Sara sat on the edge of the dressing table and shook her head. "We have too little in common. Jeff has no opinions about anything. That's dull. You know me, I have opinions about everything."

Maddie squeezed her hand. "That you do. Your passion is one of the things I love most about you."

Maddie's question reverberated through Sara's mind. She'd promised herself never to make another bad marriage—once in a lifetime was quite enough.

CHAPTER 9

Twin Falls Country Club

Country club manager, Shannon Connelly, eased behind the long bar and ran a finger along the polished mahogany grain. Brass fixtures gleamed in the subdued lighting. She mentally ticked off a checklist of stock under the counter and held several of the stemware to the light. No spots, as it should be. After completing the bar inspection, she moved on to the dining room.

Tonight's black-and-white theme carried throughout, from crisp, white linen tablecloths to the black-striped dining room chairs. Fan-folded napkins, fastened with bright, silver rings, matched the pattern on the chairs. White bone china gleamed next to sparkling Waterford crystal. A centerpiece of white roses sat on each table, blending seamlessly into the stark background.

Guests arriving at the entrance, drew Shannon's attention. Down the main hallway, she spotted Matt Foley, gazing into the trophy case. A man's man if ever she'd met one. He wheeled and maneuvered his tall frame through the crowd in her direction, with the easy grace of an athlete, smooth and confident. Shannon stood at the end of the bar and propped an elbow against the smooth surface. "You look sharper than my mother-in-law's tongue, Matt. I love a man in a tuxedo. May I buy you a drink?"

"Thank you, ma'am, and yes, you may. I'll wait here until the crowd at the dining room entrance thins a bit."

Matt took a seat, and Shannon skirted behind the bar.

"What'll it be?"

He pointed to a green bottle. "Water on the rocks, with lime."

Shannon grinned, filled a glass with ice and set both on a napkin. "I shouldn't even let you sit at my bar, Matthew Foley. You're an embarrassment to the police chiefs of America. No self-respecting cop drinks water when he's off duty." She teased him, but she knew he had an aversion to alcohol, because of his uncle's addiction to the fruit of the vine.

Matt raised the glass in a mock toast. "To each his own."

Pulling a cloth from under the counter, Shannon wiped the surface. "Date tonight? I only ask because I consider myself your best girl."

Matt laughed and shook his head. "No date. And you would be my best girl if it weren't for that pesky husband of yours."

She fluttered her eyelashes. "That offer is almost too tempting to turn down. Let me think about this for a moment. I trade a short, balding, loveable fuzzball like my Colin for a rich, good-looking cop. Sounds like a good swap." She shook her head. "But it took me years to train my main man. I have the feeling you wouldn't be as easy to manage."

Matt stared into his glass for a moment, and then shifted his gaze towards the hallway. "Tell me about the trophy in the display."

Shannon leaned across the bar. "I'm surprised you never noticed it before."

He gave a slight shrug. "I don't have occasion to spend a lot of time standing in the hallway. When the crowd stalled tonight, I saw Mary's picture."

Shannon inhaled a deep breath. "Two years ago, the day

Mary died, Sara Bradford and Dina Lambert played for the club singles tennis championship. Sara came here that morning after Mary passed away. I wish you could have seen the match. It was something to behold."

A small smile tugged at the corner of Matt's lips. "Mary used to come home after her doubles match with Sara, giggling like a school girl. They apparently annoyed Dina and her sister with their joking around. I don't think Mary and Sara ever won a match. They enjoyed irritating Dina as much as playing tennis."

Shannon refilled his glass. "Oh, yes. Dina takes her tennis seriously, and the girl has a mean streak a mile wide. I don't know if Mary mentioned it to you, but Dina spread some ugly gossip at the club, that..." She hesitated. "I'm not sure if I should say this or not."

He raised an eyebrow. "Since when have you been afraid to tell me anything?"

She laughed. "Since never. Dina told everyone that you married Mary for her money."

The muscles in Matt's jaw clenched but he didn't reply.

The buzz of conversation in the room lowered, and Shannon's eyes riveted to the club doorway. "Speak of the devil." Dina and Senator Lambert stood at the entrance. Dina paused on the top step until all eyes turned her way. Her white, beaded gown emphasized every well-proportioned curve, and silver-blonde curls floated above deeply tanned shoulders.

Shannon leaned in and whispered, "Our Dina certainly knows how to make an entrance, doesn't she? She always was the theatrical type, even in high school."

Matt glanced at Shannon, a question in his eyes. "I didn't know you went to school with Dina Lambert. I take it she wasn't your best buddy."

"You might say that. She, Sara, and I went through school together. We were in the same grade. Dina was the cheerleader, Sara the brain with a photographic memory, and I was the class clown."

A laugh burst from Matt's throat, almost spewing his drink. "I would never have guessed you were the class clown. What, in particular didn't you like about Dina, other than her vicious tongue?"

Shannon gave the bar another swipe. "She's too self-absorbed. Dina's favorite subject is Dina. The only positive thing I can say about her is she's quite a talented tennis player. Could probably have gone professional if she'd stayed with it. Apparently, it was easier to marry Senator Lambert. Instant social success." Shannon turned her gaze back to Matt. "I suppose that sounds a bit catty."

Matt set his glass on the napkin and held his thumb and forefinger a slight distance apart. "Just a tad."

Colin Connelly stepped up behind Matt and slapped him on the back, then leaned in to place a kiss on Shannon's cheek. "You hittin' on my wife?"

Matt chuckled. "Actually, she's hitting on me."

"That I can believe." Colin slid onto the barstool next to Matt.

"Tell me about the game," Matt said.

"What game?" Colin asked.

Shannon reached across and straightened his bow tie. "When Sara played Dina for the club singles championship."

One of the bartenders took over behind the bar, and Shannon moved to the empty barstool on the other side of Matt. "Before the tournament started, people were betting on the match, with Dina a heavy favorite, of course. But there was something different about Sara that day—"

"I'll say there was," Colin said.

Shannon silenced him with an I'm-telling-this-story glance. "Sara's first two serves were aces. She took over the court like a pro and never let up. I don't think Dina knew what hit her. Sara won the first set, six-two.

"Sara began to tire in the second set, and Dina won seven-six. The third set started and Sara took over again and took the set six-zero. The stands erupted with cheers, a no-no at tennis tournaments. But not many people liked Dina."

Colin took over the tale. "When they presented the cup to Sara, she dedicated it to Mary, telling the crowd she had passed away that morning." His voice lowered. "It's been in the club trophy case ever since."

Shannon patted Matt's shoulder and gave Colin a buzz on the cheek. She called over her shoulder as she walked away. "I've got to go play hostess. You guys stay out of trouble."

Dredging up the memory brought a lump to Shannon's throat. Sara had confided later, "I planned to forfeit the match, but after Mary's death, I was filled with such an enormous mixture of anger and sorrow. I wanted somehow to honor her. Winning the championship for her seemed fitting. And, in a very uncharitable way, I wanted to get back at Dina for every unkind word she ever said to Mary—hit Dina where it hurt most, in her pride. Even more than that, I wanted to win for Mary. With God's help, I did it. I knew Mary would be watching."

~*~

Mary had never told Matt about Dina's rude remarks, but that was like her. She didn't dwell on negatives. The day she died had been the worst day of his life. He'd held Mary's hand as she drew her last breath. The scene squeezed his heart until he couldn't breathe. Couldn't think about that now. The memory was still too raw.

As the evening wore on, he spotted Sara Bradford leaving her table and he excused himself from his table companions. He strode into the aisle to intercept her.

With a cop's eye for detail, he noted the slender form. She didn't look like someone who had escaped death barely twenty-four hours ago. Dark hair swept up emphasized her classic bone structure and the olive tones of her skin. He had serious reservations about her character, but had to admit she was the most attractive woman in the room.

As he drew near, she glanced up and her spine stiffened like a cat facing a pit bull.

"Sara, may I speak to you for a moment?"

She stopped, her gaze hard. "Is that an official request, Chief Foley?"

Heat bubbled just under the surface, despite his effort to suppress it. "No, but I can make it one. I'd hoped not to have to use handcuffs."

She had the grace to blush, and her tone lost its edge. "That won't be necessary. I returned your call Friday, but you had already gone for the day."

The aisle became crowded, and he guided her to a nearby alcove. "I'd like some of your time tomorrow, around one-thirty at the station, if that's convenient. I wouldn't ask you to come on Sunday, but it's important."

She consented with a reluctant nod. "Sunday will be fine."

Matt nodded. "Great, I'll see you then."

Later, as he left the country club, Matt stopped once more at the lobby display. In the enclosed case, beside the trophy and Mary's picture, sat a framed poem, written by Sara Bradford. His throat constricted as he read the words.

Mary Stanton Foley

Mary, a name known over the world,
A name given to many girls.
Name of the mother of the Savior of all.
And a repentant sinner, Magdalene so called.

The name of a wife, cherished and dear,
A friend and confidante over the years.
Someone to count on when things went wrong,
Hands that could comfort, firm and strong.

A daughter, a sister, and friend as well,
Her death brought sorrow words cannot tell.
Mary, a name as soft as an angel's kiss.
I wonder if you knew how much you'd be missed.

Matt punched his hands into his pockets and turned away. Was it possible the woman who penned those words could have killed her husband in cold-blood?

CHAPTER 10

Twin Falls Police Station

Sara pulled into the visitors parking lot a little before one-thirty, and turned into the space nearest the door. She blew out a heavy breath, glad she'd finished the bus route. The job had its rewards, but it could be tiring. The emptiness in her stomach didn't help. There'd been no time to grab a bite at a drive-through before her appointment with Matt.

Nerves tightened like violin strings over her meeting. Matt could at least have given her a hint as to the topic. Questions about the explosion? Perhaps news on Josh's murder? Could they have found the hit-and-run driver after all this time?

Truth to tell, she had her own agenda.

She exited the car and walked towards the station entrance. Halfway to the double doors, the sprinklers snapped on. Despite a sprint the rest of the way, by the time she reached the lobby, she looked like a hurricane refugee.

Inside the station, Sara strode up to the desk, shoes squishing with each step. "I have an appointment with Chief Foley."

The sergeant, safely ensconced behind bulletproof glass, tried to hide a grin. "Sorry about that sprinkler, ma'am. It must have short-circuited in the thunderstorm Friday. It's been popping off and on for no apparent reason all day. Our engineer is on his way to fix it. Have a seat and I'll tell the chief you're here."

Last night had been her first conversation with Matt

Foley since Mary's death. Memories of the night her husband died came rushing back.

On that painful evening, Sara and Maddie sat in the library. Josh had called to say he'd be home for dinner. When he hadn't arrived by seven o'clock, and she couldn't reach him on his cell phone, she and Maddie dined alone. Just another broken promise.

Later that evening, the doorbell chimed. Thinking Josh forgot his key, she opened the door and stepped back, surprised to find Matt Foley's large form filling the entrance. His SUV and a black-and-white squad car sat in the circular drive.

"Hi, Matt. What brings you out? Is Mary all right?"

"She's fine. This isn't about Mary. Is there someplace we can talk?"

She moved aside for him to enter. "Sure. Maddie and I were just having tea in the library."

He radiated tension, and a nervous flutter swam through her stomach. She led him down the hallway to the library and offered a chair.

He remained standing, turning his hat in his hands.

Muscles in her throat tightened. "What's wrong, Matt?"

"There's no easy way to say this...there was an accident on Highway 10 tonight. Josh was ...killed. I'm sorry."

Maddie gasped, and her hand flew to her chest. She rose and placed an arm around Sara's waist.

Sara's pulse accelerated as though an invisible hand closed around her heart and squeezed. Blessed numbness forced its way through her body, and her knees became too weak to bear her weight. The room swam and faded. She slid into the chair and lowered her head. This couldn't be true. It couldn't be. She'd spoken to him less than two hours ago. "A-Are you certain it was Josh?"

Matt nodded, and deep lines formed around his mouth. "I'm afraid so. We found his wallet. It was his car, and I made the identification. I'm sorry..."

To no one in particular, she said, "I spoke to him earlier this afternoon. He said he would be home..." Waves of guilt rolled over her, as she remembered the unkind thoughts when he'd failed to show for dinner.

Matt watched her, his face immobile. "Did he say what he was doing out in the country?"

"He had taken a deposition from a man about an upcoming trial, some conflict with a land title." Her voice sounded flat in her ears.

"Did he mention the man's name?"

Sara thought for a moment, then replied. "No. He would have had no reason to tell me."

"Did he tell you the route he would take home?"

She inhaled deeply, trying to concentrate on the question, and why it mattered. "No...why would he?"

He didn't answer, but asked another question. "Were you home all evening?"

"Yes, I got home about six o'clock."

He studied her face with hard eyes. "What time did you leave the office?"

She placed a cold hand to her brow, confused by his demeanor. "I left early, around three. I did some shopping and stopped for gas."

"Is your car in the garage?"

"Yes."

"May we take a look at it? Are there any other vehicles on the premises?"

"No...yes." Her mind whirled. "I mean, yes, there's another car here. Pete, our gardener, has a truck. Of course, you can look at them. I don't understand. You said he was killed in an accident. What's going on, Matt?"

"It was a hit-and-run accident. He was changing a tire when another car struck him and kept going."

Sara sat suspended in time. "Dear God," slipped out in a whisper.

Maddie stood to every inch of her five-foot stature, and the frost in her voice brooked no argument. "Matthew Foley, I believe Sara has had enough of your questions for now. She's distraught. If you need additional information, I suggest you call at another time when she's better able to assist you."

"Yes, ma'am," Matt said, and left soon after. Not before, Pete later told her, Matt inspected both vehicles, and checked her gas tank level.

After Matt left, Sara folded into the chair, buried in a sorrow so deep she thought it would crush her.

~*~

Footsteps echoed down the hallway and jerked Sara back to the present. Matt stood in front of her. "Looks like you ran afoul of our deranged sprinkler system."

She tried to smooth her slacks. "After being drenched twice in recent days, I'm beginning to think all sprinklers are deranged." She was determined to remain poised, despite her disheveled appearance. "Actually, this is the latest fashion trend. It's called the wet look."

He laughed and motioned for her to follow him. "I'd say you nailed it."

When they reached his office, Matt held the door open and allowed Sara to enter first. She stepped inside, uncomfortably aware of her appearance and the *squish* her shoes made.

Matt pointed her to a chair in front of his desk and stepped into the bathroom. He returned and tossed her a white towel. She caught it and began to wipe the water from her hair.

Self-conscious under his scrutiny, she asked, "Do you have another towel you can spare? That might help absorb some of the water from my clothes."

He returned to the bathroom and tossed her another one. "We might be able to find you something dry in one of the lockers."

She shook her head. "This will work until I get home. Before we begin, I need to ask a favor. If you can't help me, that will be okay, but I thought I'd ask. The worst you can say is no."

"Don't put words in my mouth until I've heard the request."

Words tumbled out as she explained about Danny and Poppy. "The kids lived in Arcadia Trailer Park. You know where that is?"

He nodded. "Over on the east side. One of our biggest trouble spots."

"That's the one," Sara said. "The kids' father is in prison. Their mother, Diane Morgan, has been unemployed most of the time since he went to jail. She's overwhelmed and struggling to pay the rent—even on the slum-hole trailer they lived in. The children missed church last Sunday. I stopped by today and the park manager told me they'd moved and didn't leave a forwarding address. I'm concerned about them."

"Are they related to Grady Morgan?"

"He's their father. You know him?"

Matt wrote the names on a notepad on his desk. "Yes, unfortunately. Do you think they're in physical danger? Is the mother into drugs?"

"I have no reason to think anyone would intentionally harm them. I only met the mother twice. She didn't act like a druggie, just dispirited. The kids loved going to church. I'm frightened they may be hungry and homeless."

His brow wrinkled and he wore an I'd-rather-not-be-bothered look on his face. "I can't make it a priority, but I'll see what I can find out."

Sara leaned forward. "Thanks. Now, why did you want to see me?"

His chair made a tiny squeak when he leaned back. "We discovered a child's body at Bay Harbor Thursday, and we're as certain as we can be, without further testing, that it's Penny Pryor."

She nodded. "Lily Pryor called me. Is that what you wanted to see me about?"

He looked up from his notes. "Why did she call you?"

"Penny was my best friend. Lily and Sam have never recovered from Penny's disappearance, especially Lily. Whoever took Penny destroyed more than that little girl. Lily has never gotten past it. We've become very close." Sara expelled a deep breath. "I don't understand what this has to do with me."

"Probably nothing. The Pryors identified the ring and clothing. However, the old case file listed your name. The beat cop interviewed you that night with your parents. I wondered if you could still remember anything that might be helpful. I understand it's asking a lot after such a long time and you were very young."

She shivered. "Some things you want to forget but can't. That's what a photographic memory does for you. The evening Penny disappeared is etched into my mind. It still haunts me."

"Tell me what you recall." He took a tape recorder from the center drawer and placed it on the desktop. "Do you mind?"

She shook her head.

Matt rewound the tape and pushed record, gave the date, their names and asked again if she agreed to the recording.

Leaning back in the chair, her eyes focused on a Western painting that hung on the wall behind Matt's head. It was a famous canvas of Native American buffalo hunt, but she couldn't remember the artist's name.

"We lived across the street from Penny. It was a holiday weekend—Memorial Day. Most of the families in our neighborhood were gone. Penny's parents planned a camping trip to the lake. It started to get dark, and her dad hadn't arrived home. Penny and I were playing with her new puppy in their back yard. She'd asked me to keep the puppy while they were away. My mother called me in for dinner, and I told Penny I'd come back after I'd eaten. That's the last time I saw her."

"You never picked up the dog?"

"I came out after dinner, but I didn't see Penny anywhere. I knocked on her door, and Lily said she was outside playing. I hung around for a minute or two, calling Penny's name. Then my mother made me come inside. The streets were well lit, but she didn't want me out after dark. Mom assured me Penny would bring her puppy over before they left. I waited, but Penny never showed up. I figured she decided to take her dog along."

She glanced down at her hands, the memory still vivid. "Some time later, Lily came over, looking for Penny. When she realized Penny wasn't with me, everyone became concerned and started a search. Eventually, the police arrived. They found the little dog, but no sign of Penny. I'm sure your records show the rest."

Matt rubbed his forefinger across his lower lip. "When you went outside after dinner, did you notice anything unusual—out of the ordinary?"

"Not really. As I said, the neighborhood was almost deserted."

"You said *almost.* Do you remember which families didn't go away for the holiday?"

"My family and Penny's parents were at home, of course. There were probably a few others on the street that didn't go out of town." Her fingers tightened on the chair arm, thoughts swirling. "I remember one family packing to leave. I saw a man place a sleeping bag in his truck. I thought at the time it was Penny's dad, but I later learned Sam didn't arrive until after the search for Penny began, and her parents didn't own a van."

A note of excitement entered Matt's voice. "Do you recall the color of the sleeping bag?"

She considered the question for a moment. "I can't be certain, but it reminded me of a shirt my grandfather used to wear when he went hunting. Red plaid, I think."

Matt leaned forward in his chair. "Can you remember what kind of truck, or the color? It could be very important."

"It wasn't a pickup; it was enclosed with a door in the side. I think it's called a panel truck. It was white with writing on the side."

"Do you remember what the writing said?"

She massaged her temples with her fingertips, trying to peer into the past. "No, I'm sorry. I was looking for Penny, and it didn't register. Back then, I was just learning to read."

"Was this before dinner or after?"

"After," she said.

"Did you recognize the man? Could it have been Sam Pryor?"

She shrugged. "I can't be certain. Something about him seemed familiar...but I just can't put my finger on it."

"Can you recall which house?"

"The van was parked on the same side of the street Penny lived on, just past Sam and Lily's driveway. Not in the driveway. Just past it," she said. "That's why I thought it was Sam. I'm sorry I can't be any more specific. I didn't pay close attention—I didn't know it would be important."

He closed the folder on his desk and smiled. "You did well. One more question, and then I'm through. When everyone was looking for Penny, was the truck still there?"

She shook her head again. "No, it had already gone. I didn't see it when the search began."

Matt leaned back in his chair with another squeak. "Apparently, you never mentioned the truck or sleeping bag when you spoke to the police. If you did, the cop didn't make a note of it."

He still didn't trust her. Was she being paranoid? His suspicions awakened her insecurities, even guilt when she had nothing to feel guilty about. How dumb was that?

Dredging up old memories exhausted her more than she would have imagined. She handed Matt the towels and shrugged. "Give me a break, Matt. I had just turned six and they didn't ask me a lot of questions."

He hiked one shoulder and let it drop. "Did you know Penny's uncle is Governor Brandt Ferrell?"

Sara nodded. "I met Brandt before Penny vanished. Afterwards, he and Lily's parents came by almost daily for months. I believe Brandt was just starting law school then.

I had a terrible crush on him."

She rose from the chair, and when she reached the door, she turned. "You still think I murdered Josh, don't you?"

"As an investigator, I don't know. Without the car, there's not enough evidence for me to think anything." His brow wrinkled and he blew out a heavy breath. "As a private citizen, yes, I believe you used your husband's considerable resources to arrange for his murder. Not necessarily a hit-and-run. That was probably just a lucky break."

That stung. She squared her shoulders, and her jaw tightened. "Mary always thought you were so smart. Why do you think I killed him? And if you believe I did it, why haven't you arrested me?"

His face flushed, and he glared across the space between them. "I must have two things before I can hand a case over to the prosecutor. First is intent. Second, I must place the suspect at the scene of the crime.

"In homicide investigations, there is something we call SMR motives: sex, money and revenge. If the victim was married we want to know if he or she was involved in an extra-marital affair, and if their partner knew about it. Who stood to inherit the victim's estate?"

He leaned against the desk and crossed his arms. "Statistically speaking, you are the most likely suspect. Friends or relatives commit most murders. You had motive; he was cheating on you. You inherited everything, including a hefty life insurance policy. Both are motives. I haven't arrested you because we can't place you at the scene of the crime. Yet."

She looked directly into his eyes. "Let me be equally honest with you. Josh cheated on me for the last five years of our marriage. Why would I wait so long? Yes, he left me well off, but he would have been worth more to me alive than dead. His life insurance only equaled ten years of his salary."

Matt shook his head. "That won't wash, Sara. If Josh planned to leave you for another woman, you would have lost him and his income."

"Josh played the field. He didn't have a mistress. So I'm guessing you never found such a woman."

He shrugged. "No, but that doesn't mean she didn't exist."

"Did you consider that one of the women in his life might have killed him?"

"Investigating is what I do for a living, Sara. Of course, we checked everyone your husband knew, men and women. They either had an alibi or no motive."

"I didn't murder Josh. Perhaps I was no longer in love with him because he'd lost my respect. But I had loved Josh most of my life, and I'd never have harmed him."

How could she make him understand? "Sometimes, Matt, the statistics are wrong."

Sara met his accusing gaze and realized she hadn't changed his opinion in the least.

Deputy Dawg at his most obtuse.

~*~

Matt stood at the window and watched Sara Bradford drive away. Either she told the truth, or she was an Oscar-caliber actress.

One could never be sure about murderers, though. Ted Bundy had worked a Crisis Hotline while killing dozens of young women in the Northwest.

CHAPTER 11

Twin Falls Police Station

The encounter with Sara still on his mind, Matt returned to his desk. Without knocking, District Attorney Gabriel Morrison strode into the office. He pulled a chair close, placed his feet on the desk corner, and ran both hands over thinning hair, smoothing it down against his perfectly proportioned skull.

"Don't mind me, Gabe. Make yourself comfortable."

Dressed in khaki slacks, a green polo shirt, and golf shoes, the DA flashed a grin. "Thanks, I just did. Who's the wet dish that just left your office? Water boarding one of your new interrogation techniques?"

Matt chuckled. "Sara Bradford, and no, not water boarding. Our sprinkler system attacked her on the way in. The staff has named the control panel Hal. They think it's trying to take over the station."

Gabe's right eyebrow lifted. "Hal?"

"2001 a Space Odyssey."

The light bulb when on behind Gabe's eyes. "Oh, yeah. You need to get that thing fixed."

"We're working on it."

"Guess who I received a phone call from an hour ago?"

"My first guess would be Governor Ferrell."

Gabe's gray eyebrows raised a fraction. "Good guess. Thanks for leaving me the email yesterday. As you can imagine, the governor has a stake in the Bay Harbor case. What do you know so far?"

"Not a lot. The child vanished long before Ferrell became governor. We'll have to go back to the beginning and work our way forward."

"My assistant says CBS and FOX are already camped out in the courthouse lobby. The others will, no doubt, arrive before the day ends."

The DA removed his feet from the desk, and sat upright. "What are the odds on solving a case this old?"

"Pretty slim. The timeframe certainly makes it more difficult, but we have a few leads."

"Such as?"

"The body was buried in a custom made sleeping bag. We have Sara Bradford, an eyewitness, who saw someone load a bag like the one from the gravesite, into a truck the evening the girl disappeared. Sara was very young at the time, but the information she gave squares with what we know. The truck was apparently a commercial vehicle. It had lettering on the side. I've put Hunter and Davis in charge of the case."

Gabe's brow wrinkled. "Hunter and Davis?"

Matt nodded. "Don't know if you've met them. They're the best I have, maybe the best in the state. However, you need to bear in mind, there's a possibility the killer or killers may have died or left the area. Twenty-five years is a long time."

"Or," the district attorney said, "It was some vagrant passing through. In which case, you'll never find him."

"I don't think it was an outsider. A stranger wouldn't know about the retreat grounds. Only a local would recognize the location as a great place to hide a body."

"It could've been dumb luck."

Matt shook his head. "The fact it was a commercial

vehicle lessens the odds the killer was an out-of-towner."

Gabe slapped his hands on his knees, a signal the interview had ended. "If you're as good as your reputation, you'll find this guy." He arched an eyebrow. "Are you as good as they say?"

"Don't know."

"You don't know if you're good?"

"Don't know who 'they' are. I just like to take bad people off the streets to protect the citizens. But don't get your hopes up. This is a long shot."

"Keep me informed when you have anything new. We'll need to make an official statement soon. I'd like you to be there when I talk to the press."

Matt nodded. "No problem. I'd prefer to wait until we have something concrete. Nothing worse than giving reporters daily updates when nothing's happening."

"I'll try to hold the press off as long as I can." Gabe reached the door and turned. "Solving this case would be a feather in your cap. I'm sure the governor would be grateful." He grinned. "No pressure, though."

Sara Bradford's Home

Sunday afternoon, Sara made a last-minute sweep through her home for items to donate to the church bazaar. She stopped inside the library at a shelf display that held a lead-crystal tennis ball on a matching pedestal. A trophy from the past, given to her and Josh at the Women's Tennis Tournament on Amelia Island. Their first vacation together—with a promising future ahead of them—before she found out about the other women.

The crystal orb weighed heavy in her palm as she lifted

it from the mantel and read the inscription. She turned the sphere and remembered the tournament's excitement. Horseback rides along the surf line and quiet strolls on the sandy beach strewn with jellyfish. That sense of wonder she and Josh shared for a brief time constricted her throat. She should add the souvenir to the donation box. Instead, she exhaled a deep breath and replaced the ball on the base. Unwilling to let go of the good memories.

For the next couple of hours, she and Pete picked up boxes for the sale, working from a donor list the pastor had given her. The afternoon passed in a blur as they moved from house to house. The sale started tomorrow, and she already felt the pressure. She was depending on Pastor Davidson to use his influence to keep the rain at bay.

October marked the annual event, and Pastor Davidson had tapped her the past few years to coordinate the effort, the first fundraiser the church held to send church kids to summer camp.

People often asked why she gave up a week's vacation to head up the sale. The answer was simple. The camp fund and bus ministry were her mission field. She shared pastor's passion for the project to get children into church. Most bus kids had only one parent and usually lived below the poverty level. Church once a week, and five days at camp each year, could change their lives forever.

Twin Falls Baptist Church

Sara followed Pete in her car to the church parking lot. Seth Davidson's face formed a wide grin as they pulled in. Sara smiled as the pastor waved Pete's truck into the unloading zone, like a flagman on the deck of an aircraft carrier.

The fellowship hall door stood open and cool air wafted outside into the warm afternoon. Weaving through the crowd of people and boxes, Sara left the men to unload and hurried inside. The large area bustled with energy, full of women, in loosely assembled groups, arranging tables and merchandise.

The pastor entered and placed his hand on Sara's arm. "Are you sure you're up to this? I heard about the accident Friday, but you'd left the hospital when I called. You should have let me know."

"Was it on the news?"

He shook his head. "Matt Foley told me."

She'd heard Matt was still in grief counseling at the church. "I would have called if my injuries had been serious, but I only received a few scrapes. I'm good."

Moving among the boxes, Sara joined the group of familiar faces. For the next half hour, she attached price labels and answered questions. On a trip down one aisle, she stopped. A piece of red plaid material poked out from under a stack of blankets. As she reached for it, one of the women called her name. Distracted, Sara turned away, the object forgotten.

Sara's Car, FM 2960

After evening church service ended, Sara pulled away from the parking lot, ready for a shower and bed. Her finger pressed play on the Il Divo CD *Siempre,* and the lovely, blended voices cleared her mind. She made the turn onto the two-lane county highway that led home. It was a lonely stretch of road, but lonely meant no traffic, and that was okay with her.

Headlights flashed in her rearview mirror, and a black truck eased in behind her. The brightness momentarily blinded her, and she switched the mirror tab, defusing the glare. What was this guy doing? Much too close and he had plenty of room to go around.

She lowered the car window and waved the driver past. The truck hovered behind her, suddenly increased speed, and slammed into her rear bumper. Her car skidded onto the shoulder. Turning the steering wheel into the skid, she sideswiped a tree, just off the pavement, before coming back onto the highway. Trying to keep the car from hitting the tree, she realized a sudden truth—this wasn't road rage or some crazy random assault. It was personal.

Regaining control, Sara pressed the gas pedal to the floorboard. The high-performance engine shot the sports car forward and left the truck behind.

Who was this crazy person? Why would he do such a stupid thing?

Sara pressed the red button on the OnStar control. A friendly voice responded, "Good evening, how may I help you?"

Unable to control the quiver in her voice, Sara said, "I'm on Farm Market Road 2960, headed northeast, about five miles out of Twin Falls. Someone is following me. He just rammed my car. Please send help."

"Yes, ma'am. I'll contact the authorities immediately. Let me confirm the information I have. You're driving a white Stingray coupe, Texas license..." She read off the license number.

"That's...c-correct."

"I'll stay on the line with you until we contact the local

authorities. Can you tell the make and model of the other car?"

Sara glanced in the rearview mirror and gasped. Her tormentor raced forward— mere feet separated her rear bumper from the truck.

"I'm not sure, but I think it's—" The truck again crashed into the back of her car, sending the vehicle into a tailspin. She screamed, unable to hold back the terror. The roadster careened across the highway, bounced off a railing, tipped as if to roll, then settled upright in the on-coming traffic lane.

She glanced up, just as the truck smashed into the right front fender. The impact landed her car crossways in the road, inflated the airbags, and killed the engine. Fingers trembling, she shoved the gearshift into park and turned the key. Only a futile grinding noise followed.

In a blur, the black pickup roared past her and out of sight.

Voice unsteady, Sara called, "H-hello...are you...still there?"

The operator replied, "Yes. Mrs. Bradford, are you all right?"

"My air bag exploded. It missed my face but my right arm hurts."

A new male voice spoke through the OnStar link. "This is Officer Kirkpatrick, ma'am, with the highway patrol. I'm about five minutes out. Sit tight and keep talking. Where exactly are you? Is the truck still a threat?"

"I'm stalled on the lake bridge. I think he's gone."

The sergeant said again. "Sit tight. I'm on my way."

The voice sounded calm, confident and caring, but it amazed her. 'Sit tight?' What else could she do? It was easy to be calm when a maniac wasn't trying to kill you.

Sara stuck her head out the window, inhaling a deep breath of cool air. She filled her lungs and leaned against the headrest, eyelids closed. Pain shot through her arm from abrasions left by the airbag

The roar of an engine made her glance through the window. She couldn't see the truck, but she knew.

He was back.

Anxious fingers searched for the ignition and she turned the key again—another grinding noise sounded. The black menace barreled towards her—a sinister missile she couldn't avoid. "He's back...please hurry."

Sergeant Kirkpatrick yelled, "What's happening?"

Sara whispered a prayer, "Dear Lord."

She didn't have time to respond to the officer. Her frantic fingers fumbled with the seatbelt as the truck drew closer. She bent forward straining against the belt that held her in place, and covered her head with her arms. A groan of panic escaped her lips.

Sounds of crunching metal filled the night air as the truck smashed into the passenger side. The collision slammed her against the driver-side door. Her car slid towards the guardrail as her frenzied brain tried to piece together his motives.

Was he trying to crush her inside the car? Seconds later, her mind flashed the answer. The lake lay on the other side of the protective rail.

The sports car plowed into the railing, then punched through the barrier and over the edge. Nothing but black water lay below. Sara tugged franticly at the seat belt.

Jammed.

CHAPTER 12

Lake Palmer

A brief sensation of space and time elapsed before Sara's car plunged into the lake, landing flat on the surface with an impact that sent shock waves through her body. The car tilted right. Nanoseconds passed. The vehicle settled upright and floated. Sara's fingers groped madly for the belt's release button. Before she could find it, the car's hood dipped forward and began to sink.

Icy water rushed through the open window so fast she only had seconds to grab a lung full of air before the lake's depths covered her, and the automobile continued the descent to the bottom.

Cold darkness surrounded her and she realized this might be her last moments on earth. An image of Maddie flashed into Sara's mind. Of her aunt's tender care after the death of Sara's parents in a plane crash. Without her, Maddie would be alone with no one to look after her.

Terror paralyzed her muscles. Numbed her brain. She couldn't breathe. Her preeminent thought—find the belt release. Biting cold slowed her movements. Her lungs cried for oxygen until she thought they would burst. *Please, God...not like this.*

At last, her fingers found the button. She pressed it with all her strength and the belt fell away.

Free, she kicked to the vehicle's roof, grabbed a breath of air trapped there, then maneuvered through the open window and pushed upward. How many feet was she below the surface? No way to tell. Pressing urgently upward through the cold darkness, she breathed a prayer with each stroke.

Finally breaking the top of the water into fresh air, she coughed and sputtered the foul liquid she'd swallowed, struggling for each breath. Her body felt weighted and the lake's undercurrent tried to suck her back under. She treaded water, her gaze searching the embankment. Which way to shore? How far?

Light filtered across the waves from the bridge above. Through the haze of fatigue, she could see people with flashlights moving along the shore. She turned towards the brightness that shimmered across the water, about a hundred yards away, and forced herself to start swimming. The din of sirens and shouts seemed surreal as she placed one stroke after the other, almost on autopilot. Halfway to shore, her arms grew too heavy to lift. Cold seeped into every cell of her body.

She began to slip below the surface.

~*~

On his way home, Matt Foley's radio picked up the emergency call at the FM 2960 Lake Bridge. Only a few miles from the location, Matt flipped on his overhead lights and siren, then floored the SUV. He arrived at the bridge the same time as the highway patrol car, soon followed by other emergency vehicles. No sign of the car that placed the distress call.

Matt jumped from his truck and rushed to the broken guardrail in time to see someone's head in the water. Emergency lights splayed across the surface as the swimmer struggled to reach the bank.

Matt stripped off his jacket and shoes, calling back to the patrolman, "After I'm in the water, grab a lifeline from the fire truck and throw it to me."

He dove into the lake, and biting cold invaded his body like an electric shock. Breaking the surface, he shook the water from his hair, and soon located the officer on the bridge. He tossed the lifeline, and it landed just out of Matt's reach. He swam a few strokes, clutched the collar, then slipped it under his arms, and turned towards the swimmer a few feet away. Before he reached her, the woman's head dipped below the surface.

He caught her shirt, but couldn't hold on. Dark hair spread out on top of the water. Kicking closer, Matt reached out again, grabbed the woman's hair, pulled her in close, and placed his hand under her chin. No strength left, the victim's body floated motionless behind him as he made his way to the embankment. A spotlight followed their progress as firefighters reeled them in like fish from the sea.

When they were within a few feet of the bank, men met them with blankets and stretchers. They covered the victim in blankets, and handed one to Matt. He wrapped it around his shoulders, and waved the second gurney away. He glanced at the shivering woman and recognized Sara Bradford.

Her face was ghostly pale, and lips slightly blue, she shook uncontrollably.

"What's up with you and water?"

For a moment, she gave him a blank stare. Then shook her head. "N-not even f-funny, Foley."

Ensconced on the gurney, warm cover held tight against her body, Sara studied the officer as he took out his notebook. "When they're finished with you at the hospital, we'll get your statement."

"I-I think I c-can answer your questions now." Her voice quavered. "I'm n-not injured. There's nothing the hospital can do that I can't do at h-home."

"You sure?"

She nodded, pulled the blanket tighter, and ran through the night's events as the officer scribbled on his pad.

When she'd finished, Matt pulled the officer aside for a moment. Matt turned from the trooper, then came back to stand next to her. "You okay?"

"Yes...thanks...you saved my life. I couldn't have made it to shore." She shook her head. "I can't believe someone deliberately pushed me into the lake. My insurance company will have a coronary."

Matt leaned against the ambulance door. "That's the least of your worries. Whoever shoved you over that rail meant business. You should go to the hospital. People in shock don't always realize they're injured."

Sara shook her head. "I'm not in shock, and I couldn't face another visit to the ER."

His jaw worked, and he turned away. Hands on his hips, he gazed at the gap in the guardrail. A moment passed before he swung around to face her. "You're very lucky to be alive. By some miracle, you've survived two attempts on your life." He glanced down at her. "Right now, your guardian angel is asking for reassignment."

"Has anyone ever told you your sense of humor is

inappropriate?"

"It's been mentioned." His mouth softened a little, erasing its grim set. "How do you plan to get home?"

"If I may borrow a cell phone from someone, I'll call Pete to pick me up."

"Don't bother, I'll take you. I think these guys have all the information they need from you."

"I don't want to put you out, Matt. You're wet. I can call Pete. I'm just five—"

"—Sara, I'm in no mood for a debate." His jaw seemed locked again as irritation crinkled the corners of his eyes. "I'm here and I'll take you. The way this night has gone, you may need a bodyguard, and Pete isn't exactly Kevin Costner."

It wasn't worth a fight. He was tired, wet, and probably as cold as she felt. Since he thought her a killer, he was probably regretting the rescue.

His accusation yesterday still stung. She wished she'd known Matt better while Mary lived. Perhaps he would have trusted her, realized she could never kill anyone.

Despite Matt's suspicions of her, he apparently hadn't relayed them to Mary. She would never have believed him anyway. Sara and Matt had called an unspoken truce during the last year of Mary's illness. They were civil to each other, even friendly, in Mary's presence. That ended with her death.

Were all cops suspicious by nature? She couldn't fight that. He'd have to prove himself wrong. She sat up and clutched the blanket closer, then stepped out of the ambulance. "You have serious issues."

"That's entirely possible."

Matt took her arm and guided her to his SUV, waited

until she slid into the seat, then slammed the door.

He walked around and got into the driver's seat. Why was he mad at her? She'd done nothing to raise his ire, except not follow his orders without question. Did he resent her intrusion into his professional life? She rested her head against the seat back. She couldn't worry about his feelings right now. She didn't have the strength.

Silence hung like a heavy cloud on the drive home. Sara glanced across at the stubborn set of his jaw then turned back to stare out the window. For reasons she didn't understand, tears pushed at the back of her eyelids. She held them in by sheer force of will. Why the tears now? The danger had passed and she wasn't the crying type.

Sara Bradford's Home

They stopped under the portico. Her reluctant hero got out and opened the car door. Chilled to the very core of her being, she stepped out of the car and the dam of emotions she'd held inside, broke. She gulped back a sob, and turned to flee into the house. He caught her and drew her into his arms, holding her tight against his chest.

All the anxiety and horror of the last hour overwhelmed her in a flood of tears. Minutes seemed to tick by until the tears finally stopped.

She pushed away. "I'm sorry. I don't know why I did that."

He placed his hands on her shoulders. "It's been a stressful night. I guess you're entitled to a good cry. I'd give you my handkerchief but it's wet."

He walked her to the door, took her key, opened the lock, then followed her inside.

She paused, watching as he closed the door behind him. "What are you doing?"

"Go upstairs and get into dry clothes. I'll check the doors and windows. I'm going to wake Pete, ask him to sleep here tonight. Tomorrow you'll need to see about getting some protection."

"What kind of protection?"

Matt stopped and looked down at her. "A gun, pepper spray, a bodyguard, or all of the above."

"Don't wake Pete..."

"Don't argue. The decision's made. Deal with it. Does Pete have a gun?"

Her teeth chattered. "I...t-think so."

"Where's your bedroom?"

"Upstairs...first door on the r-right."

He turned her towards the stairs. "Go change into something warm. I'll come up later to check the locks on your windows."

Her knees weak and unsteady, she moved up the stairs and made her way to the bedroom. In the shower, she turned on the water as hot as she could stand it, letting the heat evaporate the deep-seated chill and wash away the fishy smell. She grabbed a pair of flannel pajamas and a robe, then climbed into bed. Before she settled in, someone knocked on the door. Maddie rushed forward, followed by Beatrice and Matt.

Maddie sat on the bedside. "Matthew told us what happened. Are you all right?"

Sara nodded, and blinked back the moisture that welled in her eyes. She had become such a wimp. She hated it.

Beatrice pressed a cup of hot lemon tea into her hand. "*Pobre niña. Esta bebida, lo hará mejor.*"

Sara forgot her own discomfort as she watched Matt check the windows. He still wore his wet clothes. He held a steaming mug, but he must be near frozen.

Matt turned to faced them. "Those French doors need bolts at the top and bottom. Ask Pete to take care of it tomorrow." He grabbed the doorknobs and shook them, then stepped away. "I didn't see a security system. I suggest you get one as soon as possible. That's an extra layer of protection." He nodded and left the room.

Sara sneezed, then caught Beatrice's attention. "There's a thermal sweat suit and jacket in the closet that belonged to Josh. Make sure the chief changes into them before he leaves."

Beatrice nodded, took the clothes from the closet, she marched down the hallway. A woman on a mission.

Sara slid down in the bed, resting her head against the pillows. It was probably unfair to set Beatrice on Matt in his weakened state. But it needed to be done. He could be so stubborn and he wouldn't change otherwise. It would be interesting to be a fly on the wall for that confrontation.

The immoveable object and the irresistible force, set on a collision course.

She pulled the comforter up under her chin and closed her eyes. A shiver ran up her spine. Matt had been right, she should have gone to the hospital. They would have given her medicine to make her sleep. Now she faced the long night, reliving her life and death struggle in the lake.

CHAPTER 13

Matt Foley's Home

On the way home, Matt called to check on the APB that went out on the sketchy truck details Sara provided. Nothing had turned up yet. It probably landed in a chop shop somewhere in Dallas an hour after the incident.

The house stood dark when he pulled into the driveway. No surprise there. Stella, his housekeeper, usually left before nine.

He entered the kitchen through the garage, and Rowdy greeted him at the door with his happy face. Thankfully, without any dead bird offertory he'd dragged in the doggie door.

Stella left a dinner of grilled pork chops and a baked sweet potato in the microwave. She was a jewel, but he'd grabbed a sandwich earlier in the evening. She'd also made a peach cobbler. He finished off a bowl of his favorite dessert and a glass of milk before heading off to bed.

Double doors led into the bedroom he'd shared with Mary. The space was large, decorated with her impeccable taste. She'd avoided a feminine environment with a cornice board over the king-size bed, and had selected a forest green and tan color scheme in bold stripes and plaids.

He undressed and threw the clothes Beatrice forced on him into the laundry basket. The jogging suit must have belonged to Josh Bradford. Too big for Pete. It felt strange wearing a dead man's clothes, but he'd had no choice. Beatrice threatened to undress him if he didn't do it himself. From her stubborn frown, he didn't doubt she would have tried. She'd been right. The dry clothes had made him feel better.

After a hot shower, he crawled between the warm flannel sheets and tried to unwind. Sleep lurked, just beyond his reach. The old brain refused to shut down, replaying the night's events in endless, vivid color. The horror of watching someone almost drown, the fierce cold of the water, the shock to discover the victim was Sara Bradford, left him with a bone numbing weariness. Rowdy seemed to sense his angst, and snuggled in beside him.

As always, his thoughts turned to his wife. They had shared something rare. She'd been his first love. His only love. They'd planned a future, filled with children. A lifetime to grow old together.

Man plans. God laughs.

The scene outside Sara's home made him uneasy. His attempt to comfort her, feeble as it had been, disturbed him. Compassion overwhelmed him. He'd wanted to pull her close, smooth her damp hair with his hand, to reassure her that he was there. She was safe. But he hadn't.

Unbidden, Sara's poem eased into his thoughts. It amazed him how accurately the words described Mary. His throat tightened as he realized for the first time, he and Sara shared an invisible bond. They'd both loved the same woman, in different ways.

He turned over and punched his pillow. One thing he knew for certain, he could never care for anyone that intensely again.

Another thing he knew for sure. Tonight's incident erased any doubts he might have had. Someone wanted Sara Bradford dead. But who? And why? Could he have misjudged Sara? Had someone else killed her husband? It seemed a stretch, but it was possible Josh Bradford's hit-and-run was somehow connected to Penny Pryor's death. All questions that needed answers soon. Before another attempt was made on Sara's life.

He weighed the evidence against Sara's culpability in her husband's death. Even though he no longer wanted to believe it, the motive was almost overwhelming. Josh Bradford's death had been too convenient. She'd gotten rid of an unfaithful husband and inherited a bundle.

People had killed for much less.

~*~

Sore muscles and lack of rest convinced Matt to sleep in. Foul weather had kept him from his morning run for more than a week. He hated to jog in the rain. Despite the blue skies, this wasn't the day to resume his habit. He and Rowdy would get into shape tomorrow.

He filled the Yorkie's food and water bowls, made a large mug of coffee in the Keurig, and took it out to the deck.

He'd only placed one restraint on Mary using her money after they married. He insisted they live in the home he bought. In that, he'd been fortunate. Acting as his own contractor and with Joe Wilson's help, he'd built a two-story, redwood and glass structure, with five thousand square feet of living space. It sat on a twenty-acre tract of land, left to him by his grandfather.

Matt took his coffee out to the multilevel deck that flowed down to the large backyard. Heavy wooden outdoor furniture formed a conversation pit near a rock open-air fireplace. The morning air was chill and clear, but bright sunlight filtered through the fifty-foot pines to warm his face, and abate the nip in the breeze. Rowdy finished his breakfast and lay at his master's feet, eyeing a doe and her fawn, munching corn from the feeder, just beyond the tree line.

The serenity could almost make him forgot the evil out there.

Almost.

His iPhone blared the *William Tell Overture.* That would be Chuck, the station desk sergeant. Matt slid his thumb across the screen. "Foley."

"Just a heads-up, Chief. The Terror has been by twice doing his Chicken Little impersonation. Muttering that some people keep banker's hours."

The Terror was Councilman Terence Hall. The perfect way to end the start of a good day. "Thanks, Chuck. I'll be in for the nine-thirty meeting."

He finished his coffee, then went upstairs to shower, shave, and dress for work.

Twin Falls Police Station

With a wave at the desk sergeant, Matt turned right into the break room for another caffeine fix. He snatched a large foam cup from the counter, filled it with the dark brew, then took the stairs to the detective bureau to meet Davis and Hunter.

Upstairs, Matt started fresh coffee in the conference room, then checked his cell phone messages. Nothing that couldn't wait.

At nine-thirty, Hunter and Davis sauntered in and stashed two wet, folded umbrellas against the wall.

"Raining again?" Matt asked.

Hunter shook his head. "Nope. It's Hal. We tried to outsmart him with the umbrellas. One problem—the sprinkler system shoots up. We were half successful."

Obvious point. Only the bottom half of their pant legs were wet. "I thought the engineer fixed that."

"So did he. He was standing in the lobby when we came in." Davis slid into a chair. "The old guy threw a shop towel on the floor, and stalked off."

Matt spread his hands in a sorry-about-that gesture. "I'll tell him to just shut the thing down until he solves the problem."

Hunter went to the conference room coffee station, filled a cup half-full of creamer, added four packets of sugar, then filled it with coffee.

"He likes a little caffeine with his cream and sugar." Davis shook his head.

His partner shrugged and took a seat at the conference table.

From his inside jacket pocket, Davis retrieved a small black notebook. "We received the list from Sam Pryor, five people he could remember who once lived in the neighborhood and still live in town."

Davis turned a page and found his list. "Probably a few others they aren't aware of, but we'll start with these guys and add any new possible wits that come up later. We ran the names through NCIS and CCH."

The National Criminal Information System and Computerized Criminal History.

"None had a rap sheet," Davis continued. "We plan to interview old neighbors who still live in the Pryor subdivision."

Hunter picked up the dialogue. "Two guys, Charles Edwards and Donald Tompkins, work for Global. Edwards is a retail vice president. We confirmed with the Pryors that Edwards drove a white panel truck back then. He and his wife owned a dry-cleaning establishment. However, he was in the military at the time. Tompkins is a security guard for Global and former Dallas police officer. They think he drove the police van home in those days. Also something curious about Tompkins. He lives in a neighborhood pretty upscale for an ex-cop/security guard. We'll try to check his finances without getting a warrant."

Davis added, "Seth Davidson was the family's pastor. Adam Elliot is in business, somewhere in Dallas, and was in high school at the time the Pryor kid vanished. He's a former employee of Global, and both were former neighbors of the Pryors."

Hunter took the last gulp of coffee. "The final guy on the list is Jacob Jamison. He's deceased, but his widow, Maddie Jamison, still lives here. They separated years ago, but never divorced. He left her a chunk of change when he died. Neither Davidson, Elliot, nor Jamison owned a white van, of any kind, to the Pryor's knowledge. We'll interview as many of them as we can locate today."

Matt nodded at Davis. "I'll take Seth Davidson. He's my pastor and knows most of the people in town in one way or another. He might be able to help."

"We'll cross him off our list," Davis said removing a pen from his pocket. "Hunter also spoke to the church secretary at the old retreat about the stored records. They still have the retreat schedule back to the date Penny disappeared. The secretary didn't volunteer to pull the dates we need, but said we were welcome to look through the files."

Back in his office, Matt stared out the window, processing the information the two detectives presented. He pulled a yellow legal pad from his desk drawer and made two columns, listing people who lived in the Pryor neighborhood and also worked at Global. All but two made both lists.

The fact the Global security guard had been one of the Pryor's neighbors and had been at the explosion Friday was significant, as well as Adam Elliot's access to the building, despite the fact he no long worked there. The list Tompkins gave him had Elliot's name with an active access code.

Granted, Global was a major employer in Twin Falls, but he wanted to pay particular attention to those on both lists.

He reached for his phone and paged Miles.

Moments later, his phone rang. "You wanted me, Chief?"

"Stop by my office when you get a chance. I have—" Matt's office door opened and Councilman Hall stepped inside. Matt ignored him and finished the call. "As I was saying, stop by when you have a chance. I have something I want you to see."

Matt replaced the receiver and turned his chair around to face Hall. "Something I can help you with, Terry?"

Hall stood in front of Matt's desk, his feet apart. "As a matter of fact, there is. I'd like an update on the Pryor case."

Matt turned his yellow pad face down, and looked up at Hall. "I report to the city manager, Terry. And I give him a daily update. You need to see Doug. If he wants to share that information, fine."

The councilman shifted his weight to the balls of his feet. "Do you have a suspect? What are your plans to find the killer?"

"The case is twenty-five years old, and the body was discovered Thursday. It's going to take more than three days to clear the file."

Hall's face flushed red. "It won't get solved if you don't stay on top of your people. I was by your office at nine o'clock and you weren't even in yet."

Matt leaned back in his chair and looked into Hall's eyes. "My work hours are not your responsibility, Terry."

Hall planted his hands on the desk and leaned forward into Matt's personal space. "This is the most important case this city has ever covered. I won't be embarrassed by a sloppy performance by the police department. I don't want excuses, Foley. I want this investigation to run in a flawless, professional manner. If you're not up to this job, the city can find someone who is."

Matt stood and shoved his chair against the wall, his hands gripped into tight fists.

The councilman stepped back and his red face deepened to the shade of a ripe tomato.

Matt said nothing. He walked to the door, held it open, and pointed the way out.

"Wait a minute," Hall shouted. "We're not finished here."

"Yes, we are." Matt flexed his fingers to keep them from balling into fists again. "I've never needed your assistance to do my job, and I don't need it now. If you have a problem with that, I suggest you take your complaint to the city manager."

Matt waited until Hall stepped into the hallway. "And, Terry, don't ever walk into my office again without knocking."

Hall stormed down the corridor, leaving smoke in his wake.

Davis poked his head around the door. "Is it safe to come in?"

After five deep breaths to get his blood pressure under control, Matt waved Davis in. Matt ripped the notes he'd made from the scratch pad. "Take a look at this and get with Lucy. She and Cole are working the Global explosion."

Davis glanced at his partner and rolled his eyes. "Do I have to? She's as prickly as a cactus."

"The cases you guys have may be connected."

"Possibly," Davis said. "By the way, Chief, I think you should have shot The Terror. Justifiable homicide in my book."

The detective left, and Matt returned to his desk. Before he was seated, his phone rang.

Dale McCulloch's voice sounded in his ear. "Can you come down to the lab for a minute? A few things I need to fill you in on."

The CSU Chief had been with Matt since McCulloch graduated college. The best hiring decision of Matt's career. He pushed his chair back and stood. "I'm on my way."

Mac met him at the door. Counter surfaces were immaculate, like the starched white lab coat McCulloch wore. His muscular body was packed into a six-foot frame, his dark auburn hair swept off his brow. Unlike most redheads, he had an olive complexion, hazel eyes, and was considered the resident hunk by the ladies at the station.

A kind of energy flowed in the lab, along with the faint smell of chemicals. Energy, generated by McCulloch, no doubt. Matt had never seen the man sit back with a cup of coffee or for that matter, he never saw him in the break room. Not his style.

Mac plopped into his chair and kicked out a stool for Matt. "I contacted a friend at the FBI lab. They're swamped, but he moved my sample on the sleeping bag to the top when I told him the victim was the governor's niece." He pointed to the red fabric swatch. "This particular bag was an exclusive, as in expensive, model. Lightweight, thermal insulated and waterproof. The manufacturer only made about two thousand, most of which were sold locally in one exclusive sporting goods store, then went out of business."

"Trying to track down the buyer is probably a dead end," Matt said. "Most retailers don't keep sales receipts for more than seven years."

The lab man beamed at him. "But here is something I think you'll like." He turned his computer monitor towards Matt. The screen showed a lab tech in front of a large machine. Mac tapped the image with his pen. "That's a VMD chamber. It can remove fingerprints from fabric. Not sure it will work on material this old, but it's worth a try."

Matt leaned forward. "You're telling me it's possible to lift the fingerprints of Penny Pryor's killer off her clothing?"

A wide grin spread over McCulloch's face, and he nodded. "Not lifted, exactly, they're photographed. It's called vacuum metal deposition and uses gold and zinc to recover the prints. The science has been around since the 70s. However, its latest use has created a lot of excitement among fingerprint experts because it can raise prints from cloth. One of the best fabrics is polyester, and Penny Pryor's jumpsuit is a polyester blend. The VMD can even raise prints on items that have been immersed in water. How cool is that?"

"That's way cool, my friend." His smile must have outshone McCulloch's. "You're a genius, and I don't pay you enough."

McCulloch chuckled. "Don't think I won't remind you of that at my next performance review." He held up a finger. "Keep in mind, Chief, that my buddy can't put this at the head of the line. We'll have to wait our turn."

"Did you show this to Detective Davis?"

"Yeah, he and Hunter were gaga."

VDM technology had just increased the odds of closing the Pryor case. It was doable. God bless forensic science. "For this, I can wait, but see if you can bribe him."

When he returned to his office, he had a message to call Doug Anderson. No doubt what that was about. He punched in the city manager's number.

Doug answered the phone with a question. "What did you do to Hall to set his tail feathers on fire?"

"His tail is always on fire. I just refused to bring him up to date on the Pryor case. Not that there was anything to share at the moment. You know what a grandstander he is, and I don't want to read the details of this investigation in the newspaper."

His boss expelled a deep breath into the phone. "He was screaming about your coming in late, like it was any of his business. For the record, I told him you were up late saving a woman's life."

"How did you find out about that?"

"There are no secrets in Twin Falls. And by the way, it was a stupid stunt diving into the lake as you did."

"Stupid, maybe but she would have died if I hadn't. You'd be dragging the lake for her body today."

"Yeah, I know. I'll share your report with Hall to keep him out of my hair. But I'll tell him if he leaks anything, the deal is off."

"As long as you keep him away from me," Matt said. "For the record, I think it's a bad idea."

Matt hung up the receiver and mumbled. "A very bad idea."

CHAPTER 14

Twin Falls Baptist Church

Matt parked his car on the street in front of the church. A crowd milled around furniture, clothes racks, and merchandise tables in the parking lot. He made his way through the sanctuary to the pastor's office. The door stood open.

Seth Davidson sat at his desk, engrossed in paperwork. When Matt rapped on the doorframe, Seth looked up. The pastor rose and came around the desk, a big grin on his face, his hand outstretched. "Hey, Matthew, come in, come in. Did you want to have our session early this week?"

After Mary's death, Matt spent every Thursday afternoon with his pastor in grief counseling. "No. Today it's business. I'd like to ask you about the Pryor family."

"What a sad affair." Seth shook his head and moved a stack of books from a chair, then motioned for Matt to sit. "I spent Friday with Lily and Sam after they got the news. Tragic as it seems, finding her body brought closure. At the same time, they're going through a new period of mourning, wondering if she suffered, and all the pain that goes with that. How may I help you, Matthew?"

"You lived in their neighborhood when Penny disappeared?"

Seth nodded. "I had just started here as pastor. Evie and I lived one street over. When we learned of Penny's disappearance that night, we went to help search and later to pray with them. Friday was a flashback to that whole ordeal."

"Do you recall any of your neighbors who may have driven a white panel truck back then, or if they still live in town?"

"It's been such a long time." The pastor leaned back in his chair as though clearing the cobwebs from his memory. "Sorry, nothing comes to mind. The church had a blue bus-type van back then. We used it for our children's outreach."

Matt rose from the chair then shook the pastor's hand. "Thanks, Seth. If you remember anything you think will help, give me a call."

~*~

The anger management problem Sam Pryor had before his daughter disappeared, crossed Seth's mind. But he couldn't share that with Matthew. The conversation was privileged information. And it had nothing to do with the case.

After Penny vanished, the Pryors dropped out of church. They blamed God for the loss of their daughter. Distraught, Lily asked all the questions Seth couldn't answer. Questions like, "Why did God let this happen?" The inadequacy Seth felt back then still plagued him—unable to dissuade them from blaming God for their loss.

After Matthew disappeared down the hallway, Seth walked into the sanctuary and knelt at the altar, heart burdened. He whispered a prayer, "Lord, you know I will never have all the answers. I depend on you to give Sam and Lily comfort. Give me wisdom and help me teach them to hold to the promise that you will never forsake them, that you will always be just a prayer away. Especially in something as terrible as the loss of a child. Heavenly

117

Father, please help this family find peace in the face of such evil."

~*~

On the way to his car, Matt spotted Sara Bradford. He weaved around the shoppers and clutter, to her side. "If you have a minute, I need to ask you a few questions." He glanced down at his watch. "Have you had lunch?"

She shook her head. "No, but I can't leave. The school called and one of my helpers had to pick up her son."

"Okay, I'll bring lunch to you. What'll it be?"

The corners of her mouth tilted up. "I'd like a burger with everything, and fries."

"Mustard or mayo?"

"Both."

Twenty minutes later, Matt returned with the food.

Sara waved a woman over to take her place. "Let's go into the fellowship hall. It's more comfortable there."

Matt followed her inside to a table and then crossed to the coffee pot in the kitchenette. "What's your pleasure?"

"I take it black."

He poured two cups and brought them to the table. "I was surprised to see you here. You probably need a day off after last night."

"Thanks again, Matt...for what you did...I'm not sure I showed proper appreciation last night. You saved my life." She stirred the coffee with the small red stick. "Staying home would only make me relive the drama. Here, I can at least take my mind off of it for a while."

She pushed back the paper wrap from her sandwich and took a bite. "Mmm, good burger. You bought this at the Burger Shack."

"You recognized the sack."

"No, the taste. I'm a burger connoisseur."

He chuckled. "I didn't know. Is that contagious?"

A light came into her eyes. "No, but it is hereditary. My mom was a gourmet cook. She could make anything. Cornish game hens, beef Wellington, you name it. I drove her crazy because my grandfather's and my favorite meal was hamburgers and fries."

"I'll make a note of that. By the way, don't drive home alone after dark. Call me and I'll either come or send a patrol car to follow you. What are you driving?"

She took a long drink from the cup and gazed across the table at him. "Thank you, Matt. I know that's beyond the 'to protect and serve' mandate. I'm driving a blue box with four doors and four wheels. My purse, cell phone, license, and credit cards all went down with the ship."

"That bad, huh?"

She shrugged. "Pete brought me in this morning and I rented the first thing we saw. I can't replace the roadster until the insurance company settles, and that may take some time. The fact they have to pay for a rental car may speed up the process."

"Must be tough to lose such a sweet ride."

"How did you know what I...? Of course, you checked the car out the night Josh died."

"I did."

She exhaled a breath and looked over his shoulder, out the window. "The loss isn't so bad. But you didn't buy lunch to talk about my transportation problems. More questions about Sunday night? I thought we covered that."

Matt leaned forward. "I need to ask you about the explosion at Global. Tell me about the accident. Lately, it seems every case that crosses my desk has your name on it.”

Bright red spots appeared on her cheeks. “Is that an insinuation?” She shook her head. “You haven’t questioned me about the Valentine’s Day Massacre or the disappearance of Jimmy Hoffa.”

He chuckled. “You’re too young for those cases. Don’t get angry. It isn’t an indictment. Just an observation. Seems odd, after the lake incident. Tell me about Friday.”

She stared at him for a minute before she spoke. “What do you want to know?”

“Start at the beginning, when you entered the warehouse. We’ve confirmed a bomb caused the blast. Someone intended to harm you or someone else. After last night, I don’t think there’s any doubt you were the target. The next step is to determine why.”

She stopped mid-chew. “That is so unreal. There are easier ways to kill someone than with a bomb.”

“I never try to explain the criminal mind.”

“Before you ask, I have no idea how to make a bomb. I couldn’t even make a firecracker.”

He ignored the sarcasm. “Fired anyone recently who might have a grudge against you?”

“Possibly. A few months back, a supervisor terminated a woman who became violent. I don’t get involved in terminations unless it’s at the management level. Employees with that kind of grudge would go after the director or the supervisor. However, once an associate is let go, he or she no longer has access to any part of Global. If you wish, I’ll call the director to give you a list of recent terminations.” She shook her head. “I can’t wrap my brain around the fact that someone wants to kill me. Even after last night.”

Matt considered his answer before he spoke. He didn’t

want to frighten her, but she needed to deal with reality. He wadded his trash and stuck it into the burger sack. "Believe it. Get that list to me or the two detectives on the case. Have you spoken to Lucy Turner or Cole Allen?"

"Yes, over the phone." She shifted in the chair, apparently eager to return to work. "They asked the same questions you just asked."

"Be sure the list gets to Detective Turner." It occurred to Matt that one of Josh's former girlfriends might have a grudge against Sara. He'd ask Lucy to check that out. A lot of time had elapsed since Josh's death, but there was no time limit on revenge and jealousy. He pushed on. "Is there anyone who might want to personally harm you? For any reason outside the workplace? Any disgruntled boyfriends?"

A moment of awkward silence passed before she answered. "I don't have a boyfriend, disgruntled or otherwise."

He couldn't let that pass. He'd seen her date Saturday night. "What about Jeff what's-his-name? You were with him at the country club banquet."

Her demeanor shifted. Thoughtful. "Jeff isn't a boyfriend, he's a friend."

Matt grinned. "Maybe that's why he's disgruntled."

"You have a very warped sense of humor." She placed her elbow on the table and rested her chin in her hand. "Until yesterday, I would have said I have no enemies. Now, it seems an inescapable fact."

"Until we get a handle on this, you should stay away from Global. Whoever planted that bomb appears to have easy access." He checked his watch. "I have to go. It might also be a good idea to remain close to home."

She stood and tossed her trash into the receptacle. "I'm

on vacation for two weeks."

"Good, remember what I said about the escort home."

~*~

Sara hadn't mentioned her job status. That was need-to-know information, and there was no need for him to know.

After leaving the fellowship hall, she pitched back into the activity of the sale. Despite concerted efforts to keep her mind occupied, the lake experience repeated over and over in her head. She had wanted to stay home today, but what she'd told Matt was true. Besides, she'd made a commitment to the pastor to head up this sale for him. Busy hands kept the terror buried.

Lunchtime shoppers kept her occupied for the next hour. When the traffic slowed down, she collapsed in a chair, near the door, and slipped her shoes off under the table. Across the room, she spotted the red plaid material she'd seen earlier, sticking out from underneath layers of comforters and blankets. She slipped her shoes on and hurried to the display table, reached under the blankets and pulled out a sleeping bag. An exact replica of the one she remembered from the night Penny vanished.

Grumbling about the loss of her cell phone, she grabbed the bag and hurried into the pastor's office to call Matt.

The desk sergeant picked up. "Sorry, ma'am. Chief Foley hasn't returned to the station. May I have him call you?"

"Yes please. I found a sleeping bag that might be of interest to him on a case he's investigating." She left her name and number and ended the call.

She took the bag to the basement and tucked it away on a top shelf of the supply closet.

Just before five o'clock, the church secretary tapped her

on the shoulder. "Sara, call for you."

Sara took the cordless phone from the secretary. "Mrs. Bradford, this is Detective Davis. The desk sergeant gave me your message. My partner and I would very much like to look at that sleeping bag. Do you know where it came from?"

"I assume it came in one of the boxes for a sale our church is sponsoring. You can pick it up here anytime between 9:00 A.M. and 6:00 P.M."

"So you don't know who brought it in?"

"It shouldn't be difficult to find out, although it might take a little time. We have a list of all our donors, at least those from whom we made pickups. A few people dropped items off, but they were mostly church members so we can ask around." Sara checked the time. "Did you want to come this evening?"

"Yes, ma'am. I'm leaving now. Will you be there?"

Sara told him she would wait and disconnected.

Strange that a duplicate sleeping bag turned up the same week as Penny's body. Had someone gotten rid of the mate because Penny's body had been found? It could just be a common style and merely coincidence. She'd leave that for the detectives to sort out.

The church parking lot had emptied by the time the two detectives arrived. The taller and more fashionable of the two stepped forward. "Mrs. Bradford?"

She nodded.

"I'm Detective Davis. We spoke on the phone." He indicated the man next to him. "This is my partner, Detective Hunter. Do you have the sleeping bag?"

"I stored it in the basement so it wouldn't be sold by accident. I'll get it for you."

The two men followed her downstairs. She opened the

door to the supply closet, switched on the light, and glanced up at the top shelf.

The bag was gone.

Twin Falls Baptist Church

Next morning, Sara mulled over the disappearance of the sleeping bag, as she had done all last night. The disappointed detectives waited while she asked the workers if they'd seen it. No one had, and the two men returned to the station.

The janitor admitted storing a shipment of cleaning supplies after lunch, but said he'd found the shelf empty when he restocked it.

The whole scene seemed like bad television drama. Things didn't just disappear. This wasn't Hollywood, it was her church. She felt like a marionette in the hands of an evil puppet-master, controlling her life.

Before lunch, Sara checked the messages on the new iPhone she'd bought. Matt Foley's name appeared on the screen. She pulled up the message.

Matt's voice sounded in her ear. "I wanted to let you know we found your missing kids. The family moved in with Diane Morgan's parents, Mr. and Mrs. Walter Campbell. The address is 440 Harcourt Lane, in Twin Falls. A much better neighborhood for those two. Call if you have any questions."

Sara whispered a silent prayer of thanks.

At lunchtime, she left the church sale to check on Danny and Poppy.

The Campbell Home

With the help of the car's GPS system, Sara had no difficulty locating the address. The house sat on a quiet, tree-lined street in a modest neighborhood of single-story brick homes with well-tended lawns.

She pulled the car to the curb in front of a white brick structure with dark green shutters and made her way to the front door. A smiling elderly woman answered the knock.

"Hi, I'm Sara Bradford. Your grandchildren used to attend my church. I wondered if they would like to continue to do so since they moved. The church bus would pick them up."

The woman opened the screen door. "I'm Dolly Campbell. The children are in the backyard. Won't you come in?"

Dolly was a life-size Norman Rockwell painting, with her tidy gray hair pulled into a neat bun on top of her head. She wore a blue checked dress with a ruffled white apron she must have sewed herself.

Sara followed her inside. "Do the children live with you now?"

Dolly's eyes brightened. "Yes, my husband and I finally convinced Diane to come back home. We persuaded her to let us take care of the children while she returned to school. Working entry-level jobs, she simply couldn't provide for herself and the kids. We're so happy to have them here. I appreciate your offer, but the children attend church with us now."

The older woman led the way into a spotless kitchen where three plates sat on a tablecloth printed with yellow daisies and black checks. "Would you care to join us for lunch? I was just about to call the children. They would love to have you stay."

Sara couldn't keep the smile off her face. She could stop worrying about the kids' welfare. The Campbell home was a thousand percent better than the children's last dwelling, and their grandmother seemed an ideal caregiver. "I don't want to impose, Mrs. Campbell. I'm glad they're in church. I'll just say hello, and let you get on with your lunch."

"Please call me Dolly...everyone does. It will be no imposition at all. It's humble fare, but we would be happy to share it with you."

The sincerity in Dolly's voice made Sara's decision. "In that case, I would love to, thank you for asking."

Dolly selected another plate from the china cabinet then set it on the table. Lunch resided on the stove in covered dishes.

"May I help?" Sara asked.

"Of course. Why don't you put the food on the table while I get the tea?"

Sara moved bowls of golden fried okra and fresh black-eyed peas from the stove to the table, then returned for a platter of fried yellow squash and a plate of cornbread.

Dolly followed with the tea, a plate of sliced tomatoes, and red onions. "Looks like we're ready," she said with a satisfied nod. "I'll call the children."

Danny and Poppy bounded into the kitchen, accompanied by ear-piercing squeals when they saw Sara. They rushed forward, and grabbed her around the waist, almost knocking her over. The kids looked healthier and happier than she'd ever seen them.

Dolly sent the two off to wash their hands. "My grandchildren are rare for their age. They like vegetables. My husband, Walter, is a meat-and-potatoes man. Whenever he's away, I go to the market and we gorge ourselves on good old fried comfort food."

Sara drew in a deep breath. "It smells wonderful."

After seeming to inhale their lunch, Poppy grabbed Sara's hand. "Come play with us, Sara."

"I would love to, but I'm working at the church today." Sara knelt to give her a hug. "Maybe next time."

"At least stay for coffee." Dolly filled two cups and handed one to Sara. They stood at the kitchen window and watched the kids play on an apple green swing set.

Sara took a sip from her cup. "I became very attached to your grandchildren. When they disappeared from the trailer park, I became concerned. I'm so happy to find them here, well and thriving."

The older woman nodded. "I understand. Knowing they lived in that horrible place broke my heart. You can't imagine how many sleepless nights I spent worrying about them."

Sara empathized with her. The only time she'd been inside the mobile home, concern for their safety overwhelmed her. The living room furniture consisted of four wooden spools grouped around a plywood crate, the room heated by a space heater. A firetrap in the making.

"Walter and I didn't get along with Diane's husband. Grady became an addict soon after their marriage. He never took care of her and the children. When he went to prison, Diane was too proud to come home. Thank God she came to her senses."

Sara finished her coffee and placed the cup in the sink. "I brought some clothes for the children. I hope you don't mind. If it's a problem, I'll take them back."

Dolly touched Sara's hand. "It's no problem at all. We would love to have them. Growing children can always use clothes."

Sara gathered up the dishes and took them to the sink.

"I'll rinse these off and put them in the dishwasher for you."

"I absolutely won't hear of it. You were our guest", Dolly said.

Sara glanced at her watch. "If you won't let me help, I need to get back to the church sale."

She retrieved the shopping bags from her car then went into the backyard to give Danny and Poppy goodbye hugs. As she reached out to shake the older woman's hand, Sara found herself in a long, motherly embrace.

Before pulling away from the Campbell residence, Sara sat in her car for a moment, remembering where these kids had come from. Where they were now.

Finally, some good news to offset a very bad week.

CHAPTER 15

North Dallas

Weeks ago, Sara agreed to accompany Jeffery Hayden to Blain Stanton's dinner party, a political gathering of who's-who in Texas political circles. Jeff's marketing firm handled public relations for a number of politicians who would be present.

She leaned back against the headrest, as Jeff's Ferrari weaved through the narrow streets of North Dallas' most affluent neighborhood. The sun set early in October and city lights sparkled like jewels against the velvet night sky.

Jeff cruised with the traffic, finally stopping the car before an iron gate. He handed the guard the invitation. After scrutinizing it closely, the guard pushed a button and the gate swung open. The sleek vehicle moved up the tree-lined driveway to the two-story mansion ahead. The Stanton estate was the most imposing residence on a street of elegant, discreet homes.

Jeff pulled into the queue behind a limousine. At the front entrance, a valet sprang from the shadows to open their doors.

Jeff handed the kid a twenty-dollar bill. "If my car comes back without scratches, I'll give you another twenty."

The attendant almost bowed then spirited the car away.

Men and their expensive toys.

Inside, the marble entryway flowed into a great room already crowded with guests. The privileged class enjoying fine food, expensive wines, and intellectual conversation. She scanned the gathering, congratulating herself on selecting the gray silk suit for the affair. It had been the right choice.

Jeff took Sara's arm and guided her to the bar where they joined the line waiting for drinks. Muted voices and laughter almost drowned out the music of a three-piece string group nearby. When they reached the front, Jeff ordered ginger ale, with lime on ice, for both of them. Drinks in hand, they pushed through the throng to stand near the dining room entrance. Minutes later, one of Jeff's clients waved him over. Jeff excused himself and joined the group.

Feeling somewhat conspicuous, alone in her corner, Sara strolled onto the veranda. Mature oak trees blocked the north wind, leaving a pleasant calm around her. The property covered about six acres, but she could still feel the city's presence. She moved across the stone deck and stood against the rock banister. She found a prime people-watching vantage point through the open French doors. Soon bored, she turned to look out over the pool, admiring the landscape.

"It's good to see a friendly face."

Recognizing the voice, she turned around. Matthew Foley grinned down at her. He stood tall and intimidating. Perhaps intimidating wasn't the word, although he could certainly be that at times. But after two near misses on her life, his presence lent a measure of security. He looked casually elegant in a dark suit with a gray turtleneck.

His inside joke wasn't lost on her. She laughed. "What brings you to the circus?"

"Blain asked me. He never tires of trying to lure me into politics. Governor Ferrell will be here. I think he wants to pick my brain about his niece's case. What's your excuse?"

"Temporary insanity. Actually, I wanted to see the

Stantons. I haven't seen them since Mary's...I'm sorry, Matt, I didn't mean to bring that up."

"No need to apologize. It's been a long time." But his smile had disappeared. "Glad to hear you took my advice and let the squad car follow you home last night.

"After Sunday, I'll take all the protection I can get."

Jeff joined them on the terrace. He raised a quizzical eyebrow, before casting a frown at Matt. Jeff's possessiveness irked her. He knew her feelings about him so why he felt threatened didn't compute. Sara introduced the two men, just as Dina Lambert appeared.

She slipped her arm through Jeff's. Her silky voice rose above the noise. "Trying to keep all the handsome men to yourself, Sara?"

Sara ignored the jibe. "Dina, have you met Matthew Foley? He's Twin Falls Chief—"

"We've met," Dina said. The icy glare she cast at Matt said there was a story there, somewhere.

Dina took a firm hold on Jeff's arm. "I have some people I want you to meet, Jeff." She gave Sara a smug look. "I'll bring him back later."

Matt inclined his head towards Dina. "I hear her husband has presidential aspirations, but so does our governor. Between the two, I know who'd get my vote."

Sara nodded then gave a slight shudder. "I can see Dina with her eye on becoming First Lady. Her platform would probably be the benefits of plastic surgery."

Matt chuckled and lifted his glass. "Hear, hear."

"Sorry, that sounded mean spirited, didn't it?"

"Yes, but truthful."

Matt excused himself to go find Blain. He'd only been gone a few minutes when Grace Stanton joined Sara. She'd forgotten how much Mary resembled her mother.

Grace moved closer and gave Sara a one-armed hug. "It's nice out here, isn't it?"

Sara returned the hug with a smile. "Yes, I was enjoying the view. How are you?"

Grace took a sip from her cocktail glass and shrugged. "I still have some bad days where I miss Mary terribly. I guess I always will. Our son, Lee, made us grandparents for the second time last year. They named the baby Mary. She has been a godsend to me. I babysit as often as they'll let me."

"I hadn't heard about the baby. How wonderful for you. Congratulations."

"Lee asked Matt to be her godfather. We love Matt. How could we not after he cared for Mary through ..." She bit her lower lip. "Did you come with Matt tonight?"

"No. I'm with Jeffery Hayden. Dina Lambert spirited him away. Matt kindly kept me company."

Sara's old boss at Global, Adam Elliot, and his wife, Lindsey, joined them. Lindsey and Grace talked babies, and Adam turned to Sara. "Tell me about the accident at Global. Any real damage?"

"Only smoke and water, plus the loss of one high-rise lift. But we were back in business Monday morning."

His gaze gave her a professional once-over. "Obviously, you weren't seriously injured." The comment more statement than question.

The explosion had been the least of her trials. Best not to go there. "I had an angel on my shoulder."

"Any chance we can have lunch Thursday? We haven't done that in a while. I meant to call you earlier, but things are popping at the office." He'd left Global to start his own business five years ago. "I'll ask Lindsey to join us."

"I would love to. I've wanted to talk to you about the

buyout. I'm sure you've heard about it."

"Hasn't everyone?" A blank expression crossed his face. "Have you heard who made the purchase?"

"Millennium Ventures, according to Roger, although I know very little about it. I've been on vacation this week."

~*~

At the dinner table, Matt found himself seated between Sara Bradford on his right, with Charles Edwards's reed-thin wife, Marnie, on his left. Sara's escort sat across the table from her, with Dina Lambert on one side, and Pepper Parker, a large redheaded woman Matt had been introduced to earlier, on the other. Parker was a reporter for a local magazine.

The Edwards were engaging during dinner. Still affectionate with each other, Charles often smiled into his wife's eyes and she touched his hand as they spoke.

Although she consumed a mixed drink, and three glasses of wine with dinner, Marnie Edwards showed none of the effects of intoxication when she excused herself and left the table. Charles, apparently the designated driver for the evening, drank only iced tea. Matt noticed the alcohol consumption of those around him, having witnessed firsthand the carnage caused by drunk drivers.

As dessert arrived, the redhead began to tell Dina Lambert about an interview earlier that day with the leader of a national women's organization who vehemently opposed the war. "I felt fortunate to get time with her. She's very much in demand. I found her to be intelligent and well informed. We're featuring her on the cover of the *Tattler*'s December issue."

Unaware his facial expression had morphed his inner

thoughts, the woman surprised Matt when she narrowed her eyes and stared at him over the centerpiece. "You have a problem with the organization, Chief Foley?"

It would be rude to start a political debate in Blain's home. Matt shook his head.

The columnist leaned forward. "Don't be shy, Chief. I'm sure we would all be interested in your opinion."

Matt shook his head again. "I'm not sure everyone would be."

"Yes, Matt," Dina chimed in. "We'd be very interested."

Matt exchanged a glance with Blain at the head of the table. Matt didn't want to engage this pushy woman in an argument at his father-in-law's dinner table. Blain must have overheard the conversation. He gave Matt a go-ahead nod.

Matt placed his dessert fork on the plate. "Since you asked, I think this particular group consists of misguided women being used, either knowingly or unknowingly, by left wing extremists. Their presence in town, demonstrating in front of our former president's home, ties up police and wastes taxpayers' money to protect them while they engage in meaningless activities."

The woman's face turned the color of her hair. "That's unkind. They are smart, compassionate women opposed to war. In case you're unaware of a little thing called the First Amendment, they have every right to protest."

Matt folded his napkin then placed it on the table. "I'm well aware of that right. I applaud those who demonstrate responsibly. However, I don't understand why intelligent women protest at the home of an ex-president, who can do nothing to stop the war, rather than in Washington, in front of a sitting president, who can. The war continues, yet they haven't interrupted a state-of-the-union address since the administration changed."

Momentarily flustered, the woman glared at him. "May I quote you, Chief Foley?"

At the head of the table, Blain Stanton and Governor Ferrell stood. Blain nodded again at Matt.

Pushing his chair back, Matt rose. He gazed directly at the redhead. "Absolutely, as long as you keep it in context." He leaned down and whispered in Sara's ear, "This is why I don't go into politics."

Matt joined the two men. Blain lowered his voice. "Sorry about that, Matt. I think Senator Lambert brought that woman."

They followed the governor to the study where Ferrell took off his coat, loosened his tie, then took a seat on the leather sofa. He chuckled. "I guess you told Ms. Parker. Wish I could do that. I'd like to tell the media what I really think for once, just to see how it feels."

He leaned back on the couch then crossed his legs. "Thanks for agreeing to come tonight, Matt. Are you sure we can't lure you into the next senate race? We'd love to replace Lambert. You'd bring a breath of fresh air into the contest."

"I'm honored to be asked, Governor, but politics is not my game. I value my privacy and I like what I do."

The governor heaved a heavy breath. "I understand. It's not a job for everyone. I wanted to ask you about Penny. Lily is having a difficult time with this. I think she realized Penny had died, but didn't want to admit it to herself. Now that it's a reality, she ..." He rubbed his hand across his brow. "It has been so long, I had almost forgotten what a special child Penny was. Do you have anything concrete so far?"

Taking the chair next to the sofa, Matt nodded. "There

are a few leads—items taken from the grave site—that we're following up on, but I don't have anything solid to report at present."

Brandt Ferrell leaned forward. "I understand this will take some time. Let me know when you have something solid, so I can keep Lily informed before it reaches the news media."

"Of course. Be assured, we'll do everything possible to find out what happened and bring the killer to justice."

"I appreciate that, Matt."

Matt shook hands and left the two men to their political games.

~*~

Sara smiled at Jeff, as a little after eleven o'clock, he extricated himself from Dina Lambert. His face flushed as he joined the after-dinner conversation.

Later, Sara stood to leave, and said goodnight to Grace. Matt reached across the table to shake hands with Jeff, then came to Sara's side. He enclosed her hand in his. "Don't forget about the escort."

She smiled her thanks. "I won't."

In the entryway, Jeff glanced down at her. "Sorry about abandoning you for most of the evening. Every time I tried to get away, Dina held me back with questions about my business."

Sara waved off his apology. "Don't let it bother you, Jeff. No problem. I've known Dina Lambert for a long time. She can be...possessive. Matt and the Stanton's kept me company."

A flicker of irritation formed Jeff's mouth into a straight line. "I noticed the chief's attention."

Outside in the darkness, Sara tried to sooth Jeff's ego. "Matt was only being kind."

"Hmm," Jeff said. "I'm sure he was."

She cast an exasperated glance at him, but her mind wasn't on Jeff or Dina Lambert. Matt Foley's thoughtfulness throughout the evening had surprised her. Minus his usual suspicions, he could be quite charming. Had he changed his mind about her guilt since their last meeting?

His good opinion of her mattered more than she wanted to admit.

CHAPTER 16

Twin Falls Baptist Church

Matt sat beside Seth Davidson in the pastor's study for his grief counseling appointment.

"How have you been this week?" Seth asked.

Matt leaned back in the soft leather chair and stretched his legs out in front of him, to give himself a moment to think. "Better. But I still have a bad day, occasionally."

"Tell me about the bad days."

Matt paused for a moment, pulling his thoughts together. "Sunday night was the worst in a long time. I watched a woman almost drown. An attempted murder. It brought back memories of Mary's death." He shifted in the chair. "It reminded me of all the times my job kept me away from her. Time we could have spent together."

"Mary knew you were a cop when she married you, didn't she?"

"Of course, but I'm not sure she understood what the job meant in that respect."

"Did she ever complain about it?"

Matt's stomach twisted. "No. She was a realist. We often talked about it. She had the same appreciation for my job that I did. Knew that it was important. She did her part to support me by not complaining about the demands on my time. When we solved a difficult case, she felt as though she'd had a part in the success. Sometimes that made me feel worse—that she accepted it so well."

Seth tapped his lower lip with his forefinger and looked at him. "Do you think you're being a little hard on yourself? If you had spent more time with Mary, would it have changed the outcome of her death?"

Matt shook his head. "No, but it might have eased some of my guilt."

"Do you still have the anger issues at God, at yourself?"

Matt ran his hand through his hair, considering the question. "Not so much anymore. I still don't understand the why of her death. But that's nothing new. I've dealt with that in law enforcement, asking why violent things happen to innocent people."

He turned in the chair to look directly at Seth. "I've found myself becoming interested in another woman...but I haven't acted on it."

"Why not?"

"There are a lot of complications I'd rather not go into. But the major reason is it makes me feel unfaithful to Mary."

The pastor nodded in a knowing way. "It's been two years, Matthew. Do you think Mary would mind that you were getting on with your life?"

The question gave Matt pause. He knew Mary wouldn't want him to become less than he had been because of her death. "No, she wouldn't mind."

"Looking at yourself today, how far along would you say you are in your grief recovery?"

Matt gave the question the attention it deserved. Truth to tell, he hadn't considered healing in those terms. The conclusion he reached brightened his outlook. The sorrow had lessened. "On a scale of one to ten, I'm about a seven. I'm not sleeping well, but better. The job helps. There are lots of bad people out there to take off the streets. I believe that's God's purpose for my life. Doing the job well gives me a great deal of satisfaction."

Seth smiled, gave his hand a pat. "I know the feeling. Next Thursday. Same time?"

Twin Falls Police Station

Punctual as always, Davis and Hunter sat across from Matt at the conference table.

"Anything new?" Matt asked. He pulled out a chair, then propped his feet up on another one.

Davis had his notebook on the table. "We checked the old retreat files. No seminars that weekend. However, an onsite grounds keeper, Robert Cook, lived in the apartments. He wasn't on duty that weekend, but he could have been there." He shook his head. "We'll never know for sure."

"Why's that?" Matt asked.

"He's dead. Died last week," Hunter replied.

Matt leaned forward in his seat. "Foul play?"

"No. Lisa says complications from alcoholism, cirrhosis of the liver, et cetera," Hunter said. "We're running a background check on him."

"I'll ask Joe Wilson to tape the place off, and Hunter will write up a search warrant, see if we can find a judge to sign it tonight. If we pull that off, McCulloch's people will be out to tag and bag everything in the morning."

Hunter turned to Davis. "How come I always get the easy jobs like writing up the warrants and making a judge mad for calling him away from his dinner?"

Davis slapped him on the back. "Cause you're better at the details than I am."

"Anything else?" Matt pulled his feet off the chair and stood. A thought occurred to him. "Which retreat apartment did Cook live in?"

Davis gave him a knowing grin. "The one with the great view of the burial site."

Pryor Neighborhood

Davis and his partner left the station. The Pryor neighborhood was first on their list. Sam gave them the names of two people who still lived there.

This was the routine of most investigations. Foot soldiering, from house to house, asking questions. To be honest, he preferred it to sitting in the office making phone calls. The real action was on the street.

Hunter finished off a bagel then wiped his mouth with the small white napkin the vendor provided. "We couldn't afford to live in this neighborhood."

"With my single status, I don't want a house. Condominium living is great. No yard work. But I know what you mean. These places sell for five to ten times their original value."

Davis tugged his tie closer to his neck, then centered the perfect Windsor knot as they reached the first home on the list, Mrs. Elsie Kaufman.

The Kaufman home, a Tudor style two story, sat back on the lot with a manicured lawn on a curved driveway.

When they neared the front door, a woman's shrill voice shattered the morning's silence.

Hunter glanced at Davis. "What's that?"

Davis grinned. "Maybe the princess found the pea under her mattress."

Hunter cast a quizzical glance his way. "Should we intrude?"

Davis walked up the steps and rang the bell. "That's what we do, partner."

The shouts stopped. The door jerked open. A woman glared at them from the entryway. Her upper lip wore the tale-tell wrinkles of a smoker. Her angry scowl erased any beauty she might have possessed.

It only took a second for Davis to realize this couldn't be Elsie Kaufman. Too young. Elsie Kaufman would be in her late sixties.

The woman looked at Hunter, then at Davis. "What do you want?"

Davis flashed his badge. "I'm Detective Davis, this is my partner, Detective Hunter. We'd like to speak to Elsie Kaufman, if she's available."

The woman's face relaxed as she focused on him. "My mother doesn't live here anymore. She's in Serene Acres Rest Home. I'm her daughter, Dora Hastings. Is there anything I can help you with?"

"We understand your mother lived in the neighborhood at the time Penny Pryor vanished."

Dora stood aside, inviting them in. She led the way to the living room. They followed her into a large room with a warmth, inconsistent with Dora Hastings' personality.

A man of about forty, with a dark receding hair line, sat in a rose-print chair near the window, legs crossed, a newspaper open on his lap, a frown etched grooves in his brow.

Davis let his gaze roam around the room. Beige drapes printed with delicate pink roses covered the windows. The fabric pattern continued on chair covers and throw pillows on the earth-tone sofas. Furniture formed a conversation group around the focal point of the room, a huge cream-colored fireplace. Too feminine for his taste, but beautiful.

Dora failed to introduce the man. He stood, holding out his hand. "I'm Todd Hastings. Please, have a seat."

She shot Todd a cold glance, then turned to face Davis. "We were about to have coffee. Would y'all care to join us?"

Hunter shook his head. "No thanks, but don't let us stop you."

"That's okay, no hurry." She leaned back against the couch. "It's been all over the neighborhood that the police found Penny's body."

Davis nodded. "We're questioning anyone who lived in this area when she vanished. Your mother's name came up on our list."

"Yes, my mother lived here when it happened. So did I. I knew Penny. We weren't friends, but I babysat her once. Really sad. Her folks were always fighting. Sam slapped Lily and Penny around. I never trusted Sam Pryor. He always seemed too quiet to suit me."

Todd Hastings lowered his paper. "Dora, you shouldn't say such things. Those poor people have enough—"

"—you don't know anything about this, Todd. It happened before we were married."

Hastings folded the paper, slapped it down on the end table, and left the room. Minutes later, a back door closed with a bang.

Davis returned his attention to Mrs. Hastings. "Did you ever see Sam actually strike Penny?"

"Never saw him hit Penny." Dora pulled her thin lips into a smirk. "I heard that he slapped Lily once. I saw the bruise on her cheek."

Through the picture window, Davis watched Todd Hastings as he got into his car, the tires spinning on the cement as he backed out of the driveway.

Further conversation with Dora ranged from her suspicions of Sam Pryor to her concerns about her neighbors. Davis threw a glance at Hunter before heading to the door. "Thank you for your time, Mrs. Hastings. We'll let you know if there are any further questions."

Back in the car, Hunter turned to him. "You remember in Proverbs, where King Solomon said that it's better to live in the wilderness than to live in a palace with an angry and contentious woman?"

Davis shrugged. "So?"

"In case you missed it," Hunter said. "He had Dora Hastings in mind."

Davis grinned. "It's a wonder Todd Hastings hasn't murdered her."

"That's easy," Hunter said. "The only way to get rid of that one is to drive a stake through her heart, then shoot her with a silver bullet."

Davis pulled into the street and glanced over at his partner. "She did give us one useful piece of information, provided what she said is true. It's a stretch, but we can add Sam Pryor's name to the list of suspects.

CHAPTER 17

Serene Acres Rest Home

The scent of disinfectant burned his nose, as Davis strode to the information desk and asked for Elsie Kaufman. The receptionist directed them down the hallway to room 232. The smell of cleaning chemicals intensified as they made their way down the wide corridor.

At Elsie Kaufman's room, the door stood open. Davis knocked on the doorjamb. "Mrs. Kaufman?"

A woman sat near a bed, by the window. She looked up, a smile on her face. "I'm Mrs. Kaufman."

The area was small, about twelve by fifteen. The section near the door held standard industrial furniture. An ancient woman lay on the bed, her thin body curled into a fetal position her breath came in open-mouth gasps.

On the other side, someone had crammed a few small pieces of elegant furniture into the room.

Elsie Kaufman stood when they entered, shook hands with both men, then returned to her chair.

She reminded Davis a little of her daughter, but her eyes held a serenity he didn't think Dora would ever possess.

At about five-foot-seven, Elsie Kaufman stood tall. Gray hair swirled into a knot at the back of her long graceful neck, her skin looked pale and smooth. She wore a simple blue dress that seemed incongruent among the housedresses of the other residents.

Intelligent blue eyes seemed to appraise him and Hunter. "Come in. Please have a seat, gentlemen. I'm afraid

I can't offer you refreshments. Unfortunately, that's one of the many luxuries my new home doesn't provide for guests."

Davis introduced himself and his partner. "We're fine." He pulled over a chair from the other side of the room. Hunter sat on the side of Elsie's bed. "Have you heard Penny Pryor's body has been found?"

"Yes, Dora called me with the news."

"Can you tell us what you remember about the night she vanished?"

Hunter took out his notebook as Davis spoke.

"Actually, I saw very little." She pushed a strand of gray hair back into the hair clasp. "My husband and I helped with the search that night and again the next day. Most of the neighbors joined in to help. A terrible night for the Pryors. My heart broke for them. We kept a close eye on our children after that, afraid the monster would return. Thankfully, that nightmare never came to fruition."

Davis leaned forward. "Do you know anyone from your neighborhood that drove a white panel truck back then?"

She hesitated for a moment. "A policeman lived a few houses down from me. As I recall, he drove a white police van. I ran into him at the market last year before Dora brought me here. I remembered him because he and his wife used to walk past my house on their evening stroll. They would stop to chat. I hadn't seen him since he moved. He said his wife passed away some time ago."

"Do you know his name?" Hunter asked.

"Not his last name, but his first name is Don. He's a security guard at Global Optics. It was stitched on his uniform when we met at the market."

Hunter caught his eye, then jotted something down in his notebook.

"Anything else you remember about that night that could help us find Penny's killer?" Davis asked. "Was Don a member of the search party?"

She shook her head. "I don't recall seeing him, but there were a lot of people there. I did see a van similar to his a little earlier that evening, but I don't think it belonged to Don. I only remember because the police asked if we'd seen any strangers in the neighborhood. Of course, it was getting dark. I could be mistaken." She folded her hands in her lap. "I'm sorry I can't provide you with more useful information."

Davis shook her hand when they rose to leave. "On the contrary, you've helped quite a bit. Thank you for your time. May we come back if we have further questions?"

"Of course. It's good to talk with someone, even if the subject is unpleasant. I don't get many visitors, other than Dora and Todd. He brings me lunch from McDonald's from time to time."

On their way out, a small black woman inched down the hallway in a wheelchair. Someone had removed the footrests and she walked the chair with her feet. A snail could have outrun her.

Davis smiled down at her. "May I help you go somewhere, ma'am?"

"Yes, sir. Thank you. I want to go to the front to visit for a spell."

"Sure. Hold up your feet. I'll take you there." In the vestibule, he helped her onto the sofa and left the wheelchair where she could slide into it when she wanted to leave.

"Thank you kindly, young man."

"Yes, ma'am, glad to help."

Outside, Davis remarked, "From all outward appearance

Elsie Kaufman's mental ability is above average. Not everyone would have noticed where the security guard worked. And Don Tompkins' absence from the search party could mean he'd taken the body to the retreat."

Hunter nodded. "Yeah, I saw where you were headed with that question. Anybody who didn't join in to find Penny could be our murderer. It's a place to start. However, the killer could have hidden the body in the van, then joined the search. Wouldn't be the first time."

"I hear you, pal, but I think Tompkins would be too smart to do something stupid."

"Why do you say that?"

"They used bloodhounds in the search. As a cop, Tompkins would know better than to hang around the neighborhood with a body in his truck the dogs could sniff out."

Sara Bradford's Home

Hunter twisted Davis' arm to go to a barbeque rib joint for lunch. Davis hated the messy hands, but he had to pacify his partner from time to time. Hunter wasn't into bean sprout sandwiches. Davis filled his plate with beans, coleslaw, and grilled chicken, without the sauce.

After lunch, they drove under the overpass to Highway 75 and turned left, headed to the outskirts of town to talk to Jacob Jamison's widow.

Davis rang the doorbell. A plump, smiling Hispanic woman answered the door. After introducing him and his partner, he asked to see Maddie Jamison. The housekeeper disappeared for a moment. Her slight accent drifted through the doorway.

"Miss Maddie, two police detectives are here to see you."

"Show them into the library, Beatrice, please."

Beatrice returned to lead them down a spacious hallway to a large, mahogany paneled room, one wall filled with leather bound books. A healthy fire blazed in the hearth.

A small well-dressed woman sat in a brown leather chair near the fireplace. She waved them in, indicating the matching sofa across from her. "Thank you, Beatrice."

Maddie Jamison turned her attention back to them. "Have a seat, gentlemen. You must be the detectives looking into Penny Pryor's disappearance. Lily said you might stop by. I suppose I should call it a murder now. It's difficult to think of Penny in that way."

Davis handed her his card. "Yes, ma'am. What can you tell us about that night?"

"I'm afraid I won't be of much help. My husband and I were out of town when it happened. We knew the family. Penny and my niece, Sara, were best friends. Penny was a sweet child, energetic, always with a smile on her pixie face. Such a tragedy. Not the sort of misfortune that usually happens to people you know."

Hunter pulled a notebook from his pocket.

"Did you ever know Sam Pryor to abuse his wife or daughter?" Davis asked.

"Nonsense. If I'd suspected anything of the kind, I would have reported it. Let me guess. You spoke to Dora Hastings. Sam Pryor worshipped his daughter. He would never have harmed her. He did spank Penny, but I didn't have a problem with that. Penny could be very strong-willed. In my personal opinion, if there were more spankings, there would be fewer Dora Hastings in the world."

She stood and walked to the hearth. "Dora's vicious innuendos can cause real trouble for Sam and Lily. Which they don't need to deal with while they grieve for their daughter."

Davis listened politely, but Maddie couldn't know for sure what had happened in the Pryor home. How many times had he heard people become incredulous to learn a neighbor was a killer? Evil people were adept at blending into society.

"I'm a little over-sensitive where Dora is concerned." Maddie returned to her chair, a slight frown wrinkling her brow. "Dora's mother, Elsie, is a good friend of mine. About a year ago, Elsie had pneumonia. For some reason, she started to hallucinate, became confused. Dora took advantage of the situation. She placed her mother in a rest home. Elsie didn't fight it, even gave Dora power of attorney. I think Elsie feared she had Alzheimers. As it turned out, she had a simple reaction to a medication her doctor prescribed. Once off the meds, she returned to normal.

"Dora took control of Elsie's home, automobile, and bank account. Elsie Kaufman doesn't belong in Serene Acres any more than I do. Dora refuses to let her leave. I've tried to intervene, but my attorney says there's nothing I can do.

"I'm sorry, gentlemen. I didn't mean to go off on a tangent. But the mere thought of that woman..." She took a deep breath. "Please continue."

"So you never saw any evidence that Sam Pryor hit his wife?" Hunter asked.

"I'm aware of one occasion. Lily came to see me after it happened. She said it was the first time he'd struck her. She asked my advice. Since there was no regular pattern of abuse, I suggested they go to their pastor for counseling. I believe they did so. Lily never told me of another incident."

Hunter cast an impish grin at Davis. "The situation with Mrs. Kaufman is out of our jurisdiction, you understand. However, off the record, there is a possibility that if you contact Todd Hastings, away from his wife, he might help you. No promises."

Maddie patted his hand. "Thank you. Perhaps I'll do that. Todd always liked Elsie."

The housekeeper showed them out. When the door closed, Davis turned to his partner. "You know you shouldn't have said that."

Hunter shrugged. "Probably not. I liked Mrs. Kaufman...and I'm not at all fond of her daughter. And God works in mysterious ways."

Davis expelled a deep breath. "Hunter, I don't know how to tell you this, but you are not God."

CHAPTER 18

Twin Falls Police Station

Matt arrived at the station at half past eight Saturday morning, giving him time to prepare for the nine o'clock meeting with Davis and Hunter. The desk sergeant waved him over as he walked through the lobby. "Ralph Simmons, from Custom Body Works, called a few minutes ago. Sounded excited about something. Wants you to call him."

Matt took the note to his office. He called Davis. "Any updates for the meeting?"

"No. We're going back out to the Cook place with a search warrant later. Why?"

Matt read the phone message the desk sergeant gave him. "Then let's postpone until tomorrow."

He disconnected with Davis, then called Simmons.

A receptionist answered and put Simmons on the phone. "Chief Foley, do you remember the BOLO notice you sent out a few years back, about the red Mustang with damage to the driver's side?"

After the accident, they'd towed Josh Bradford's car in. Paint smears, left by the hit-and-run vehicle, allowed McCulloch to identify the make, year, and model. The detectives sent out the notice to all the body shops in the area.

Simmons continued, "This morning, we received a car that matched your bulletin. A miracle we caught it. I hired a new man who read the old memo posted in the break room. It had been there so long the other guys ignored it. Anyway, the new guy noticed the vehicle he was about to work on matched the description."

Matt sucked in a breath. "Good catch. Who brought the car in?"

Papers rustled in the background. "Lance Cushing. He dropped it off. Asked to have the body repaired and wanted the car made ready for state inspection. The sticker and license plates were both outdated. I have his phone number on the worksheet."

"Hold on to the car. I'll send someone over right away. Give me the license and VIN numbers." Matt jotted down the numbers as Simmons read them off, then called McCulloch to have him pick up the vehicle.

Matt ran the license plates through DMV. The car's outdated Louisiana tags, listed the owner as Margaret Manning. She purchased the vehicle at an automobile auction in that state six years ago.

He dialed Sergeant Kennedy and gave him Cushing's telephone number. "Ask him to come in for questioning."

Later, he located Lucy Turner and asked her to take the interview. He gave her the background information on the kid. At four-o'clock, she buzzed to say she had Cushing in room one.

"Be right there." Matt strode down the corridor to watch the proceedings from the room next door. He closed the door and switched on the monitor in the corner. Detective Cole Allen joined Lucy and took a seat at the table.

Cushing looked nervous. The blond soul-patch under his lower lip gave a slight quiver. "Am I in trouble?"

Lucy didn't answer. She leaned back in her chair, across from Cushing. "Mind if we record this?"

Cushing placed both hands on the table. He looked around the walls as if the answer might appear. "No...I guess that's okay. Do I need a lawyer?"

Lucy shrugged. "We just want to ask a few questions. We're not charging you with anything, but I'm gonna read you your rights." Lucy switched on the recorder and read the Miranda warning. "Do you understand these rights as read to you?"

Cushing nodded.

"You'll have to answer yes or no, Mr. Cushing," Turner said.

Cushing leaned forward. "Yes."

Cole reached for a pen in the table drawer to hide a smile. He slid a waiver form across the desk for the man to sign. Cushing hesitated, but signed, then slipped it back to Cole.

"Do you want to waive your right to an attorney?" Lucy asked.

Cushing mumbled, "Yes."

Lucy resumed the interview. "Okay, let's get started. Did you take a red Mustang to Custom Body Works this morning?"

Cushing nodded. "Is there a problem? I have the title. Just haven't had time to transfer it."

"When did you purchase the car?"

"I didn't buy it. My uncle passed away and I inherited it. The title was in my uncle's papers, the last owner signed it over to him."

"What's your uncle's name?"

"Cook, Robert Cook. I don't understand. It's not a stolen car, is it? Like I said, the previous owner signed the title. I didn't know—."

Matt moved closer to the monitor.

"Did you ever drive the car while your uncle owned it?"

"I didn't even know he had a second car. When Uncle Bob passed away, I found it in a storage shed on the property. The car seemed in good condition, except for the body damage. It started right up when I jumped the battery. I decided to fix it up for my wife to drive. I don't—"

"We confirmed the car was involved in a hit-and-run accident four years ago. Attorney Joshua Bradford died in the crash. Paint smears on the Mustang match the paint on Bradford's car. Did you know Mr. Bradford?"

Visibly shaken, Cushing's eyes widened. He sat up straight in the chair. "No, no, you don't think I—my uncle drank a lot, but I don't think even he would leave an accident."

Matt walked back to his seat. Cushing apparently decided not to take the rap for something Uncle Bob might have done. Cushing could be telling the truth. It would be difficult to prove otherwise with the uncle dead.

Lucy continued. "And you never drove the car before today?"

"No, like I told you, I'd never seen it before yesterday when I took over the property he left to me."

"Do you have any idea where you were in August, four years ago?"

Cushing paused for a moment. "Uh...four years ago I was still in college at the University of Tennessee. I can't be sure, but I think that's the summer I stayed on campus to take some summer courses."

Lucy pushed back her chair and stood up. "That will be all for now. Thank you for coming in. If we need anything further, we'll call you. By the way, we'll have to hold on to the car for a while, and I'll need to see that title."

After Cushing left, Matt caught Lucy in the hallway. "Joshua Bradford interviewed Robert Cook the night he died."

Lucy lifted an eyebrow. "I checked Cushing's driving

records before he arrived. He has a few traffic tickets. Nothing else. We'll check Robert Cook's record, then contact the college to confirm Cushing's story."

"Bring Davis up to date when he gets back." Matt massaged his neck muscles on the way to his office. He stood at the window behind his desk, running the interview details in his mind. Outside, gusts of wind whipped red and orange leaves in circles on the sidewalk, finally settling them in piles on the grass.

After four years of investigation, could the solution be this easy? Had Cook followed Bradford and run him down? For what reason? Accident maybe?

Detectives had interviewed Cook after Bradford's death. According to the casebook, the man had been drunk, almost incoherent, that evening. Cook had a number of DUI's. The state had revoked his driver's license. Reason enough for Cook to leave the scene. Especially a fatal accident. No Mustang had been registered to Cook at the time and the case went cold. Now Cook looked good for both murders, Penny and Josh Bradford's.

~*~

When Matt returned to the station after lunch, a crowd of soccer moms, with their embarrassed kids filled the lobby, all trying to out-shout each other. The usual fight between parents, coaches, and referees had broken out at the game.

Amazing. Sometimes kids were more mature than their parents.

He strolled down the hall to the crime lab. Dale McCulloch sat on a stool, peering into an elaborate microscope.

Matt cleared his throat.

McCulloch looked up and gave him a lopsided grin. "Help you, Chief?"

"Find anything on the vehicle?"

"We pulled it in. You already know the paint smears on both cars matched. I also found minute particles of blood in the dents. It's the car, all right. No question.

"I did a computerized reconstruction of the accident. The damage to both vehicles matched. You may remember from the crash site, there were no skid marks on the road. An intoxicated driver might not have braked. No way to tell whether it was deliberate or alcohol confusion."

Matt pulled out a stool and sat down. "There's a good possibility Robert Cook is responsible for Joshua Bradford's death. What about the car's interior?"

McCulloch turned from the microscope to face Matt. "Not much, except four years of dust. Someone wiped the inside clean before the dust settled. That's not something an innocent person does. There were recent fingerprints on the steering wheel, gearshift and car door. I assume they belong to the nephew, placed there when he drove it to the repair shop. I'll check the prints against the ones the detectives got from Cushing."

The CSU Chief picked up a bagged leather-bound book from the lab table and tossed it to Matt. "We did find a day timer under the car seat. Didn't you say the car belonged to Margaret Manning? If so, the book can't be hers. The initials don't match."

Matt caught the bag. He looked down at the embossed gold initials and almost dropped the container. The initials *S B* were stamped on the cover.

Sara Bradford.

The monogram's significance slammed him like a punch

in the gut. The notebook proved a connection to the car that killed her husband. Proof he'd been looking for over the past four years. It should make him happy, but it didn't.

Had Sara hired Cook to kill Josh? Certainly a possibility. Sara must have been in the car at some point to have left it there.

Matt held up the day timer. "Any fingerprints?"

McCulloch nodded. "A few, all belonging to the same person." He pushed his glasses up on his nose. "Something strange about that, though. There were no prints on the leather cover, someone had wiped it clean. All the prints I found were on the inside. And, the calendar dates were two years after Bradford's death."

Matt's gaze shifted to the notebook. "From that we can assume we have a murderer who is smart enough to wipe the prints off the cover. But dumb enough to leave it in the car with her initials on it?"

"Sounds right to me. Her?"

"Yeah. Bradford's wife's name is Sara."

Mac whistled. "Wow. I can verify ownership of the notebook by the fingerprints, make sure they're hers."

"Do that as soon as you can." Matt bounced the book against his palm. Sara Bradford might be many things, but she wasn't dumb. "You sure none of the prints in the car match those in the calendar?"

McCulloch shrugged. "If there are, we haven't found them. We gave the car a thorough going over. The only prints inside belonged to whoever drove the car last and they don't match those in the notebook."

Sara Bradford's Home

The church sale finally behind her, Sara had spent the afternoon boxing the leftovers for the Goodwill and Salvation Army before heading home.

As she got out of the car, Matt Foley's Expedition pulled in behind her. His solemn expression gave her a *déjà vu* moment. He wasn't bringing good news.

Sara grinned anyway. "Hi, Matt. I came home to grab a bite. I missed lunch. Come in. If you haven't eaten, I'll repay you for the lunch you bought."

"Thanks, I've eaten." Matt didn't return the smile. A moment of silence followed before he spoke again. "Sara, there's something important I need to discuss with you. Where can we talk?"

A nervous quiver lodged in her stomach. "This sounds serious. Let's go into the kitchen. You can talk while I eat. Whatever it is, you can tell me in front of Maddie."

Sara led the way down the hallway. She pulled cold chicken and fruit salad from the refrigerator, then set them at the island.

Maddie entered from the hall. "I thought that was your voice I heard, Matthew. What brings you out?"

He pulled a stool from under the counter and sat across from Sara. Her aunt eased into the one beside her.

"We found the car that killed Josh earlier today. It belonged to a man named Robert Cook," Matt said.

A welcome relief flowed through her body. Sara inhaled a deep breath. "That's great news. Have you arrested him?"

"Can't. He died from natural causes a few days ago. Do you know him?"

She plumbed the recesses of her memory. After a moment, she locked in on the name. The name had been among those Josh's law firm had requested from the notes in his briefcase after his death. "Cook, wasn't that the

159

name of the man Josh interviewed the day he died?"

Matt nodded. "Have you ever met or had any dealing with Cook?"

She scanned the stoic expression on his face and it hit her. He'd known about Cook all along. He'd been testing her. "Not to my knowledge."

"The car wasn't all we found." He held out a photo of a desk calendar. "We found this inside the vehicle. Does it belong to you?"

Disbelief and a touch of anxiety crept up her spine. She recognized the notebook. "It's mine. It went missing ages ago from my desk. I assumed I'd lost it or someone took it by mistake. How could it turn up in that car?"

He didn't speak, just stared straight into her eyes.

Realization dawned. She could feel the blood drain from her face. Unable to suppress the tremor in her fingers, she replaced the fork on the dinner plate. "Good heavens, Matt. Did you come here to arrest me? How can you think...? The automobile doesn't belong to me."

He looked down at his hands. "It wasn't registered in your name, and I didn't come here to arrest you. But I may have to, unless the DA thinks we need more evidence before filing charges. He may go with Cook's bad driving record, but the notebook connects you to Cook. Are you sure you've never spoken to him?"

Sara shook her head. "I can't say with absolute certainty...but not to my knowledge."

Maddie spoke for the first time. "You can't believe Sara had anything to do with Joshua's death, Matthew. I remember you as being smarter than that when you were in school."

He glanced at Sara then back at Maddie. "If I believed her to be guilty, I would arrest her." He picked up the photograph. "But this is evidence that can be used against her."

He walked across the room and stood in the doorway. "I shouldn't tell you this, but this case has re-opened. You should find a good attorney. If you are arrested, with your clean record, a lawyer can get you out on bond. You might also want to consider if there's anyone who dislikes you enough to frame you for murder."

His footsteps echoed down the hallway, the door closed, and he was gone.

The sound of the car engine faded into the night. Lunch forgotten, Sara laid her head on her arms and closed her eyes. Her job was in turmoil, someone was trying to kill her, and now the police had evidence to tie her to Josh's murder. Matt had said he hadn't arrested her because there'd been no proof. Now he could connect her to the hit-and-run vehicle. All the terror demons from the past were unleashed, and it surprised her that she could handle it.

For the past four years, she wondered what would happen if this moment came. Odd, but a sense of calm washed over her. Uncertainty had kept her off balance. Now, at least she had something to fight against.

When she opened her eyes, Maddie's troubled gaze met hers. "You need to call Harold Golden. He'll know what to do. No one in their right mind would believe you were involved in Joshua's death."

Sara nodded. "You're right. Harold can tell me how to proceed from here."

She'd met Harold Golden through her husband. Josh introduced Golden as "the foremost criminal attorney in the country." In the early days of her marriage, she and Josh spent no less than two evenings a week in Golden's company.

161

Harold Golden's home had been a Mecca for young lawyers. Invitations to join one of his late-night sessions were coveted by young attorneys, and Josh had been Golden's favorite. She dialed his private number. "Hi Harry, it's Sara Bradford."

His tone came across a little stilted. "Yes, Sara. How may I help you?"

"I'm sorry to say this isn't a social call. As of a few minutes ago, I'm a suspect in Josh's death. I wanted you to know that before you decide to defend me, if you can fit me into your caseload."

"Why is it, after all this time, they've decided to pin this on you?"

Sara told him about Matt's visit. The scratch of his pen sounded as he took notes. When she finished the story, he spoke, "I don't think you have a problem. The evidence they have is circumstantial at best, not enough for an arrest warrant. I'm swamped with other cases. I don't think I could do your defense justice. I can send you a list of good attorneys..."

"I'm sorry you're not available, Harry, but I understand."

Sara replaced the phone on its base. Did Harry think her guilty?

Her mind flashed back to Josh's funeral. Harry had seemed distant and quiet. She assumed his silence was grief. Never for a moment did it occur to her that he'd considered her somehow responsible. Did he know of Josh's extra-marital affairs? Assume she had killed him in a jealous rage?

Her chest felt vacant, as if someone had slammed the breath from her body. "Looks like you're wrong, Maddie. Some people do think I could have murdered Josh. Harold Golden, for starters."

162

CHAPTER 19

Sara Bradford's Home

After her conversation with Harold Golden, Sara took a mug of hot tea into the library. The aromatic steam had already begun to relax her frayed nerves. She needed that. It would make it easier to fall asleep later.

She settled into a chair in front of the fireplace as bright embers floated out of sight up the chimney, resting her head on the soft leather back. She sipped the tea, trying to unwind. Heaven knew her muscles had good cause for tension. Her body had more than its share of trauma the past few days. The phone rang and she placed the cup on the end table, then reached to answer it.

"Sara Bradford?" the voice on the phone inquired.

"Yes, this is Sara."

"Sara, this is Gaye, I'm the ER nurse who took care of you earlier this week. Do you remember me?"

"Of course, Gaye. How are you?"

"I'm fine, thank you. The reason I called is we have a patient, Dolly Campbell, in emergency. She's asking for you. She was involved in an accident, and insisted we contact you before she'll let us take her into surgery. She needs treatment immediately and we can't locate her relatives. Would it be possible for you to come right away?"

"I'm leaving now." Sara grabbed her car keys and rushed out the door. Gaye hadn't mentioned the children. Perhaps they were at home with their mother. *Please, let them be safe.*

Twin Falls Memorial Hospital

The nurse met Sara at the entrance to the emergency ward and led her into a curtain-covered cubicle where Dolly Campbell lay on a gurney, her face pasty white, wrinkled with pain.

Sara moved to Dolly's side and took her hand. "Dolly, it's Sara."

The frail woman's eyes fluttered open. She tried to lift her head but the effort seemed too much. Dolly clutched Sara's hand. "Thank God you came. We were on our way to our lake cabin...a car crossed the median...hit us head on." She took a shaky breath. "I think Walter and Diane are dead." Her voice caught. "I couldn't tell for sure...the nurses won't tell me if Poppy and Danny were hurt or how badly."

Sara's heart plummeted. The children were in the car. She moved closer. Dolly still gripped Sara's hand. "Don't talk now, Dolly. Let the doctors take care of you. Afterwards, you can tell me whatever you want."

"No." Dolly's voice grew insistent. "I must say this. If anything happens to me...promise you will take care of the children. If Walter and Diane are gone, there's no one to care for them. Please."

Sara squeezed her hand. "Of course I will. You have my word. Now please let them attend to your wounds."

Dolly nodded as two nurses wheeled her out with an urgency that frightened Sara.

In ER, Sara stepped down the hall to the waiting room. Ahead, she spotted Gaye and stopped her. "There were two children and two other adults in the accident with Mrs. Campbell. Can you tell me how they're doing?"

Gaye's face scrunched into a pained expression. She

shook her head. "I'm sorry, Sara. I can only give that information to the nearest relative. It's HIPPA rules."

Sara gulped a shaky breath. "I understand, but I don't think there is a nearest relative. Dolly said the whole family was in the accident."

Gaye touched her arm. "Believe me, I would help if I could."

Tears stung the back of Sara's eyelids. She pulled her new cell phone from her bag and punched in the number on the business card Matt gave her.

A few seconds later, a tired voice came on the line. "What is it now, Sara?"

His voice sounded weary with a touch of irritation. She swallowed her pride. "I need your help. I'm at the hospital—"

The volume of Matt's voice increased. "I told you to let us know when you left home. Why didn't you listen?"

Her voice caught, despite efforts to remain calm. "It isn't me. It's the children, Poppy and Danny."

"Who?"

"The children from the trailer park you found for me."

A long pause followed. "Tell me what happened."

When she finished, he said, "Hold tight. I'll be there in a few minutes. The hospital will talk to me."

~*~

Before he left home, Matt called the highway patrol and got a run down on the accident. It wasn't pretty. Afterwards, he made the twenty minute drive to the hospital. He stepped into the ER and Gaye met him at the nurses' station.

"Hey, big guy. What brings you in?"

He pulled her aside. "I heard about the expressway accident. How bad are the victims?"

Gaye shook her head. "Two of the family members, the grandfather and children's mother, were DOA when we got them. The grandmother is in surgery with massive internal injuries. Both kids are alive, thanks to their seatbelts, but they have broken bones. The driver in the other car survived with a broken leg and a concussion. Texting and driving. He's in recovery now. Are the family friends of yours?"

Matt shrugged. "In a manner of speaking."

He gave Gaye a half wave and went in search of Sara. He found her in the surgery waiting room, her gaze fixed on some point in the darkness beyond the window. She brought to mind a big-eyed doll he'd seen in store windows. Fragile and vulnerable.

Why did this woman keep intruding into his life? Had his guardian angel turned sadist? He kicked himself mentally. That wasn't fair. Sara had her own major problems. He cleared his throat.

She rose and hurried to him. "Have you found out anything? Are the children alive? Are they okay?"

"The kids are fine. A couple of broken bones." He paused. "The grandfather and mother died in the accident. The kids are sedated, they don't know."

Sara wrapped her arms around her body and turned away, as if to shield herself from the news. "Oh no...poor...
"

Matt touched her arm and led her back to the sofa, then sat beside her. "The doctor will let us know as soon as Mrs. Campbell is out of surgery."

He sat with Sara until one o'clock, when a young doctor came. He introduced himself as Dr. Dietz. "Are you both

166

family members?"

Matt stepped forward to meet him. "No, I'm Police Chief Foley." He nodded towards Sara. "This is Sara Bradford, a friend. The children's only other relative is their father. He's in prison."

"I see," Dr. Dietz said. He turned to Sara. "You're the one Mrs. Campbell asked for before the surgery?"

Sara moved close to Matt. "Yes. How is she?"

"She suffered extensive internal injuries, which were made more difficult by her age. The prognosis is not good. She's in recovery now. She'll go from there to ICU. You can visit her for fifteen minutes, every two hours."

"How are the children?" Sara asked.

"Danny has a broken arm. Poppy has a broken foot and some bad bruises. They'll be fine. You can look in on them, but they need rest. Tomorrow will bring them some very bad news."

~*~

While she waited for ICU visiting hours, Sara looked in on the kids. They were sleeping, probably sedated for the pain.

It was early morning before Sara and Matt got in to see Dolly. She was conscious, and glanced up at Matt, questions in her eyes.

Sara tilted her head in his direction. "This is Police Chief, Matt Foley. A friend."

Dolly tried to lift her head. "Walter...Diane?"

Sara clasped the injured woman's hand. "I'm sorry..."

The old woman closed her eyes. "It's okay. I knew. Chief, you are my witness. If I don't...make it, I want Sara to take Danny and Poppy. There's no other family. Will you tell whoever needs to know that this is my verbal will? I can't bear to think they might go into foster care." She took a shaky breath. "Or to their father."

"Yes, ma'am," Matt said, his voice husky. "I'll take care of it." He pulled a small notebook from his pocket and wrote out a rough will, then called one of the nurses into the room and asked her to witness Dolly's verbal instructions and her signature on the page.

Sara listened to Dolly's life story in fifteen-minute installments throughout the early morning as life support monitors beeped incessantly in the background. Nurses wandered in and out of the room. Worry lines creased their brows as they read the instruments. Dolly reminisced about her life with Walter. They'd met in an orphanage and married when they finished high school. Dolly inhaled deeply between each sentence, her voice becoming softer as the hours passed.

Sara leaned close to catch each word.

Finally, the older woman drew in a shuddering breath. "Sara...remember your promise."

At seven thirty Sunday morning, the grip on Sara's hand loosened, the green band on the heart monitor flat lined, and bells went off. Sara backed from the room as it filled with emergency response attendants to no avail.

Dolly Campbell had slipped away.

Moisture trickled from under Sara's lashes onto her cheeks. She stumbled into the corridor and braced against the wall.

Just down the hall, Matt waited between two IV poles and a portable blood pressure monitor, his arms folded, waiting.

"I didn't mean to keep you up all night, Matt."

He cleared his throat, then reached and took her arm.

"Not a problem. Come. I'll follow you home."

Matt Foley's Home

Monday morning, Matt started his three-mile run with a warm up on the back deck before breakfast. With Rowdy at his heels, he started a slow run then built up speed until his blood pumped madly and adrenalin flooded through his body, giving him a runner's high.

After a shower and shave, he dressed for work then went downstairs and warmed a bagel, added cream cheese and poured a cup of coffee.

Taking the food to the deck, he stood and ate, gazing across the lawn into the woods as a graceful hawk soared above the treetops. The deer were gone. Too late in the morning for them. They were early risers.

He found Stella in the laundry room. "Don't make dinner tonight. I'll eat in town."

She turned towards him with a smile. "Fine, Chief."

"See you later."

He returned to his bedroom. He'd dropped his holster and weapon in a chair here when he came home. He headed out the door and paused as a thought hit him. "Rowdy, come here boy. Want to go for a ride?"

The dog skidded around the corner, his nub of a tail wiggling. Matt got the leash from the closet and hooked him up.

"Stella, I'm taking Rowdy with me today."

She acknowledged his statement with what sounded like "fine".

He settled Rowdy in the backseat and drove to the station.

Bringing the pup along had been an inspired idea. The

hospital told him they'd release the kids today, around three o'clock. He wanted to be there when Sara told them about their family. She would need backup for that dirty job. In his own special way, Rowdy could help.

Twin Falls Police Station

The misty autumn air hung low and mild, as Matt pulled into the station. He went in search of Hunter and Davis and found the two detectives in the break room. "Sorry I missed the nine o'clock meeting. Couldn't be helped."

Rowdy jumped into Hunter's lap. They were old friends. The dog intuitively knew Davis wasn't a dog-man. Hunter accepted Rowdy's wet kisses. "What are you doing here, buddy?"

Matt took a seat by Davis. "I have a death notification. Two kids lost their family last night. He's my backup. What's new on the Pryor case?"

Hunter stirred his coffee, and petted Rowdy with the other hand. "The victim is officially the Pryor girl. Lisa received the dental records late yesterday." He took a printout report of yesterday's activity from his inside pocket and handed it to Matt. "My wife said to thank you for installing the laptop computer in the car. I got the paperwork done without having to come back to the office."

"Tell her she's welcome. That was the purpose for the installations. Let you people spend more time on police work—less time with written reports. How's the legwork going?"

Davis blew across his cup. "We've finished all the interviews." He ticked off items on his fingers. "What we know so far, Charles Edwards is a Vietnam vet. Don

Tompkins retired from the bomb squad in the Dallas Police Department. Elliot was away with his parents that weekend. Jacob Jamison's widow said they were also out of town that Memorial Day. Seems Jamison amassed quite a fortune after he moved to Arkansas."

Hunter added, "And when Jamison died, he left the money to his widow. He and Maddie Jamison separated, but never divorced. Lucky break with her handicap."

"What's your next step?" Matt asked.

"We're still working the panel truck angle." Davis glanced at his partner. "And we also need to go through all the junk Mac collected at the Cook place. But that's on the back burner for now. Spoke to Tompkins and Edwards yesterday. Both admitted they used a panel truck at the time the girl disappeared. Since they lived in the neighborhood and had access to a white truck, we moved them up in rank on the list of suspects."

"And," Matt said. "Tompkins' bomb squad experience makes him suspect in the violence at Global."

Davis' easy grin disappeared. "There's also the possibility Sam Pryor may have abused Penny. Two people confirmed he slapped his wife, which could have extended to the child. I don't want to believe it, but we need to put the question to Sam and Lily."

"Do what you have to do, but I suggest you go to their home. Since Lily Pryor is Governor Ferrell's sister, we don't want him on our backs for police harassment. Be sensitive to the family's ordeal. This has been one long nightmare for those two people."

Davis tugged on his tie. "Unless Sam's responsible for his daughter's death."

Matt nodded. "Point taken. I'll try to reach Governor Ferrell. Let him know that angle is part of the investigation, and hope he understands."

Sara Bradford's Home

A thin wisp of clouds floated overhead in the buttermilk sky as Matt pulled into Sara's driveway.

Beatrice opened the front door, a red tinge to her cheeks. Apparently, she remembered their last encounter when she threatened to undress him. Without a word, she led him to the library where Maddie Jamison sat before a black-faced computer monitor.

Maddie turned when he cleared his throat to announce his presence. "Hi, Matthew, how may I help you?"

"I didn't know you used a computer," he said.

"Most computers have a handicap feature that makes it easier for people with vision problems. The black screen with white letters is easier to read. I use it to make out the weekly menus for Beatrice. Are you looking for Sara?"

"Yes, ma'am," Matt said. "Is she at home?"

Maddie nodded her head towards the hallway. "You'll find her in the kitchen. She's washing dishes."

Matt started towards the door, then turned back. "Did you say washing dishes?"

"Yes, Matthew. It's one of the dark sides of her personality. I'll let her explain it to you."

He walked down the passageway into the kitchen. Sara stood at the large country sink, up to her elbows in soapy dishwater. She looked over her shoulder when he entered the room. "Hi, Matt." She gave him a bright smile. Reaching into a drawer, she withdrew a dishtowel and threw it at him. "Come on in. You can dry."

He caught the towel. "What is all this? I know you have a dishwasher."

Sara dunked a plate into the water. "It's soap-suds therapy. Whenever I have a difficult decision to make, I wash dishes. It clears my head. A little trick I learned from my mother. I'm sure she just wanted me to do the dishes, but somehow, it works for me."

"I will be happy to assist you. It is a little known police fact that no husband has ever been shot while helping his wife with the dishes. I say that with all the limitless resources of my profession."

Sara gave him an impish grin. "Is that a proposal?"

He placed the towel over his shoulder, took her by the arms and turned her to face him, ignoring the water that dripped from the rubber gloves she wore. "Do you want it to be?"

He hadn't a clue where that question had come from.

Tears welled in her eyes. She leaned in to him and placed her brow on his chest. "Oh, Matt, I'm such a mess. I don't know what I want right now. You heard Dolly ask me to take care of her grandchildren. I have to pick them up in an hour. I can't let them go into foster care, but I'm scared to death to bring them into my life. You, of all people, know how dangerous that could be with all that's happened lately. Not to mention the issues of adding active children to the mix of people here in their fifties."

He nodded. "Ah, I see your dilemma. The funeral is scheduled for Wednesday?"

She sniffed and tried to wipe her eyes with the wet gloves and deposited a glob of suds on her nose. "I made the arrangements as soon as I could. Delaying it will only prolong the inevitable. No one has told the children about their family. I must do that today." Her voice caught, her lower lip trembled. "Matt, those little guys have nobody, besides me. I care for them so much. It breaks my heart to think what they might have to endure if I don't take them..."

He helped her remove the gloves, pulling at the oversized fingers as she worked her hands free, then gave her a paper towel to wipe her nose. Taking hold of her arm, he led her to the table bench in front of the bay window. When she was seated, he slid into a chair beside her. "Would you like me to tell them? That's why I came by. It's not a job I like, but sometimes, I have to deliver bad news to families."

She shook her head. "I couldn't ask you to do that. Besides, the kids don't know you. I think they'd handle it better if it came from me. Could you just be there? I can't mess this up."

He leaned across the table and looked into her eyes. "Raising two children alone is not to be taken lightly. Kids need both parents, and a stable home life. Especially these two. I don't think they've ever had stability in their lives. It'll be a big job."

She placed her elbows on the table, resting her chin in her hands. "I know that. That's why I'm in such a quandary. I've always intended to quit work when I had children. I would like to home school, or at the very least, send them to a Christian school. I know they should have two parents. Right now, I feel that one parent is better than foster care."

"So what's your plan?" he asked.

She took a deep breath. "I've prayed hard for wisdom. God's given me peace about bringing them here." She gave a sardonic laugh. "But He hasn't been forthcoming with any of the details. I called an attorney earlier today to see if I could get custody. He doesn't think there'll be a problem. I asked him to meet me at the hospital at three. He'll also check out the Campbell's property, since the children are their legal heirs."

Tears welled in her eyes. "I want to take care of them—give them as much love as they need until their wounds, physical and mental, heal. The big issue is how to make sure they're safe"

Matt rose, walked to the counter, and brought back another paper towel. "I'll work on the safety part. For what it's worth, I think you made the right decision."

"That's easy for you to say," Sara replied with a tear-stained grin.

"Do you have car seats?"

She nodded. "I purchased one for Poppy and a booster seat for Danny. That's what the sales clerk recommended."

"Since Danny is six, you wouldn't be ticketed for not having him in a booster, but it's safer to use one. Where are they?"

"In the portico entryway. I haven't put them into the rental car yet." She led the way.

"You all set to go?" Matt asked.

"Give me a minute to freshen my makeup. I don't want them to see I've been crying."

She headed upstairs and he strode to the entryway and picked up the car seats. "I'll put these in my car and wait outside. I brought Rowdy with me."

CHAPTER 20

Twin Falls Memorial Hospital

The sun set high in the sky, a bright ball of fire in the blue canopy. Thankful for the good weather, Sara glanced at Matt. She didn't understand his motives. Not that she didn't appreciate his help. Matt Foley was a good man. She knew that from talks with Mary before her death. But she and Matt had gotten off to a bad start. He'd told her he still considered her guilty in Josh's death. What had changed his mind? Or had it changed? Was he just thinking of Danny and Poppy? The man was an enigma.

Matt parked the car, leaving the window down halfway for Rowdy. As they reached the entrance, her attorney, Blaze Baxter, met them. Blaze looked nothing like his name. Fifty, thin and balding, he looked more like an accountant than a lawyer, but he came highly recommended.

She made introductions as Blaze led the way past the double doors to the reception desk. This place had become much too familiar for her tastes. Getting well acquainted with a hospital wasn't a habit she wanted to encourage.

She cast Matt a grateful glance, then followed Blaze to the admissions' office and signed all the forms to get the children released. It would have taken all day without Blaze's authority behind her.

After they'd finished the paperwork, she thanked him for his help, then she and Matt went up to see the children. The hospital had put them together in a semi-private room.

Sara gave the door a light tap then stepped into the

room. The children stared, with blank expressions, at cartoons on the television. Their eyes lit up when they saw her.

Danny's left arm had been secured in a camouflage cast, while Poppy's foot sported a pink one. Sara gave them a long hug and introduced Matt.

Wide eyed, Danny looked at Matt. "Are you a real cop?"

Matt grinned. "Yep, 'fraid so."

"Can I see your badge?"

Matt removed the shield holder from his pocket. He handed it to the boy.

"Wow. Why don't you wear a uniform?" Danny asked.

"When you're the chief, you get to choose. I only wear it for special ceremonies. You guys ready to go home?"

A nurse and an orderly appeared in the doorway with wheelchairs, and Matt loaded the children on board.

Sara caught the woman's gaze. "We want to take them to the hospital chapel before we leave, if that's okay."

She gave an understanding nod. "Call me when you're ready to go."

There were six pews in the small chapel, all empty. Light filtered through stained-glass windows from one wall that made colorful patterns on the light blue carpet.

Sara had prayed most of the night for the right words to inform these children. She'd asked God to let her be the kind of parent her dad and mom had been to her. They'd handled parenthood with easy grace. She'd been an only child. Her parents praised her talents, which were few, but never pushed. Letting her find her own way, in her own time. Losing them had placed a permanent scar on her heart.

Poppy sat on Sara's lap, and she drew Danny's chair close to the pew. Matt took a seat in front and turned sideways to face her.

Heart lodged in her throat, she inhaled a deep breath. As simply as possible, she tried to explain the complicated concept of death. "Your mommy and grandparents are in heaven with Jesus now. They were sad to leave you. They asked me to take good care of you."

Danny's eyes welled. He knew what she meant. Poppy, unaware, played with the gold locket Sara wore.

She pushed on. "Our bodies are temporary containers. A vessel God gives us to keep our souls safe until we die. When death comes, the soul leaves its earthly shell. It goes to heaven in a brand new body. This new body doesn't feel pain, or grow old. It lasts forever. Someday, when you are very old, you can join your mom and grandparents in heaven for a grand reunion." She pulled them close. "Do you understand what I'm saying?"

Danny's chin dropped to his chest, but Poppy just stared at her with big teary eyes.

Sara cast a pleading glance at Matt.

Matt lifted Danny onto his lap, then gave Sara a nod of encouragement. "You're doing great. It may take some time for them to understand."

Sara's gaze searched the children's faces. "Do you have any questions?"

Danny leaned back against Matt's chest. "Does it mean that Grandy's 'ritis doesn't hurt anymore?"

"That's right, Danny. She feels no pain, not ever."

He nodded. "Good. She'll like it there." He paused, then a worried frown wrinkled his small brow. "Where will we live?"

Sara held back her tears by force of will. "With me, in my home. Do you think that will be okay?"

A look of relief washed over his face. "Yes, ma'am."

Outside, Matt strapped Danny in the car seat while Sara did the same with Poppy.

Rowdy seemed to sense the children's sadness. He didn't jump or wag his tail. The pup placed his head on Danny's knee, gazing up at him with soulful eyes.

Sara gained a new respect for Matt as he drove them to a child-friendly fast food chain. He had good instincts with children, bringing Rowdy and taking them to a restaurant with a playground had been the right choices. The children barely touched their meals, but the toy captivated Poppy on the drive home.

When they arrived at Sara's, Matt helped her get the children into the house and removed the car seats from his SUV. Afterwards, she walked him to the door. "Thank you for today, Matt. I don't think I could have done this alone."

He put his hand on the door and looked down at her. "No problem. Call me if you need help."

He closed the door behind him. Already, she found she missed the comfort of his presence.

Maddie, Beatrice and Pete met the children at the door, a group of loving new grandparents. They couldn't replace the Campbell's, but they could love them just as much.

"Want to see the flowers?" Pete asked.

Danny nodded. He took Poppy's hand in his, very much the protective big brother. They followed Pete outside.

Sara stood at the window and watched the little boy trying so hard to hide his pain.

Later, Sara took Poppy upstairs for a short nap before dinner. The little girl had looked at her new room, and cast a frightened glance at Sara. She couldn't make Poppy go into the room alone. The little girl needed time to adjust to the house and sleeping alone. Sara turned back the cover on her own bed.

Danny might be experiencing the same phobia. However, he said nothing when she asked him if his room was all right. Perhaps he wanted to impress her by being a big boy.

There had been too much chaos in his young life that forced him to grow up too fast.

A sudden panic attack hit Sara. The kids had no clothes here. She'd have to go by the Campbell place to pick up some necessities until she could shop for them. And she didn't have a door key.

Global Optics

Matt spent most of the drive back to the station with Sara and the two kids on his mind. He'd involved himself in her personal affairs. Considering their history, that was a bad idea. The past four years he'd considered her a murder suspect. Now, she seemed to be everywhere he turned, with him playing the role of knight in shining armor. Perhaps those two kids had drawn him in. Children had always been his weak spot. And those two had never caught a break. Whatever. He needed to proceed with caution.

He made an abrupt u-turn and headed to Global Optics, organizing his mind around the few facts he had on the explosion. He wanted to ask Tompkins a few questions.

Outside the Global building, he stood on the pavement, admiring the monument to modern architecture. Its mirrored presence reflected the sun but diffused the light in a way that didn't blind him.

Two uniformed men sat behind the security desk before a bank of six monitors. One faced the screens with only the back of his head visible. The other guard, Don Tompkins, stood at the counter. Ahead of Matt, a young woman marched to the counter, three-inch heels clicking on the tile. Her type made him uncomfortable. Very self-assured, with the expression of a petulant child, who'd never had anyone tell her no. "I'm back from lunch. Someone parked in my space. I want the car moved."

The eager young guard in front of the monitors sprang to his feet. "Right away, Ms. Dean."

The older man reached out and placed a steady hand on the young man's shoulder, then turned to Ms. Dean. "I'm sure you have important things to do, Emily. Why don't you give my partner your car keys? We'll locate the individual in your space and park your car for you. Ben will return your keys within the hour."

She slapped the keys into the young man's hand. "You people need to get your act together. You should prevent these problems. That's what we pay you for." She whirled then stalked towards the elevators.

Tompkins turned to Matt. The guard nodded in Ms. Dean's direction. "Actually, we're paid to protect company property, but I thought it best not to remind her. She's the CEO's secretary. The executive parking area is a sacred cow. I hope you're not the culprit in her space."

Matt held up both hands. "Not me. I'm in visitors' parking. They taught me to read signs in grade school."

"Glad to know someone can still read. Now, how may I help you, Chief?"

"I have a few follow up questions about last Friday. Do you have a minute?"

"Sure, let me take care of Ms. Dean's problem first. I'll be right with you." He turned to his partner. "Ben, call Nancy Warren in the distribution center. A sales rep went back to see her a few minutes ago. He's probably parked in

Emily's spot. If so, tell him to move it. I'll be in the office if you need me."

Mission accomplished, Tompkins led Matt to the office he'd previously visited. Matt didn't sit down. "This will only take a minute. What do you know about making bombs?"

"A lot less than I used to. There are websites with systematic instructions on how to build a bomb if you know where to look. Bomb cults and chat rooms with all kinds of crazies. I keep an eye on them, a holdover from my old job. When I see a scary post, I let my pals on the squad know. Bombers are the worst kind of cowards."

He shook his head. "I helped with the Oklahoma City bombing in '95. Worse than anything I witnessed in war."

How much of what Tompkins said was his true feeling or just a good act, Matt couldn't tell. But he sounded sincere.

"I can't disagree with you there," Matt said. "You're telling me there are cults out there who share that kind of information?"

Tompkins laughed. "Scary, isn't it? You can spot the amateurs by how many fingers they have missing."

Matt shook his head. "The bomb unit folks picked up all the pieces to reconstruct the bomb. This guy wasn't an amateur."

"That's not good," Tompkins said.

"Any pros on those websites? Do they brag about their success stories?"

"Probably, and maybe a few al Qaeda protégées. And yes, I've seen some bragging but nothing specific enough to track them down."

Matt stepped back to the door. "If you see anything helpful, give me a call. While I'm here, I'd like to speak to Charles Edwards, if I may."

The guard picked up the phone on the desk. After a

short interval, he turned to Matt. "Take the elevator to the top floor. Edwards's secretary will meet you there."

Matt left the reception area and marched across to the elevators. He hadn't obtained much information from Tompkins. At least the security guard knew investigators were on the job.

The elevator stopped on the fourth floor. As the door slid open, an attractive woman waited for Matt in the hallway.

"Chief Foley, I'm Gail Barnes, Mr. Edwards's secretary. Please follow me. He's waiting for you in his office."

She led Matt to the end of a wide hallway and opened the door to a spacious secretarial office. Ms. Barnes picked up the phone. "Chief Foley is here, Mr. Edwards."

A few seconds later, the inner door opened. Edwards came out, his hand outstretched. "How are you? You impressed my wife, Marnie, at Stanton's dinner." He gave Matt's hand a firm grip. Edwards pointed him to a chair. "How may I help you?"

Matt let his gaze roam around the office as he took a seat. The space was elegant, like the man, filled with contemporary office furniture with smooth, graceful lines. Modern artwork was tastefully placed around the walls. Bookshelves covered one wall with a faux fireplace in the center, complete with an electric log. "I came on another matter and decided to update you on the explosion while I was here. It appears someone planted a bomb in the forklift."

Edwards's eyes widened. "I hadn't heard. I appreciate your letting me know." A slight frown wrinkled his tanned forehead. "Who could have done such a thing, and why?"

"I'd hoped you might have some ideas. We have lots of theories but little else. I suppose there's the possibility someone tried to squelch the buy-out."

Matt threw that out there, already convinced Sara Bradford had been the intended victim. He wanted to watch Edwards's reaction. "Can you think of any motive for what happened?"

"I wish I could. It's extraordinary. I've been in the optical business for more than twenty years. Nothing like this has ever happened. However, I can't imagine it was to sabotage the buyout. That's a done deal."

Matt nodded. "I won't take up any more of your time. If you come up with any ideas, call me."

"Certainly, certainly." Edwards walked him to the door. "This seems to be my week for police visitors. Two of your detectives questioned me about my whereabouts when the Pryor child disappeared. I'm afraid I couldn't offer much help. I was on tour of duty in Cambodia at the time. What a tragic business for Sam and Lily. Marnie wrote me when it happened. We knew the family."

Hunter had checked the man's Army record on his whereabouts that weekend. Edwards had not been in Cambodia, but on a month long furlough. Most troops went to Hawaii, but he could have come home. Hunter was checking that out. Bad memory or an outright lie? Matt didn't know, but he hoped to have the answer before their next meeting.

County Court House

District Attorney Gabriel Morrison stopped in the men's room after he left the judges chamber. He set his briefcase on the edge of the sink, smoothed the well-trimmed hair above his ears with both hands, then straightened his red power tie.

All in all, a good day.

He'd gotten a ten-year sentence for an abusive husband. Not the sentence he'd wanted, but perhaps enough time behind bars to keep the man from killing his wife for a few years. If she was smart, she'd change her name and leave the state.

Pride was sinful, but he couldn't help the sense of accomplishment that welled inside him after a satisfying win. It was why he did what he did. The law ran through his veins. He loved the justice system, its fairness, its dignity. There were some notable exceptions, but most of the time, the rule of law prevailed.

Grandfather Morrison survived Auschwitz. After liberation, he came to America, earned his law degree, and eventually sat on the New Jersey Federal Court bench. He had instilled in Gabe a deep sense of right and wrong.

To Gabriel Morrison, the job wasn't about conviction rates, it was about putting the right people away. He'd known Matt Foley for a little over six years, and he knew Matt felt the same. When Matt Foley gave him a case, there were never any loose ends to prove embarrassing in front of a jury. Matt thought like a lawyer.

Gabe smiled at his reflection in the mirror, then hurried back to his office.

A few minutes after he arrived, his secretary walked in, closing the door behind her. "Gabe, Harold Golden is in the foyer. He wants to see you. Shall I send him in?"

Gabe sat up straight in his chair. What could one of the foremost criminal attorneys in the state want with him? To his knowledge, Golden didn't have a client on the court schedule.

In college, Gabe once watched Golden in action. He didn't relish facing the man in a courtroom. Golden had earned his nickname, the Golden Tiger, in what seemed to be impossible-to-win courtroom battles.

Gabe stood and buttoned his jacket as his secretary ushered the distinguished lawyer in. "Harold, good to see you. What can I do for you?"

Harold Golden looked exactly like what he was, a $500-an-hour lawyer in a tailored suit and handmade Italian shoes. His flawless tan and gray hair accented his patrician good looks. Golden stuck out his right hand. "I apologize for dropping in, but I wanted to discuss a case with you. I took a chance you might have a few moments to visit with me."

The man stood two inches taller than Gabe's own five eleven. Golden oozed charm that could sell sandcastles to Arab tribesmen. Gabe motioned him to a chair. "No problem. Which case in particular?"

Golden took a seat in the chair next to the desk and crossed his legs. "The Joshua Bradford case. Do you remember it?"

Gabe leaned back in his chair. "Yes, hit-and-run, a few years back."

"That's correct. I understand you have new information on the case."

Gabe hadn't heard about any new evidence, but he would never let Golden know that. "What's your interest, Harold? Are you representing a suspect?"

"No, on the contrary," Golden said. "I want to see the killer prosecuted to the fullest extent of the law."

"That's the way I always work. Did Bradford work for your firm?" Gabe didn't like vendettas, especially when he didn't know what in blazes was going on.

"No, Josh's field was civil law, but he was like a son to me. He had one of the finest legal minds I'd run into. He would have been brilliant in criminal law." Golden's brow wrinkled into a frown. "Someone took his life much too soon. I want to see his killer punished. I believe that person is his wife, Sara Bradford."

Golden explained about Sara's call the previous evening. "I think there may be a conflict of interest between your police chief and Mrs. Bradford."

"How so?"

"If you've met Mrs. Bradford, you know she's an extraordinarily beautiful woman. She could turn the heads of many men." Golden brushed a spot of invisible lint from his pants leg. "I wondered why, after four years, Foley hasn't made any attempt to arrest her."

Gabe didn't like any part of this. Didn't like this man casting aspersions on his police department, specifically, Matt Foley. "If Matt hasn't arrested her, it's because he doesn't feel he has enough evidence to prosecute. When he does, he'll bring the case to me to make the final decision. This isn't news to you, Harold. You know how the system works. What is it you want me to do?"

The muscles in Golden's jaw flexed and his voice became defensive. "One of the reasons I've gained a measure of success is due to my ability to read people. I've had doubts about Sara Bradford since the accident. I meant no disrespect to Chief Foley. Just wanted to make sure this case gets all the attention it deserves."

Lawyer-speak for "I'll be watching your sorry behind." Gabe leaned forward. "I can assure you that it will."

Golden rose from his chair and held out his hand. "That's all I ask. Thank you for your time."

Gabe walked him to the door, then turned and strolled back to his desk. He rubbed his palm across the bald spot on his head. A very strange interview to say the least. Did Golden have a hidden agenda behind the meeting? Was he infatuated with Sara himself? Wanted to punish her for rejecting him? Whatever the reason, he obviously had the woman in his crosshairs.

Gabe picked up the phone.

He needed to talk to Matt Foley.

Sara Bradford's Home

Over dinner that evening, Sara watched the children pick at their food, unsure if they didn't like it or if it was because of their grief. She made a mental note to find out what they liked in addition to fried vegetables.

Maddie tried to keep the mood light. She asked the children about their favorite television shows and games. A pang of conscience hit Sara, realizing she'd never told Maddie of the talk with Roger Reynolds and the Global incident. Things Maddie should know for her own safety.

At least Maddie knew about the lake episode. However, she would not be happy that Sara kept secrets about her life being in danger.

She also needed to find out who'd donated the sleeping bag to the church sale. It might not be important, but she had to make sure, starting with the copy of the donor list.

After dinner, when the children were watching a Disney DVD and she and Maddie had settled in the library with tea. Her aunt sat in a chair by the hearth. Sara took the chair facing Maddie, cleared her throat, then plunged into the events of the past week.

As the confession unfolded, Maddie's eyes widened. "I can't believe you narrowly escaped death twice, and you didn't tell me. Don't coddle me, Sara. I assure you, I can take bad news. You may recall I've had a few disasters in my life."

Maddie gazed into the fire for a long moment. After a few minutes, she spoke again. "I won't fuss over you, Sara, if that's what you're afraid of. We are family. You're like a daughter to me. You don't keep secrets of this magnitude from family."

"You're right, of course. I just didn't want to worry you. I'll do better. I promise."

Maddie placed her teacup on the saucer, a slight tremble in her hand, her face drawn.

Time to lighten the mood.

Sara picked up the church's donor list. "Want to help me do a little detective work?"

The serious expression slipped from her aunt's face. The corners of her mouth turned up. "I think you're changing the subject, but of course I'll help. I always wanted to play Miss Marple."

A Residence in Twin Falls

The man's gaze followed the ceiling fan's revolutions. He spoke in a friendly, conversational tone. "Not from our donations, Sara. I've never had much use for camping equipment. Sorry."

After he hung up, questions raced through his mind. How much did she know? Could they trace the bag back to him? There must have been hundreds sold. He bought them so long ago there should be no record of the purchase. The housekeeper must have added the bag to the church collection box. Bad timing. Should have destroyed it years ago.

Curious, Sara called him, rather than the police. Had she realized who she had seen that night? Was it possible she knew the sleeping bag came from him and called merely to confirm it? If so, he had made a fatal error. She would know he lied.

He shook his head. Too many questions, too few answers.

Bad luck that the bomb, and shoving her off the bridge, hadn't worked. No more time to devise elaborate schemes. He must take care of Sara. This time, permanently.

He walked across the room, opened the bar cabinet, and pulled down a large crystal snifter. With the brandy bottle uncapped, he filled the glass a quarter full, then swirled the liquid before moving it to his lips.

He stopped, then poured the liquid down the stainless steel sink.

What he had to do called for a clear head.

CHAPTER 21

Twin Falls Police Station

Matt placed the last sheet of paper in his out-box, leaned back, and stretched. He'd forced himself to run again this morning, Rowdy at his side. Hard to get back on track when he'd missed a few days. Pushing himself to the limit on the lonely, rural road prepared him to face the emotional and physical demands of the job.

He scanned Hunter and Davis's reports from the previous evening. Flipping through the pages, he expelled the air from his lungs. Nothing new. But he wasn't expecting a breakthrough this early. Police work resembled the tortoise more than the hare.

The case had stalled, and Penny Pryor's face haunted him.

Perhaps he should call the *Herald*, plant a rumor the police had new leads and expected to close the case soon. See if that unnerved any of their suspects. If something didn't break, that old chestnut would be worth a try.

He'd finished filing the one-sheet report in the folder on his desk when Gabe Morrison stuck his head in the door. "Got a minute?"

Matt waved him inside. "What brings you out of your lair?"

Gabe slid into his favorite chair in front of the desk. "I had a very interesting meeting with Harold Golden yesterday."

"Golden? The hot-shot attorney?"

"The same. He wanted to talk about the Josh Bradford

191

case. Any new developments I need to know about?"

"We found the car yesterday. The vehicle belonged to Robert Cook. He lived in the area where Bradford died. Bradford met with Cook earlier that day. Cook had a string of DUI's. Lost his drivers license ten years ago. He seems to be the logical suspect, but he passed away a few days ago."

Matt explained about the car with Sara's notebook inside.

Gabe smoothed the crease in his trousers. "Do you think she's involved?"

An underlying tension in Gabe's voice meant this was more than idle curiosity. "I haven't ruled it out, but the evidence is shaky." Matt told him about the dates and fingerprints. "What is Golden's interest in the case?"

"He's after Sara Bradford's scalp. Thinks she killed her husband. Wants to ensure the long arm of the law keeps a tight grip on her. He also thinks you're covering up for her."

"I hope you know me better than that."

Gabe rose from the chair. "I do. That's why I'm telling you. Besides, I don't like Golden. He's arrogant and self-righteous. Nothing I'd like better than to prove him wrong. But a word of caution—watch your step. Golden has powerful connections."

Italian Restaurant, Plano, Texas

Matt left the station at one o'clock. As he pulled onto the freeway, the cell phone on the dash trilled the *William Tell Overture*. Matt glanced over and Blain Stanton's number reflected on the screen. Blain never called just to chitchat. "Hey, Blain. What's up?"

"Where are you?" he asked.

"On my way to lunch. Why?"

Blain cleared his throat. "Meet me at that Italian restaurant in Plano that you like. We need to talk."

"Sure, see you in twenty minutes, traffic permitting."

A line had formed outside by the time Matt arrived. Inside looked like standing room only at the bar. He didn't worry. Blain Stanton had a way with restaurant hosts. When Matt mentioned his father-in-law's name, a white coated waiter led him to a secluded booth in the back where Blain sat, drink in hand.

Ice cubes clinked as Blain shook his glass at the waiter for a refill. The server gave a nod of acknowledgement. Blain glanced at Matt. "You still a tee-totaler?"

"Bring me an iced tea," Matt said to the waiter and slid into the booth across from Blain. "What's on your mind?"

"You want the bad news before lunch or after?"

"Before. I couldn't enjoy the food with a black cloud over my head."

The waiter returned with the drinks. Blain ordered a steak while Matt opted for the house special, veal in a lemon butter sauce.

When the waiter left, Blain took a long sip from his glass. "Remember the red-headed reporter from the party, Pepper Parker?"

Matt grinned. "How could I forget?"

Blain didn't return the smile. "Well, you won't find this funny. You're her cover story in the January edition of *Texas Tattler*, the rag she works for."

"How did I rate that honor?"

His father-in-law shook his head. "Believe me, it's no honor. It's an expose'. She should be on the *National Inquirer's* payroll. Rumor has it she's digging up everyone who ever held a grudge against you. Then she'll print it as the gospel truth. You seriously ruffled her feathers."

"So it would seem. How bad can it be? My police record is squeaky clean."

Blain stirred the ice in his drink with his finger and snorted a laugh. "She won't let that stop her. Her type is more interested in innuendos than facts. My source says it will be ugly. She's going for your personal life, insinuating you married my daughter for her money and may have been culpable in her death. That'll be a stretch, since Mary died of cancer."

The tea in Matt's mouth turned to acid, and a deep-seated weariness settled in his chest. His wife didn't deserve to have her name dragged through tabloid filth, nor did her parents. "Is there anything we can do to stop it, short of shooting her?"

A red flush of anger colored Blain's cheeks with a touch of sadness that furrowed his brow. "Nothing short of buying the magazine, which I thought about. But she'd peddle the story somewhere else. I'm sorry about this, Matt."

Matt pushed his salad plate back. "Not your fault. I guess I could sue her for slander, but that would only give the story more media coverage."

"If you want to take her on, I'll back you all the way."

"I just might do that." Matt repositioned the napkin on his lap as the server brought their main course. "Sometimes we have to call these people out. Hit them where it hurts. In the pocket book."

"The governor asked me yesterday if there was anything new on his niece's murder. You might consider keeping him updated."

Matt had expected to hear from Ferrell before now. "I would be happy to send him a copy of the reports I send to

Doug, but I'm sure all correspondence goes through ten people before it reaches him. I don't want my investigation played out in the evening news."

His father-in-law gave a thoughtful nod. "Brandt has a private, secure fax in the governor's mansion. I'll get you the number."

~*~

The drive back to the office seemed longer than usual, his mind troubled. He wished Mary were here to talk to. She could always find the positive aspects in dark situations. It didn't bother him so much that the unprincipled woman would tarnish his name. He didn't like it, but he could handle it. But Mary? How could he fix that?

The day started bad and had gone downhill. He'd dealt with a lawyer and a reporter with an axe to grind, neither of whom had his best interest at heart. And the day wasn't over yet.

Sara Bradford's Home

Sara slipped into a pair of jeans and a sweater. The Campbell funeral loomed tomorrow afternoon. Before then, she had to shop for the kids.

"Focus," she told herself. She'd only picked up a few necessities yesterday. The visit to the empty Campbell home had been an ordeal, filled with images of her last visit. She'd have to make another trip. Another time. She'd also have to settle the children's financial affairs, but that would have to wait. This had to be done right—get the children settled into their new environment for the sake of the precious lives now in her charge. And for her promise to Dolly Campbell.

She closed her eyes. Where did one buy a suit for a six-year-old boy? *Lord, a crash course in being a mommy would be a big help.*

After a moment, she picked up the phone and called Shannon Connelly. Her friend didn't have children, but she was a storehouse of information. Skipping the small talk, Sara dove right into her problem. "Shannon, I'm now the mother of two children. I need your help."

A long silence filled the phone line. "Fancy that, and I didn't even know you were expecting. I think you'd better start at the beginning."

Sara emitted a shaky laugh. "That came out a little blunt." She gulped a deep steadying breath and told her friend about the Campbell's' death. "Shannon, do you think I should take them to the funeral? Would it scar them for life to go through that?"

"Girl, you've come to the wrong person," Shannon said. "My parenting skills are non-existent. All I can give you is my opinion. Heaven knows, I'm no shrink."

Sara leaned back against the pillow on her bed. "I'll take any advice I can get. Besides, I value your rational thinking."

Shannon asked. "How old are the children?"

"Danny is six, Poppy is almost five."

"Okay, for what it's worth, I think you should take them. Otherwise, someday they might resent you for not allowing the closure that would bring. Do you really intend to adopt these two kids?"

Sara pushed the cordless phone closer to her ear. "That's the plan. I fell in love with them long before this happened. I won't send them into child protective custody."

Sara's throat constricted, an ache deep inside squeezed her heart into pulp. "Burying one family member would be hard on an adult. There will be three caskets on that dais. You don't think the trauma of the funeral would be emotionally harmful?"

"I hope not." Shannon's voice sounded softer. "But as I said, I'm not an expert. When the time is good, I'd like to meet these amazing youngsters."

"Will do. Thanks, Shannon. By the way, you don't know where I could pick up a suit for a six-year-old boy, do you?"

Shannon gave her the names of two department stores that had dress clothes for children. Sara hung up and hurried out to her car.

~*~

When Sara returned from the shopping trip, she passed the kitchen. Danny's small form came into view. He stood on a chair at the island. She set the packages down in the hallway and walked up behind him. "Whatcha doing, Champ?"

He tossed a grin over his shoulder. "Making me and Poppy a sandwich. We like biscuits with chocolate syrup, but I couldn't find the biscuits."

A loaf of bread lay on the counter with four pieces of bread set in a straight line. Danny had done his best, despite one arm in a sling. He busied himself, pouring dark, sticky liquid on the bread. More hit the counter than the bread. "I can see that. May I help you?"

He shook his head, swinging his blond bangs with the movement. "Naw, I'm 'bout finished."

She winked at him. "I'm not sure that's a nutritious snack, and it sure looks messy."

He glanced up at her, wide-eyed. He wiped his sticky hands on his pants leg. "Yeah, it's messy all right."

"How about I get you some peanut butter and crackers, and an apple? Tomorrow, I'll make sure you get biscuits and chocolate syrup for breakfast. Deal?"

"Yes, ma'am. That's our favorite."

She took his hand. "Right now, I need to get you cleaned up."

Beatrice entered the kitchen with Matt Foley in tow. She looked at the mess on the counter and rolled her eyes. But bless her, she didn't say a word. Sara gave her an apologetic glance. "Sorry, Beatrice. I'll clean this up after I get Danny scrubbed down."

Beatrice smiled. "Is okay. I have grandkids."

"I hate to ask," Sara said, "But would you cut up an apple then make a few crackers with peanut butter? They didn't eat much lunch earlier." She grinned at Matt. "Hi, I'm enjoying the fruits of motherhood. Do you need to see me?"

He didn't answer but followed her as she led Danny upstairs. She made a mental note. Make sure mid-morning and afternoon snacks were available when the kids got hungry.

~*~

Matt stood in the bathroom doorway as Sara lifted Danny onto the closed toilet seat. She pulled a washcloth from the cabinet, wet it with warm water, and washed chocolate syrup off the boy's hands.

With all her other problems, Sara didn't need a lawyer with a grudge to add to her woes. Matt had debated with himself all the way here whether to warn her of Golden's visits with the DA, but she needed to know.

She stood the little boy back on the tile floor. "Go get a clean pair of pants and shirt, then find Poppy. Beatrice will have your snacks ready."

They walked downstairs behind Danny and turned right into the library. She sank into a chair in front of the hearth as though relaxing took effort. "From the look on your face, you don't have good news for me."

He stood at the mantel, appreciating the glow the fire cast against her skin. "Sorry to say, you're right."

Her brow furrowed into a tired frown. "Now what? Did you come to arrest me?"

"Not as bad as that. I stopped by to give you a heads up. Harold Golden went to see the DA. Tried to pressure Gabe into filing charges against you. Why is he so sure you killed Josh?"

She shrugged. "For the same reasons you were—maybe still are. I'm sure he knew Josh was unfaithful, and in a male, chauvinistic way, he approved. When Josh died, he assumed I killed him out of jealousy." Sara dropped her head in her hands. "Can my life possibly get any more complicated?"

"On a positive note, the DA blew Golden off." Matt waited in silence for a moment. "I have to get back to headquarters. Call if you need me."

She lifted her head and nodded. "I appreciate your letting me know, Matt."

"No problem. I'll let myself out."

Back in his car, Matt shook his head. He owed Sara the benefit of the doubt. And he'd learned one thing today. Circumstantial evidence could lead to the wrong conclusion.

CHAPTER 22

Sara Bradford's Home

Sara, Maddie and the children were ready Wednesday morning when the limousine driver pulled under the portico and rang the bell. The small group headed to the car.

While the driver helped Maddie and the kids into the backseat, the front doorbell rang. Sara changed direction to answer the summons.

Matt Foley stood in the entrance in a tailored black suit and crisp white shirt. "Thought you could use some backup."

Funeral Chapel

Matt rode in the limo with the small family to the funeral home. Sara had arranged to have the services held there since the cemetery was on the grounds. A sizeable crowd of friends and neighbors jostled each other in the foyer.

Inside, flowers banked the dais and flowed around the three caskets, filling the air with a sweet scent of roses mixed with the fresh fragrance of lilies. Matt held tight to Danny's hand. There weren't enough flowers in the world to brighten this occasion.

In deference to the children, Seth Davidson kept the service short. When it ended, the crowd moved to the front to pay their respects, finally leaving the family alone in the sanctuary. When the last mourner had gone, Sara gave

Matt a this-is-going-to-be-tough look as she lifted Poppy into her arms. He picked up Danny, holding the boy's thin frame close. Danny looked down at the faces of his mother and grandparents, tears welling in his eyes. He took a deep gulp of air and smothered a sob against Matt's shoulder.

A lump the size of a boulder formed in Matt's throat, and the back of his eyelids burned. So much courage housed in Danny's small body. Matt tried never to question God, but it seemed unfair to give such a burden to small children.

When the family had time to gather their composure, they stepped out into the sunlight and walked the short distance to the gravesites.

After the interment, Matt spotted Joe Wilson in a small crowd waiting to offer his condolences. Joe stopped under the canopy to shake hands. Matt introduced him to Sara and Maddie.

Joe gave a solemn nod. "I covered the accident. Just dropped by to pay my respect." He moved on with the line of people and disappeared into the crowd.

The limousine drove them to the church fellowship hall for the wake. The small party found a table, and Sara filled plates for herself and the children. Matt followed Maddie and filled a plate for himself.

When Danny and Poppy joined some other children outside, Matt asked, "Did you notify Grady Morgan?"

She placed the fork beside her plate with a solemn nod. "Blaze notified the prison officials."

"Grady didn't want to come? I know he's a scumbag, but his kids could have used his support." Matt shrugged. "Maybe not. It's probably better this way."

Sara watched the kids through the double glass doors. Danny stood on the sidelines, watching Poppy play chase, his face solemn. "Blaze said the prison officials at Huntsville would have let Grady come, but he refused. Apparently, he's still angry with Diane for divorcing him. And there was no love lost between him and his in-laws."

"When he gets out, he won't let those kids go if he believes he can squeeze a dime out of the situation," Matt said. "Tell Blaze to insure there are no loopholes in the adoption papers."

The color drained from Sara's face. "I pray you're wrong. Those kids couldn't handle a long court battle. They've been through too much already. How much longer will he be in prison?"

"He's served five years of a ten year sentence. Unless, of course, he gets paroled."

Matt Foley's Home

Matt shed the suit as soon as he arrived home. Dressed in jeans with a long sleeved polo, he inserted a "George Strait's Greatest Hits" album into the CD player connected to the intercom's stereo system. He tossed Rowdy a couple of treats then took a fresh cup of coffee out to the deck, and left the French doors open. The romantic strains of "You Look So Good in Love" drifted through the portal.

A light breeze whispered through the live oak trees, sending a shower of rust colored leaves swirling to the ground. Before too long it would be too cold to sit out here without a coat. He'd have to add to the stack of wood for the outdoor fireplace.

He'd brought home a file on the Global explosion Lucy gave him, that included a copy of the Fort Hood bomb techs report. The residue left behind had been military grade plastic explosives, meaning someone had stolen it from a base supply depot or in transit. Lucy and Cole were working with the Fort Hood bomb squad to track down any missing inventory.

The doorbell interrupted his reflections. He placed his mug in the chair's cup holder to answer the summons. Joe Wilson stood outside. "Come in, Joe. What brings you by?"

Joe grinned and stepped into the doorway. Out of uniform, he wore a red plaid shirt and jeans. "I got tired of waiting for you to buy me that steak. Thought I'd remind you."

Matt led the way into the kitchen. "I've been up to my backside in alligators, my friend. But you're in luck. I bought a pack of T-Bones on the way home. You want some coffee?"

"Had my quota for the day. You have anything stronger?" Joe parked on a barstool at the island.

Matt reached into the cabinet and pulled down a large mug. "Hot apple cider or hot cocoa. Choose your poison."

"The cider sounds good," Joe said. "Your CSU team cleaned out the Cook house. Find anything helpful?"

"I haven't had a chance to ask. Like I said, I've been busy."

The barstool squeaked under Joe's weight. "What's happening with that case? The victim was Governor Ferrell's niece, right?"

"True. The case seems to be connected to a bombing at Global Optics. How, I haven't figured out yet."

While the cider heated, Matt removed the steaks from the fridge. He added a marinade, put two large sweet potatoes into the oven, and pulled out a bunch of fresh asparagus. "I'll let the steaks set while the potatoes cook."

They carried their drinks out to the deck with "Amarillo by Morning" playing in the background. Joe took the chair next to Matt and watched Rowdy cavort with the fawn. "You've got a sweet set up here, Matt. I could get use to this. You ever want to sell, give me a shout." He blew across the cup before he took a tentative sip. "What makes you think the two cases are connected?"

"Couple of things. Sara Bradford witnessed Penny's abduction. There have been two attempts on Sara's life this past week after we found the child's body. The explosion at Global was the first."

Rowdy charged across the lawn and jumped into Joe's lap. He scratched behind the dog's ear. "That's the pretty lady I met at the memorial park today?"

"That's the one," Matt said.

"Is she married?"

"Spoken like a true bachelor." Matt grinned. "Widowed. Remember the hit-and-run on highway ten, four years ago? That was her husband."

"I remember. You don't soon forget a scene like that." Joe stared out at the darkening sky as a pink and orange sun set behind the forest. "When I gave the nephew the list of search warrant items taken from the Cook home, he mentioned you had confiscated his car."

"I did. It's the car that ran down Josh Bradford."

Joe seemed to think about it for a moment. He whistled. "Curiouser and couriouser."

"Tell me about it," Matt said. "Throw a log on the fire while I get those steaks going. I'm hungry. Then you can pick holes in my theory."

CHAPTER 23

Twin Falls Police Station

It was seven-thirty Thursday morning when Matt Foley turned onto Highway 75. With sunshine, and the temperature in the mid-fifties, it was a pleasant drive to the station. Tall evergreens stood like sentinels along the roadway, and added a wintergreen scent to the breeze.

Traffic around the square flowed smoothly, uncluttered for once. Halloween banners in black and orange shouted their wares in shops. Not his favorite holiday. A national excuse for mischief from the crazies.

He made a stop at his office to check messages before he headed upstairs to meet Davis and Hunter in the conference room. Nothing in the emails that couldn't wait.

As he passed Davis' desk he picked up the Pryor murder book. He thumbed through the pages then put it back in place.

Three cases. Sara's name involved in each of them. Penny Pryor's death, Josh Bradford's murder, and the explosion in the Global Distribution Center. She could be criminally culpable in one of the cases, but not all three. A child could not have been responsible for the Pryor girl's disappearance, and Sara wouldn't expose herself to a bomb she had planted.

Instinct told him the three cases were connected. He'd learned to trust his intuition. A God-thing that had never failed him.

Removing Sara as a suspect gave him a different perspective. What if she was the catalyst? The victim—the link that tied it all together? She had seen the killer, even if she couldn't identify him. Did the killer know that? Was he trying to kill Sara before she remembered who he was?

Josh Bradford's death didn't fit the scenario. No obvious reason for his murder. The evidence pointed to an accident caused by a drunk driver who'd fled the scene, but Matt wasn't ready to close that chapter yet.

The two detectives walked in, snapping him back into the moment.

Hunter poured a cup of coffee and leaned against the counter. Davis settled comfortably in one of the chairs. "We hit a blind alley on the sleeping bag Mrs. Bradford found. No one has seen it since she placed it in the basement. We've run background checks on everyone involved with the old retreat at the time Penny Pryor disappeared. We located the church treasurer. She remembered Robert Cook. Gave us the name of his drinking buddy in those days. We're interviewing him this afternoon."

Davis leaned back, a pleased look on his face. "This is the same Robert Cook who died in the last few days after years of alcoholism."

"Looks like you guys have everything covered. Just FYI, Cook owned the car involved in the hit-and-run that killed Joshua Bradford. And before Bradford was run down he interviewed the old man."

"The woman who found the sleeping bag, any relation to that Josh Bradford?" Davis asked.

"She's his widow."

"Is it possible one perp is responsible for both deaths?" Hunter asked.

Matt stood to leave and then turned back. "Too early to say for certain. But it's always been my opinion there are no coincidences in police work."

WORKS OF DARKNESS

Forest Hills Mobile Home Park

Hunter glanced over at Davis. "Exactly what do you expect to find out from Casey Bosworth?"

"According to the church secretary, back in the day, this guy was Robert Cook's best buddy." He switched off the engine and opened the car door. "I hope he can fill in the gaps in what we don't know about Cook...better known as a fishing expedition."

The mobile home park was a rarity compared to others in Twin Falls. Lots were well tended with live oak trees shading the property. Individual homes had skirts around the foundation, and steps with handrails that led to the entrance, and an attached carport.

The Bosworth's doublewide was no exception.

Davis led the way to the front door and knocked. A woman he assumed to be Bosworth's wife answered. She pointed them to a back sundeck where a stout balding man, in Bermuda shorts and a loud Hawaiian shirt, grilled hamburgers.

The older man flipped a burger with practiced ease. "What can I do for you fellows?" He nodded towards the grill. "You're just in time for lunch or a glass of iced tea."

Davis fought the temptation to say yes. Instead, he flashed his badge and introduced himself and Hunter. "Thanks for the invitation, but no. We have a few questions about a former friend of yours, Robert Cook."

The man waved them to a couple of seats at a table shaded by a green and white striped umbrella. "Sure, ask away. Haven't seen him in years, though, so there's not much I can tell you. Saw his obit in the newspaper. Can't say it surprised me."

Davis admired the man's handiwork with the spatula. "You knew Cook when he worked as groundskeeper at the Baptist retreat?"

Bosworth removed the burgers from the grill. He placed the platter on the table and sat across from them. "We used to hang out together, before I quit the sauce. Bob always drank like he had a hollow leg. After I quit the bar scene, we drifted away from each other." He nodded toward the house. "I had to quit or lose my wife. I'd already been divorced twice. Didn't want to go through that again."

He held up a glass of ice tea. "This is what I drink these days. I heard his nephew Lance brought the booze to Bob after he lost his driver's license. I think Lance hoped Bob would drink himself to death. Lance was Bob's only kin. His place didn't look like much last time I was there, but property values have increased, big time. Folks looking to move to the country."

Hunter removed his notebook from his pocket. "How is it that a maintenance man could afford to quit work and buy his own place?"

"All I can tell you is that one day Bob showed up at the bar in a new pickup and said he'd quit his job. He bought drinks for everyone that night. I asked him if he'd won the lottery. He just smiled. Never would say where his sudden wealth came from."

Davis shook Bosworth's hand. "Thanks for your time. We won't keep you from your lunch any longer."

"No problem. I hope what little bit I knew will help," Bosworth said.

Back in the car, Hunter waited until he'd closed the car door before he spoke. "Sounds like blackmail."

"Yep. This means we move him from suspect to eyewitness. Cook knew the killer. Bosworth substantiated what Cook's bank statements revealed."

Matt Foley's Home

Matt showered, dressed, and switched on the local news as he loaded the Keurig for his first caffeine fix of the day. The newscaster's announcement made him pause. The legend at the bottom of the screen read, *breaking news.*

"An unnamed source inside the Twin Falls Police Department has named long time Twin Falls resident, Robert Cook, as the prime suspect in the murder of Governor Ferrell's niece. The source claims that Cook is responsible for the twenty-five year old kidnapping and murder of Penny Pryor whose body was discovered last week on the Bay Harbor development site."

The screen flashed a picture from Cook's driver's license, followed by an aerial view of the construction site.

The report continued.

"Cook had been employed as a groundskeeper at the retreat, formerly located on the property. We'll keep you updated as this story develops."

The newscast had Terry Hall's name all over it.

Matt reached for the phone and punched in Doug Anderson's number. He answered with, "I heard it a few minutes ago."

Matt couldn't quell the anger in his voice. "Doug, I'm beyond livid. You know as well as I do the story came from Terrance Hall. This is the reason I didn't want him in the loop. The story is premature and it's a distraction we don't need."

"Calm down, Matt. I'll handle it."

"Calm down! I promised the governor I would keep him informed. Now he gets this in the news. There's no proof

Cook was responsible. Now, I have to tell Ferrell this is a bunch of BS and it leaked from my department."

"I said I'll take care of it, Matt," Doug said. "It won't happen again. That's a promise."

Matt slammed down the phone and tried to pace off the rage that surged through his system. He took five deep breaths before his blood pressure returned to normal. Bad information was out there. He couldn't erase it. All he could do was damage control.

He picked up the phone again to contact Blain Stanton

CHAPTER 24

Twin Falls Police Station

A crowd of reporters waited in front of the station when Matt arrived. He drove to the back entrance. Wading through the media hounds yelling questions would do no good. He couldn't call out Terrance Hall for putting out bad, or at best, incomplete information.

He found Hunter and Davis waiting outside his office.

"Where'd that news story come from?" Davis asked.

"You don't want to know." Matt unlocked the door and waved them inside.

Davis took a seat then leaned forward with a grin. "It looks like the news media got it wrong...again. We spoke to Cook's buddy yesterday. Cook came into some big bucks right after Penny Pryor disappeared. He bought land, a truck and built a house on the property. Quite a status change for a guy making minimum wage. It also tells us that whoever the killer is, he or she has some serious money."

"He was blackmailing the killer," Matt said. It was a statement not a question.

Davis nodded. "That's my guess. The timing is too coincidental."

"You checked out his bank statements?" Matt asked.

"We're ahead of you, Boss," Davis said. "We went through about six years of statements Cook had stuffed into a drawer in his home. He had steady cash deposits of three thousand dollars a month, plus his social security check. My guess is one big payoff with monthly installments."

Matt sat on the corner of his desk. "Bank records from all the suspects to see who pulled that kind of money on a monthly basis might solve this case."

Hunter growled, "And to do that, we'll have to get warrants. Don't think we have grounds for that."

"I know, but if you guys come up with an easier solution, go for it."

"We'll try to get a warrant on the top two suspects and pray for a judge who isn't big on the right to privacy," Davis said.

Hunter stood and pushed back his chair. "I love to go through other people's financial records. Lets me see how the affluent half lives."

After the detectives left his office, Matt picked up the phone and brought Doug up to speed.

Sara Bradford's Home

Sara spent the first hour of Thursday morning on the phone with Pastor Davidson, arranging enrollment for Danny and Poppy in the church school. She'd found their inoculation records and birth certificates when she brought clothes from the Campbell home. Now, she needed to buy school uniforms before tomorrow. A top priority on her to-do list.

School would help to keep their minds off the loss of their family, at least for a little while. Nothing could erase that pain, but getting into a routine would be a start towards putting their lives back together. When she'd disconnected from the pastor, the phone rang.

"You free for lunch?" Jane Haskell's cheery voice greeted her.

"I'm free, and I'd love to. I need to do some shopping in town. How about The Tea Shoppe on the square?"

"Sounds great. See you at 11:30." Her secretary's voice hinted this wouldn't be just a social luncheon.

The Tea Shoppe

Sara pulled into a spot in front of the whitewashed brick building that housed The Tea Shoppe. Laura Ashley window treatments and table settings catered to female clientele. She could never imagine a man in this feminine environment.

Jane breezed through the doorway looking like a ray of autumn sunlight in a red A-line dress, topped with a fall-hued scarf. "Hey, Sara, I wasn't sure you were here. Didn't see your car."

"I'm in the blue sedan, two cars down from you."

"Why would you trade your dream car for that?"

Before Sara could reply, the waitress approached.

Sara scanned the menu. "Bring us the sandwich assortment." She glanced at Jane, who nodded. "And Earl Grey for me."

"And add a few scones and lemon tea cakes," Jane added.

When the server had gone, Jane turned to Sara. "Now, tell me about your car."

She couldn't give Jane the facts about the lake incident, at least for now. It still frightened her to think about it. "It's out of commission for a while." She hadn't lied, exactly. It was out of commission. Permanently. "So, how are things at work after the explosion?"

"Everyone's still a little shook up, but the place seems to run like a well-oiled machine. The old 'when the going gets tough, the tough get going' spirit prevailed. Roger had the minions bring in a crew to get the place in order. I heard the battery exploded, and you were almost killed."

Sara shrugged. "As you can see, I'm fine. The police are still looking into the explosion." She'd become a master at evading the truth.

Jane sat, wide-eyed. "I worried about you until Don told me the hospital released you. There's something else I wanted to talk to you about. I heard what happened with Roger. When I saw the boxes in your office, I knew the rumor was true."

Sara fought the urge to let her mouth drop open. "How could you know that? Is the executive suite bugged?"

"There no secrets at Global." Jane chuckled. "You should know that by now."

The conversation was interrupted when their lunch arrived. After the waitress left, Sara stared across the table at Jane. "Well, I know it now. Please, keep this to yourself. I don't want my people to become upset. I'll be in Monday to tell them about the job change. At least, I hope Roger will allow me to do that."

Her secretary's eyes took on an excited twinkle. "Sara, I have information that will guarantee you walk away from Global with a golden parachute."

Sara patted her hand. "Don't worry about me, Jane. If I'm terminated, I'm sure they'll give me a severance package of some kind. Besides, I won't have to worry for a while. I haven't touched Josh's life insurance money."

Jane shook her head. "Be quiet for a minute. Listen to what I have to tell you. A few months ago, I attended a party with the personnel director, who was quite..." Jane hesitated, "Drunk to put it bluntly. She let slip that Global could be in a lot of trouble with EEOC if they ever checked her records. It seems there is some disparity in the salaries between men and women. So yesterday, I hacked into the payroll records."

Sara almost spewed tea from her nose. "You did what...how?"

Jane munched a bite of her sandwich and held her hand up. "Don't get your tidy-whities in a bunch. My dad sold software for a living. I cut my teeth on a keyboard. I felt justified after the way Roger treated you."

"Jane, you can't—"

"I can, and I did, girlfriend. Now let me finish. You know Chance Cummings came in as an intern the same time you did."

Sara nodded, afraid to hear what would follow.

Jane lowered her voice. "What you don't know, is that they brought Chance on board for ten thousand more per year than your starting salary. The gap between his and your pay range has grown larger, even though you have more people and more responsibility. Why? Because he's male and one of Roger's chosen few. You can sue for enough to keep you in champagne and Chanel for a very long time."

The tea in Sara's mouth turned bitter. She held up a finger. "You risked your job to help me, which I appreciate. But I would never file a discrimination suit against Global. I don't approve of what they did. However, I agreed to work for the sum Global offered me. The firm gave me a fair wage. I can't complain now because they offered someone else more who happened to be male."

Jane rolled her eyes. "Girlfriend, you need a keeper. When you find another job, you need to hire me. Somebody has to keep this little lamb from being sheared."

Sara sunk back against the chair. "I guess it's a deal.

Somebody has to keep you out of jail for hacking into confidential records."

Collin Creek Mall

When Sara left the Tea Shoppe, she picked up Poppy and Danny for a shopping trip to buy their school uniforms. Excited chatter and questions about the uniforms filled the car on the way to the mall. Sara experienced the same thrill with the new responsibilities of motherhood. The winter uniforms were adorable, with a green, gray and purple plaid skirt, white sweater, and green blazer for Poppy. Dark gray slacks, white turtleneck sweater and green blazer for Danny. Sewing the school emblem on the jackets would be a new skill, but Beatrice was handy with a needle. She would help.

Sara left the store with four large bags and the two children in tow when her cell phone rang. Maneuvering the bags as she fished out the phone, she guided the kids to a nearby seating lounge.

The caller ID reflected the name of the church secretary. "Sara, you remember the sleeping bag the detectives wanted? We found it."

"When? Where?" She glanced around to make sure the kids were close.

"Today. Someone had returned it to the sales tables upstairs where one of the workers bought it for her son. She's returning it here in about an hour."

"That's wonderful news. Tell her to bring it to you. Please hold on to it until I can contact the detectives. They'll be happy to hear it turned up."

After such a long time, she wasn't sure how meaningful the sleeping bag would be, but if it could help the police find Penny's killer, so be it. There could have been thousands sold in sport shops across the country.

After returning the phone back to her handbag, she gathered the shopping bags and headed to the exit.

"Sara, it's the chief!" Danny shouted as he dashed to meet Matt Foley headed in their direction.

He picked up the boy and joined them.

"What are you doing here? Are you following me?"

He responded with a raised eyebrow. "Hardly. I don't have time to act as personal bodyguard. One of the department stores had a shoplifting complaint. I was close and took the call. A fourteen-year-old girl. The kid's first offense, and the store manager agreed to let me give her a warning. Since she's so young, I didn't want her to get a record."

He grinned. "I'll probably live to regret it. Why are you here?"

"School uniforms for my new charges. They start tomorrow."

His being here would save her a call. "The church found the missing sleeping bag. The church secretary is holding on to it. Would you let Detective Davis know?"

"I'll do better than that. I'll pick it up on my way back to the station. You headed home?"

"We were just leaving when I got the call," she said.

"Good." He took possession of the packages. "I'll follow you home then stop by the church."

Sara Bradford's Home

Danny and Poppy finished their favorite breakfast of buttered biscuits and chocolate syrup. Not the most healthy diet, but today was special. She wanted to make it as easy as possible for them on their first day at a new school. A small concession to ease their anxiety.

The other kids were bound to ask questions that would be painful for them to answer.

Sara sent Danny off to brush his teeth, then followed Poppy to assist with her dental hygiene and to help her dress.

Poppy twirled around in her new finery, admiring her reflection in the mirror. "Do I look pretty, Sara? I hope so. I want to be pretty, just like you."

Sara pulled her into a hug. "Kitten, when you get older, you'll make me look like the Wicked Witch of the North."

A smile lit her tiny face. "Really?"

"Really."

On the drive to school, the children were silent, watching out the car windows. A white Chevy followed too close on her bumper, distracting her from the road. She tapped her breaks. The driver backed off and she brought her attention back to her driving.

Poppy seemed nervous about school. Facing an unknown experience for the first time. Her insecurities were an issue Sara intended to work on. But Danny would handle it well. Already a pro, since this was his second year.

Sara pulled into a parking space, got out, and released Poppy from her car seat. Danny had already unfastened his and opened the door.

She walked Danny to his class, then Poppy to her Pre-K 4 class. Outside the door, Poppy looked up at her with wide, teary eyes. "Sara, c-can I stay with you?"

Kneeling down to Poppy's level, Sara took both of the child's hands in her own. "I tell you what, Kitten. Let's give this a week. Then, if you still don't like it, I'll homeschool you. Just give it a try. Many of the children in your class you already know from Sunday school. Okay?"

Poppy gave an uncertain nod.

Sara kissed the top of her head. "Good girl."

After she'd introduced Poppy to her teacher, Sara handed over the school supplies and walked away, blinking back the tears that threatened.

CHAPTER 25

Twin Falls Baptist Church

Late Friday evening, Sara sat at the pastor's desk finalizing the receipts from the garage sale. The quiet after everyone left felt a little creepy, but she pushed it out of her mind. Nerves reacting to the tribulation of the past weeks.

She leaned back in Pastor Davidson's chair. A neck cramp made her wince and she massaged it until the tension eased. Parenthood required an enormous amount of energy, especially since she was new at it. To ease the cramp, she moved her head in circles, first right, then left. The exercise worked, relaxing the muscles.

She took a quick glance at her watch. If she hurried, she could get home in time for dinner with the family.

After she counted the money and filled out the deposit slip, she placed the checks and cash inside a moneybag, and smiled. This year's fundraiser had been a huge success. They'd earned enough to pay for summer camp for the church member's children, and to finance the trip for a number of bus kids.

After zipping the bag, she placed it into the middle desk drawer. Mission accomplished, she dialed Matt's number as he'd instructed, to have a patrol car escort her home. He would be upset if she didn't.

Feeling a bit foolish, she punched in the station number. "Hi, this is Sara Bradford. Chief Foley told me to call and ask for an escort home."

"I beg your pardon?"

Great. New man on the desk. She repeated the request.

"Sorry, ma'am, I can't do that without instructions directly from the chief."

"Can you contact him? He left instructions at the desk...never mind. I'll call him myself."

She disconnected and dialed Matt's cell number. The call went to voicemail. Fingers drumming on the desk, she considered her next move. If she didn't reach Matt soon, she'd miss dinner with the kids.

She could make the call from her car. If she didn't reach him, when he saw her number on his caller ID, he'd call her back.

While waiting, she auto-dialed home. Maddie's soft hello sounded through the connection.

"Hi, how'd the afternoon go with the children?" Sara asked.

"So far, great. We've managed to keep them occupied. You need to pick up some educational toys and games."

"I know. That's at the top of my to-do list." She fumbled for the car keys in her handbag. "Wanted to let you know I'm leaving the church now. See you in a bit." She disconnected the call, then tried Matt's number again.

Still no answer. Where could he be? She dropped the phone into her sweater pocket and closed the office door.

The air bit cold and crisp through the thin layer of her clothing and she hurried to her car. A blue-northern had blown in late that afternoon and dropped temperatures to the low thirties. She sucked the cold air into her lungs, enjoying its freshness and the smell of pine that rode in on the brisk breeze. The moon hung low, like a giant yellow balloon in the night sky, making the church steeple gleam white and pure in its brightness.

She pressed the automatic unlock-button on her key fob

then opened the door.

The crunch of gravel on the pavement drew her attention. She tossed her handbag onto the carseat and turned.

Before she completed the movement, a thousand sharp needles jabbed at the base of her skull, and a well of darkness sucked her down into its inky black depths.

Outside Twin Falls, Texas

Consciousness returned in bits and pieces. Sara's eyelids seemed weighted and a wave of claustrophobic panic crashed over her. Total darkness surrounded her. Darkness so thick and impenetrable it pressed against her skin. Suddenly, she couldn't breathe. Her mouth felt dry, as if stuffed with sand. She ran her tongue over cracked lips.

The darkness reawakened memories of the lake, the cold, the need for oxygen. Disjointed thoughts flashed through her mind. Why couldn't she see? Another thought even more terrifying. Had the blow that knocked her unconscious blinded her?

The next sensation came as pain that shot through her skull, followed by penetrating cold from the hard floor beneath her. A flat surface, like marble or smooth stones. Terror built inside her chest—a volcano poised to erupt.

Alone. Completely alone. Like after her parents' death. Her last year at college, they'd flown her back to school. Their plane went down in a storm on the way home. Her whole world ripped out from under her in a flash of lightening that destroyed the aircraft's navigational system.

Breathing in quick nervous gasps, vivid memories from the present swam by. The forklift explosion, Dolly's death, and the children. All paraded across a wide screen behind her eyelids. Until, once again, she slipped into the welcome comfort of nothingness.

Matt Foley's Home

Too many late hours this week had caught up with Matt and he'd turned in early. He tried to ignore the sound of a distant telephone that pierced his sleep-fogged brain. With a punch to his pillow, he turned over, but the annoying ring persisted. Eyes half-closed, he threw his legs over the side of the bed, and picked up the phone. "Foley. What do you want?"

"Uh...sorry to wake you, Chief." Duly chastised, the desk sergeant's voice sounded cautious. "A Mrs. Jamison called, sir. She insisted you get back to her right away. Her niece hasn't come home. The niece called about six o'clock. Said she was on her way, but she never arrived. I explained the twenty-four hour wait period before filing a report, but the lady wouldn't take no for an answer."

Now wide-awake, Matt looked at the clock. 11:07 PM. "No need to apologize. I know Mrs. Jamison well. She's a force to be reckoned with. Call her back. Tell her I'm on my way."

Anger bubbled inside as he slid warm feet into cold slippers. He'd told Sara not to be out after dark without an escort. Considering the recent attempts on her life, he couldn't ignore Maddie's concerns. Logic told him she had reason to sound the alarm. Most missing persons showed up unharmed. He could only pray that would be the case in this instance. But he couldn't quell the apprehension that settled over him.

Sara Bradford's Home

Twenty minutes later, Matt arrived at the Bradford home. Lights glowed from every window, a testament to the vigil within. A couple of cars he didn't recognize sat under the portico in the driveway.

Matt swung his SUV in behind a black Mercedes.

Before he could ring the bell, Shannon Connelly opened the door, her face ashen. "I'm so glad you're here, Matt. Come in. Everyone's in the den."

Shannon led him down the hallway into the library where Maddie, Colin, and Jeffery Hayden, the Greek god who'd accompanied Sara to the Stanton party, waited.

Palpable silence hung over the distraught group. The two men stood in front of the hearth, backs to the embers of a dying blaze. A pot of coffee and a plate of sandwiches rested on a teacart. Three pairs of eyes became alert when he entered the room with Shannon.

"Thank you for coming, Matthew." Maddie Jamison rose from a chair to greet him, her pale skin drawn tight across the cheekbones. "I...need your help. I'm afraid something terrible has happened to Sara..." Maddie lowered herself back into the chair. "Help yourself to the coffee and food. Beatrice insisted on making them. Keeping busy helps her cope. She's concerned, as indeed, we all are."

Shannon moved to the cart and filled a cup. She handed it to Matt. "You look like you could use this."

He took a grateful sip. "Tell me why you're sure Sara is in trouble. Could she have stopped off somewhere, forgotten to call?"

"Not Sara," Maddie said.

Maddie continued, "She always calls if she's delayed for any reason. She wanted to be home for dinner with the

224

children. Matthew, you know about the recent attempts..."

"I'm afraid it's serious, Matt," Colin said. "Jeffery and I went to the church. We found her car, still in the parking lot, the door open, and her purse in the front seat. The cell phone lay on the ground by the vehicle. As a cop, I'm sure you know what that means."

Maddie sat small and still, apprehensive lines creased her normally smooth brow. Matt touched her shoulder. "Try not to worry. I'll put my people on it immediately. Have you called any of her friends?"

"Most of them are here." She nodded at the others. "Except for the people in the bus ministry and I'm sure she isn't with any of them."

"Humor me. Give Shannon a list of Sara's friends and their phone numbers."

The task would give Maddie a chore to do. He wanted to ask Colin some questions but not in Maddie's presence.

After Maddie left the room, Matt pulled Colin aside. "There were definite signs of a struggle in the church parking lot?"

Colin nodded. "As I said, the car door was open, her cell phone was lying on the ground. It appeared someone surprised her."

With a motion for Colin to follow him, Matt led him through the front entrance and outside. Jeffery Hayden followed.

Matt stopped near his car. "Colin, did Maddie tell you we found the car that killed Josh?"

Colin nodded.

"I didn't want to ask this in front of Maddie, but under the circumstances, do you think it's possible she may have staged the scene at the church. Decided to run rather than face murder charges?"

For the first time, Hayden spoke. "Not Sara. Never." Hayden's jaw clenched. "She wouldn't leave without telling Maddie, and she wouldn't kill anyone. I've known Sara for a long time. She's no coward. She'd face any charges against her and prove them wrong."

"It's my job to look at this from all angles. Because of the past attempts on her life, I'll treat this as a kidnapping. We'll pull her car in; ask questions of the neighbors, see if they saw or heard anything."

Colin nodded. "I think you should. I have to agree with Jeffery on this. Sara wouldn't leave, not when she knew Maddie would be worried sick about her. And don't forget, she just brought those kids home."

"Where are the children?" Matt asked.

Colin stuffed his hands in his pockets and nodded towards the house. "Shannon read them a bedtime story and put them to bed. They don't know what's happened. We didn't think they needed anything else to upset them. If we don't find Sara soon, they'll have to know. Not a job I want to tackle."

Shannon walked out of the house to Colin's side. She slipped her arm through his. "I called two of Sara's friends. They haven't seen or heard from her. Find her, Matt. She's in danger. I know it."

Matt walked around his car and got into the driver's seat. The reflections of the three friends were outlined in his rearview mirror as he drove away.

He had worn a confident demeanor in their presence, but he was more than a little troubled. The woman he'd comforted in the kitchen wasn't the type to run.

Stopped at a red light on his way back to the station, Matt glanced at his cell phone. He'd missed two calls from Sara, about the time she'd vanished.

CHAPTER 26

Outside Twin Falls, Texas

The touch of the tile floor sent needles of cold piercing into Sara's body. She shivered uncontrollably as she tugged the sweater tight around her body. The vicious pain in her head caused her stomach to roll.

The icy dungeon mocked her. Her own fault she'd landed in this situation. Matt warned her. She should have waited inside the church until Matt or a patrol car arrived. If she had insisted, the desk sergeant would have located Matt.

Couldn't think about that now. The damage was done.

She faced death. If not from thirst and exposure, then from the hands of her abductor when he returned. But she also knew she couldn't give up. Maddie, Danny, and Poppy gave her reasons to fight this predicament with everything in her power. The children couldn't lose another caregiver. Not this soon. Not this way. She had to suck it up and find a way out. If she waited until her captor came back, she was dead. That reality spurred her into action.

The first step towards escape would be to find a light source so she could explore her prison.

No way to tell how long she had lain unconscious. A day? Hours? Urgency consumed her as she fingered the useless watch on her wrist—unable to read the time in the dark. She jerked upright, and gulped a breath of air as pain shot through her head.

She extended her legs as far as possible. Physical activity might at least provide some warmth. Her foot bumped something solid. Closer examination revealed a wooden column that braced the ceiling.

With her back pressed against the partition, she straightened and slowly rose to her feet, fighting the vertigo washing over her. She grabbed hold of the beam and regained her balance, but still a little shaky.

From the column, she reached out and touched the wall. Moving around the room, she ran her hands up and down the partition in search of a light switch. Nothing.

As she continued the circuit around the area, her shin connected with a sofa and a small table. Her heart leapt as she touched a refrigerator and her fingers made a frantic search for the door handle. With a steady hand, she opened the door.

Only more darkness.

The panic-demon gripped her again, until the warm air emanating from inside the appliance, told her the power was off. Probably worked from a generator that had been turned off.

She closed the door and pushed her fingers into the sweater pockets. The iPhone was gone. Either her assailant had removed it or the phone had slipped out during the attack.

That cell phone would solve all her problems. Even if she didn't know where she was, the authorities could find her with the phone's GPS feature.

Continuing exploration around the wall, she bumped into a desk. She groped through each drawer and fingered every item, trying to identify the objects by touch. Pliers, a hammer, a few nails. After searching four drawers, she had nothing but tools, which she might be able to use later. If only she could see.

The items she'd hoped for, she found in the last drawer.

A box of four candles. But no matches. Success urged her on. There should be matches or some means to light the candles. She searched the drawers again. Still no matches.

"Arrrrrgh," she slammed the last draw closed and groaned in frustration.

A tight one-handed grip on the precious candles, she continued the search, wincing as an object jammed into her leg. Something made of wood protruded from the wall. She rubbed the bump that formed, just above her ankle, then reached out. It was a stairwell in a basement or cellar.

No handrails on the stairs. She moved up them like a child, sitting on one-step and pushing up to the next level with her hands and feet.

At the top, she found a metal door. The discovery gave her added strength. She pulled against the doorknob with every ounce of power that remained. Before long, her breath came in exhausted gasps, her head throbbed and the queasiness returned. For the moment she conceded defeat.

Her dungeon—locked securely from the outside.

Twin Falls Police Station

By one o'clock Saturday afternoon, Matt's people had inspected the pavement where Sara's car was parked, and Dale McCulloch had gone over every inch of the rented sedan. The search yielded no clues as to who her abductor might have been.

Two patrol officers had interviewed neighbors in the church vicinity. A senior citizen out walking his dog around six-thirty Friday evening saw a man and a woman in the church parking lot, but he couldn't describe either.

Despite efforts to keep Sara at a distance, she had become more than just another missing person. But she was still a suspect in a murder case. For that reason alone, Matt had to cover all the bases.

With every hour that passed, Matt's frustration mounted. He'd had her picture flashed on local news outlets, and two of his men checked car rentals, taxicabs and flight schedules. Part of his responsibility as a cop. He'd known it was a wasted effort. And he was right.

Matt called Seth Davidson to meet him at church that morning, before services. They'd knelt at the altar and prayed for Sara's safety. No time to stay over for church. The first forty-eight hours after abduction were crucial. Each minute that passed lessened the odds of finding her alive.

~*~

Sara whacked the doorframe with her palm in frustration. The salty taste of blood on her tongue told her she'd bitten her bottom lip. Fighting back tears, she lowered herself to the last step. Panic and despair was the enemy. Remain calm. Stay focused.

Maddie or Matthew Foley would start a search for her. How they would find her, she had no clue. Even she didn't know where she was.

Chin in her hands, she refocused on the problem at hand.

Someone placed candles here, for power failures. They must have provided some means to light them. She just had to find the matches, a lighter, or whatever. No matter how long it took. She rose to her feet, using the wall for support, and started back around the room.

Sara slipped the candles into the sweater pocket and retraced her steps, checking above her head for shelves. She felt along the partition as high as she could reach until her arms ached, then felt stupid. A light switch would do her little good. It would be useless without the generator.

She passed the table and sofa again, finally drawn back to the refrigerator. On impulse, she stopped and checked the top. Her fingers closed around a large square box.

"Yes!" She slid the top back and fingered the wooden sticks.

For a fraction of a second, she paused—afraid to strike the match. What if she felt the heat but couldn't see the flame? She removed the candles from her pocket, gripped the match in her other hand, and sat on the floor.

Pushing her fear deep inside, she drew the matchstick across the side of the box. The light flared in a bright blue and yellow flame. Nothing had ever looked so beautiful. With a trembling hand, she lit the wick.

Hope welled inside her. She had a fighting chance to survive this trial.

The candlelight renewed her courage. Things were looking up. A glance at her wristwatch gave her the time, 8:15. Morning or evening? No way to tell.

Since Josh's death, she had gone through the motions of living. Going to her job, working the bus ministry, just putting in her time. If she survived this ordeal, she would do better. She'd raise those wonderful children, God had brought into her life, with unconditional love and understanding.

As her eyes adjusted to the light, Sara scanned the room. The frosty dungeon was a storm cellar, about twenty by fifteen feet. One room with a door to a small bathroom she'd somehow missed earlier. The switch she couldn't find was a cord tied to a bare bulb in the ceiling. As expected, when she jerked the string, nothing happened.

On a bathroom shelf, she found a small battery operated radio. She pulled it down and pressed the *on* button. Static filled the small space. She tuned in to a local talk show. The familiar voice of the host, dispelled her sense of isolation. It also gave her the time and day. Saturday evening. She had been here since Friday night.

Knees weak, she moved to the cabinet, pulled down a cup, and filled it with water from the sink. The cool liquid soothed her parched throat, but it made her colder. She'd give a thousand dollars for a cup of hot tea with honey to ease her frayed nerves and warm her body.

Thirst quenched, she let the tallow drip into another cup, then set the candle inside. The wax would hold it upright after it hardened.

Sara moved towards the hide-a-bed sofa. She pulled the bed out and found two blankets and a pillow on the mattress. She retrieved the cover, and let the bed drop back into the base with a cloud of dust that filled the close space with the musty smell of rat droppings and damp fabric. She brushed away as much dust as possible from the couch, and wrapped the blankets around her shoulders. Please don't let there be spiders, she thought.

Now to see if there was food in the cabinets. When she opened the doors, a fair stock of staples appeared. At first glance, it looked to be mostly soup and beans. Unappetizing, but she could exist on them for a while.

Satisfied that her survival needs were met, Sara's mind raced with possibilities. Perhaps she could dig out with the tools, or maybe unlock or pry the door loose.

She tackled the door again. Using the tools at the top of the stairs, she began to work on the doorknob. The screw heads on the knob were Phillips, and the only screwdriver she'd found was a flat-head. She gave it a try anyway, before finally admitting defeat. With the claw end of the hammer, she tried to pry the knob plate off. No luck.

After an hour, exhaustion overcame her. The knob had loosened but was nowhere near ready to come off. She stopped. Her head throbbed and nausea swept over her. She'd try again after she rested.

It was after midnight when disappointment slowed her steps as she walked back down the stairs. She lay on the sofa, and wrapped herself in the covering. Welcome warmth seeped into her body.

The need for rest overshadowed the smell of the blankets.

~*~

The muffled sound of thunder filtered into the cellar along, with the sounds of raindrops splashing against the ground above her. She had slept eight hours. Her eyelids seemed weighted. She let them close, sleepy in the soft candlelight. Her mind drifted off into a gentle, quiet place.

She awoke hours later to the sound of *drip, drip, drip*. Her fingers touched the floor.

Water.

The cellar had a leak somewhere.

What next? Along with darkness and cold, she could now add wet. Could pestilence be far behind?

A glance at her watch told her it was Sunday evening. Grabbing the candle, she made her way to the bathroom on shaky legs. She washed her face in the cold water and dried it off with toilet paper. Her reflection in the mirror was a pitiful sight. Dark hair, matted with blood, her face pale as the ghost of Christmas' past.

An urgent need to work on the door surged through her, but the strength needed to climb the stairs just wasn't there. She must find a way out before her captor returned. If not, perhaps she could convince him Matt Foley knew who he was and had the entire Twin Falls Police force on his trail. Trouble was, she'd never been a convincing liar.

Her head pounded and the dizziness returned, along with a rolling stomach, signaling she had a concussion. Weakness forced her to lie down again and pull the covers close. If she could get warm and rest, she would feel better.

She closed her eyes. Unbidden, she fell asleep.

Sometime later, she awoke to a blast of thunder that accompanied the drip of water. A sound outside, above the tempest, erased her concerns about the water. Over the storm, the distinctive crunch of gravel drifted into the cellar. Footsteps moved closer.

Her nemesis had returned.

CHAPTER 27

Twin Falls Police Station

Matt's stomach growled. Too busy to stop for Sunday lunch, he wished he'd taken Davis up on the offer to bring him a sandwich at noon. He grabbed the phone and dialed Joe Wilson's number, tapping his pen on the desk while he waited for his friend to answer.

When Joe picked up, Matt didn't bother with formalities. "How about joining me for an early dinner?"

Slight pause. "Sure. Where?"

Matt clutched the telephone under his chin while he adjusted his shoulder holster, and pulled on his jacket. "Meet me at the Steak Out in twenty minutes."

"I'm on my way."

Steak Out Restaurant

Matt arrived at the restaurant before Joe. The Steak Out was one of the oldest restaurants in Twin Falls, supposedly opened by an ex-cop. It was the place to come when he wanted a great steak. They didn't serve anything else. Just prime beef, potatoes, a salad bar, and two kinds of pie, apple and cherry. Simple and reasonable. There were only a few customers scattered around the room, the evening crowd hadn't arrived yet. He commandeered a quiet table in the smoking section in back. His friend liked a cigar after dinner.

Joseph Dawson Wilson had been one grade ahead of Matt in school. An old soul, born mature and wise. He'd taken Matt under his wing after Matt's family was murdered, tried to protect him from his abusive uncle. More times than he could count, Matt had gone home with Joe after school, sleeping over many nights.

As a skinny kid, with a big nose and ears before he'd grown into them, Matt's classmates would have made his life unbearable, had it not been for Joe.

When Matt joined the Army, he'd gone to the Federal Building in downtown Dallas to be sworn in. Alone, in a crowd of recruits surrounded by family there to see their sons and daughters off, he felt a little sorry for himself. Trying to read the book he'd brought to read, he glanced up to see Joe smiling down at him. "Mind a little company, kid?" Joe stayed by his side until Matt got on the bus.

His friend stepped into the breach again after Mary's death, moving into Matt's home to keep him from being alone. Made sure Matt ate, showered, shaved, and when he was able, sent him off to work. Joe had put his life on hold for six months, until he knew Matt could handle the grief. He owed Joe Wilson more than he could ever repay.

Matt waved at Joe when he entered the restaurant. His long strides brought him quickly to the table. He slid into a chair and glanced across the table at Matt. "You're buying, of course."

Matt grinned. "Of course. I wouldn't expect you to release the tight grip you have on the first dollar you've ever earned. However, it's going to cost you in another way."

"I knew there had to be a catch when you called." Joe placed the single-sheet menu the waitress handed him on the table. "So what do you need?"

"We'll discuss it after we eat."

They placed their orders and Joe leaned back in the chair. "How are you doing? I know this is a bad time of the year for you."

Matt shrugged. "This year's better than last."

"That doesn't tell me much."

Matt fingered the coaster under his tea glass. "Better. I sleep most nights. The job keeps me busy. I'm getting there."

Joe nodded, satisfied. He glanced over Matt's shoulder and muttered. "Uh oh."

Matt leaned forward. "What?"

Before Joe could answer, Terrance Hall stood beside their table. He planted his feet wide, his arms crossed. "Robert Cook."

"What about him?" Matt asked.

The councilman wore a satisfied smirk. "You missed it, Foley. He killed the Pryor girl and Josh Bradford. And you never had a clue."

"I wouldn't spread that rumor too broadly, Terry. At the moment, all we have is circumstantial evidence. If your theory proves wrong, you'll lose face with your media cronies."

"Finding the hit-and-run vehicle on Cook's property isn't proof? The fact Cook was custodian at the place where he buried the girl isn't conclusive? What do you want, bloody footprints leading to his front door?"

Restaurant patrons had begun to notice the confrontation. Conversations stopped.

"All circumstantial, Terry," Matt said calmly. "You keep riding that dead horse and you could wind up with egg on your face."

Hall's hazel eyes narrowed, and some of his bravado slipped away. The doubtful expression lasted only a moment. "Don't try to bluff an old card shark, Foley. Who else could it be?"

"What about I'm-not-going-to-discuss-police-business-with-you, don't you understand?"

"Maybe you'll have to explain your actions to the governor." Having issued his exit line, Hall marched to his table and for the first time, Matt noticed Hall's dinner companions. Pepper Parker and Harold Golden. Nothing positive could possibly come from a gathering of the Matt Foley Fan Club.

Joe stared at the trio and shook his head. "Do you think Hall was born a jerk, or is it a learned behavior?"

The councilman was like an annoying fly that kept coming back no matter how many times he'd been swatted. "Both."

"Is he right?"

"I don't think so," Matt said. "At the time, we didn't consider Cook a suspect in Bradford's murder. No reason to. The murder vehicle wasn't registered to him, and we had no motive or grounds for a search warrant. Now we know he was connected to the murder vehicle and to the retreat, he's certainly high on our list of suspects. But other evidence points to Cook as a witness, rather than Penny's killer."

The waiter brought their food and they lapsed into small talk. Joe made short order of the steak and pushed his plate back. "Okay, so what's up?"

"I'd like you to go with me to the Cook place tonight to look around."

"I assume you have a good reason." Joe pulled a cigar from his pocket. He offered one to Matt who declined. "You know your people came back with a warrant and took everything that wasn't nailed down."

"I'm on a scouting expedition," Matt said. "Probably nothing there, but I want to look around. Do you guys have it taped off?"

Joe lit the expensive cigar then took a couple of puffs to make sure it was burning. "Yep. Only because I haven't gotten around to removing it and notifying the nephew he can take possession. You lookin' for anything in particular?"

Matt didn't have a clue what he hoped to find. "I'm just following a cop-hunch. It could be the mother of all wild goose chases. Do you have flashlights with you? It will be dark by the time we get there."

Joe laughed. "I don't know about you city cops, but the sheriff's office is always prepared for emergencies."

Matt chuckled, reached into his money clip, and placed three bills on the tray.

Outside, the heavens displayed a fantastic light show. Joe shot Matt a questioning look. "You sure you want to do this tonight?"

"Don't worry, Wilson. You won't melt."

"That's not what the girls tell me." Joe slapped Matt's back and walked towards the county SUV. "Let's take mine. I'll bring you back to pick up your car when we're finished."

Robert Cook's Place

They drove west as the last glimmer of light faded on the horizon. Joe talked fishing on the trip out, the major passion of his life. He spent most of his off-duty time on the lake or on one of the off-track rivers nearby. His hobby yielded a ton of fish. An invitation to Joe's annual Labor Day fish fry ranked right up there with Super Bowl tickets.

A full-fledged thunderstorm raged as Joe swung the county vehicle into the circular, gravel driveway.

Somewhere in the distance, a tinny sound sneaked through the roar of the storm.

Nature flaunted her power through the heavy downpour, with lightning flashes, and rolls of thunder that reverberated the ground under their feet. The rain slowed a little, and they made a mad dash for the house, stopping to step over the yellow tape.

Joe sent him a disgruntled glance as they reached the covered porch. "Only for you, pal, would I come out on a night like this."

"I know. I owe you, big time."

"Don't you forget it. Because I won't."

Once inside the house, Joe flipped the light switch. Brightness filled the room. "Well, well, well. The utilities are still on. Wonder if the nephew plans on moving in when we release the property."

Matt extinguished the flashlight and let his gaze sweep the room. The place was almost empty. Joe took one side of the room, Matt took the other.

"Okay," Joe said. "What am I looking for?"

"A written confession to Penny Pryor's murder would be nice."

Joe scowled at him. "Besides that."

"You'll know it when you see it. Or not."

Opening drawers in a nearby desk, Matt found them empty. McCulloch had packed up everything but the dirty dishes in the kitchen sink.

For now, Matt wanted to see if anything obvious stood out, maybe take a look in the shed where the Mustang had been stored.

After a quick look over the premises, he had to write off the search as a wasted effort. At least he'd tried. He wasn't good at waiting in his office for something to break. Not when Sara's whereabouts were uncertain.

Joe sifted through a few old newspapers on the coffee table. "Doesn't look like there's much to see."

"I had just come to that conclusion," Matt said.

Joe switched off the interior lights and opened the back door, letting the beam of his flashlight sweep over the yard.

Matt stood behind Joe as the light illuminated an old car and the vent of what appeared to be a storm cellar.

Joe shut the door.

"Wait a minute, Joe. Is that a radio? Where's it coming from?"

Joe swung the door open again. "Sounds like it's coming from the storm cellar, but that doesn't make any sense."

"Let's check it out." Matt stepped around the rain puddles, moving towards the cellar, Joe behind him. The sounds became louder with each step.

Someone had jammed a crowbar through the metal rings on the door and lintel.

Reflex action made Matt remove his gun. He glanced behind him to see that Joe had done the same.

Matt slid the crowbar out with one hand and yanked the door back with the other. Rusting hinges screamed in protest. Matt took cover beside the door and raised his weapon. He peeked around the doorframe. Inside, a candle glowed in the darkness.

"Police, we're coming in," Matt yelled.

He descended the steps, aware he made a perfect target for anyone inside. Noise from the radio filled the small space as he reached ground level.

He stepped onto the floor, and the beam of Joe's flashlight swept across the cellar, then stopped.

Illuminated in the brightness, Sara Bradford stood, with a hammer raised in defiance.

CHAPTER 28

Robert Cook's Home

The man made a slow pass by the Cook place not liking what he saw. He drove a mile down the road, made a u-turn and came back for another slow pass. The windshield wipers struggle to clear his view of the sheriff's car in the circular drive. He pulled over and doused the headlights. Through the rain, he watched as Joe Wilson and Matt Foley stood in front of the storm cellar door. He should have come earlier.

No doubt they'd found Sara alive. The blow he'd struck hadn't been hard enough to be fatal. The woman had more lives than a cat.

How had they found her so soon?

He pounded the steering wheel. Getting rid of Sara had just become immeasurably more difficult. If she were smart, she'd hire a fulltime bodyguard. He certainly would in her situation.

Getting rid of her would be more difficult, but not impossible. He knew where she lived, and he had copies of her house keys. He'd have to wait for the right opening—when she let down her defenses.

He smiled as he pulled away from the Cook place. After he rounded the curve heading back to Twin Falls, he switched the car's lights back on.

~*~

Relief swept over Matt as he holstered his gun. He took a tentative step towards Sara. "Are you all right?"

She dropped the hammer and collapsed on the sofa, lowering her head into her hands.

Concern for her wellbeing twisted his gut. Dried blood matted her hair. Tears and dust stained her cheeks, her clothes were wrinkled and covered with dirt.

She looked into his eyes, and her voice caught in her throat. "How did you find me? Who brought me here, and where am I?"

Matt knelt beside her. Tortured visions of what might have happened if they hadn't found her made him tremble. It had been a long time since he'd felt such helpless anger—fury at the unknown assailant responsible for Sara's condition. "You're in a storm cellar on Robert Cook's property, the man who owned the car that killed Josh. We were about to leave when we heard the radio and followed the sound." He smoothed the hair away from her face. "You're giving that guardian angel of yours a workout."

She rose to her feet. "I know."

Joe Wilson interrupted. "It would be best to leave the questions for later, Mrs. Bradford. You need to have a doctor look at your wounds. Can you walk? Perhaps we should call an ambulance."

"I can walk. Just take me out of here." Her speech was fast and disjointed, her breath coming in quick gasps. "I don't want to spend another minute in this horrid place. Please."

Joe caught Matt's eye. "You shouldn't move someone with a head injury."

"It'll be okay. She's already been moving around. Let's do as she asks."

When she stepped forward, Matt lifted her into his arms.

Her head rested against his shoulder. A tremor ran through her body, whether from cold or the long ordeal she'd suffered, he didn't know. He needed to get her somewhere, warm and safe.

The rain had slowed but still soaked their clothes as they trekked back to Joe's SUV. Matt placed Sara in the backseat while Joe opened the hatch, returning with blankets and a pillow.

Sara's teeth chattered as Matt wrapped her in the thick covering and placed the pillow under her head. Joe handed him a barf bag. "Just in case."

"You are prepared, aren't you?" Matt passed the bag on to Sara.

"Just like the Marines. Now let's get this girl out of here." Joe opened the driver's side door and got in. As they spun out of the driveway, he switched on the strobe lights and siren.

After opening the vents in the back, Matt turned the heater on high. He grabbed Joe's radio and called Twin Falls Memorial. "This is Police Chief, Matt Foley. I'm on my way in with a woman who has a head wound. ETA twenty minutes."

He glanced back at Sara. "You okay?"

She pulled the cover up tight under her chin and closed her eyes. In a barely audible voice, she said, "Matt, I don't want you to think I'm some wimpy, weepy female. I'm not like that at all. It's..." She paused and took a deep breath. "This has been a really rough week."

Just happy to have found Sara alive, Matt glanced over at Joe and couldn't suppress a grin. "Your secret is safe with us."

Don Tompkins' Home

Late that afternoon, Don Tompkins shut off the television and paced. He couldn't keep his interest on the game. Giving in to the impulse that plagued him all day, he picked up the phone to call Maddie Jamison.

They'd spent a pleasant evening together at the country club dinner. Don found her easy to talk to. They'd shared some common interests, playing bridge, hiking, and reading.

That wasn't the only reason Don wanted to make the call. True, he enjoyed Maddie's company, but he also needed to stay close to the Bradford home.

He had qualms about beginning a relationship with Maddie. She impressed him as a very shrewd lady. She would know if his intentions were not sincere. Quite possibly, she would see through his pretext.

After the death of his wife, Don seldom dated. No one would ever accuse him of being a player. Not only were his skills rusty, they were nonexistent. An occasional dinner with a female friend was the extent of his social life.

The hole in his heart left by Debra's passing still ached. He missed the companionship, the oneness. Still, a relationship with Maddie Jamison would involve a commitment he might be unable to make. Muttering to himself, he cast doubts aside and dialed the number, rehearsing what he would say.

A woman with a slight Mexican accent answered. He gave his name and waited. A minute passed before Maddie came on the line.

"How are you, Don?" Her voice sounded strained.

"I've picked a bad time to call, I know, but I wanted to see how you're doing. I saw the news bulletin about Sara. If you'd rather not talk, I can call back later."

"No, it's okay. There won't be a good time until Sara comes home." Her voice broke followed by a moment of silence. "I'm sorry. I'm just so frightened for her."

"You haven't heard anything?" He knew the answer, but he had to ask.

"There has been no word. Matthew Foley promised to call me the minute he finds out anything."

"If you have no objections, I'll come over. Two heads can worry better than one."

"You may come over, if you wish. A few friends are here now keeping vigil with me. But I warn you, I'm not going to be a very good hostess."

Sara Bradford's Home

Don tuned in to the Cowboy game on his way across town. It was the third quarter and the Pokes were behind three points. He'd become a more avid fan after retirement from the force. He had more time on his hands.

Twenty minutes later, he parked in front of the Bradford residence. He'd run into heavy rain on the drive out, but the worst of the storm lay to the north. The sweep of his headlights revealed the three-story brick Tudor design he'd seen when he followed Sara home after the explosion. It was impressive, sitting in the middle of what looked like a hundred acres of rolling meadows and trees. A four-foot white rail fence went as far as the eye could see.

Maddie answered the door. She was dressed in gray slacks, white blouse, and a gray and green plaid jacket, her gray-blond hair casually styled. Her face was scrubbed clean but tired, with the same pretty features he remembered.

He followed her into the den where she introduced him

246

to her pastor, Seth Davidson, and Colin Connelly. The other two, Shannon and Jeffery Hayden, he'd met at the banquet.

Worry lines creased the pale faces of the women. Dark circles under their eyes testified to the strain they were under.

"Have either of you eaten anything today?" He directed his question to Shannon.

She shook her head. "Pastor Davidson has tried to get Maddie to eat something, but she won't. I don't think she's eaten since lunch yesterday."

Don turned to Maddie. "Well, I won't take no for an answer. I make a mean omelet, and if your housekeeper doesn't toss me out of her kitchen, I'll have a mouth-watering concoction ready in about twenty minutes."

To Shannon he said, "Can you point me in the direction of the kitchen?"

"I'll do better than that. I'll take you back and introduce you to Beatrice." Shannon slipped her arm through his. "I love a man who takes charge."

A large kitchen opened up before him, and the faint scents of cinnamon and yeast filled the air. The floor was brick with a long island in the center where copper-bottom cookware hung within easy reach. Someone who loved to cook had designed the space.

The faithful Beatrice welcomed him into her kitchen. She provided everything he needed to make his omelet "a la Tompkins", a cholesterol nightmare. But the occasion called for good ol' comfort food.

He sizzled bacon, ham, and sausage while Beatrice chopped red onions, tomatoes, cheese, and mushrooms. He beat the eggs until they were light and fluffy, added spices, and then assembled individual omelets for everyone.

While he worked, Beatrice made coffee and toast and set warm plates at the breakfast nook in the bay window.

Still wearing one of Beatrice's frilly aprons, Don went into the den. "Food's ready, folks. Come on while it's hot."

The group trouped into the kitchen with Pastor Davidson and Maddie leading the way. After the pastor blessed the food, the somber party began to eat. The meal was consumed in short order. Even Maddie finished most of her omelet.

The small group remained at the table, long after Beatrice cleared away the dishes and refilled coffee cups. It felt like a wake as they spoke of good times shared with Sara.

Later when they returned to the den, someone had built a glowing fire in the hearth. They scattered into nearby chairs, silently watching Beatrice bring in fresh coffee and place the tray on the teacart.

At seven o'clock, the phone next to Maddie's chair rang, making her jump. She hesitated for a fraction of a second before picking up the receiver. Don understood. She feared the call brought bad news and didn't know if she could handle it.

Maddie straightened in her chair, inhaled, and lifted the phone. Don scanned her face as worry lines disappeared, and then re-formed as she ended the call.

"That was Matthew...he found Sara." Her voice caught with a near-sob. Maddie leaned back and sank deeper into the chair. "Sara's injured but he doesn't think it's serious. He and the sheriff are taking her to Twin Falls Memorial. He'll fill us in when we get there."

Don and Shannon brought their cars under the portico. They loaded the passengers and headed to the hospital. He had watched Maddie's ashen face as she spoke to Matt Foley. Had he told her the truth about Sara's condition? He hoped so, for Maddie's sake.

CHAPTER 29

Twin Falls Memorial Hospital

Matt waited outside the emergency room bay. His gaze followed Maddie as she weaved towards him, past the IV machines and a stretcher that cluttered the hallway. Don Tompkins followed behind her.

"How is she, Matthew?" Lines of concern creased Maddie's brow as she placed her hand on his arm with a gentle touch.

"She seems to be okay. They took her for a CAT scan on the head wound a few minutes ago. We'll know more after the doctor has a chance to read the results."

"Can you tell us what happened, Chief?" Tompkins asked.

"I haven't questioned her and she hasn't said much. We had to take care of her injuries first. She's had a pretty bad ordeal."

"Can I see her?" Maddie asked.

"Of course, as soon as she returns from x-ray."

Maddie lowered her gaze to her hands. Tension tightened the muscles around her mouth. "I can't believe some maniac is running around Twin Falls trying to harm Sara. Do you have any idea who's responsible?"

"We're hoping Sara can fill in some of the blanks."

Based on the questions Sara asked when they'd found her, she hadn't recognized her assailant. But he wasn't about to divulge that information in front of Tompkins.

Twenty minutes later, an orderly wheeled Sara back into the emergency bay. He returned the bed to its previous position in the exam room, and left. Maddie hurried forward and clasped her niece's hand.

Sara tried to sit up, but winced, then leaned back against the pillow. "Hey."

"Hey yourself. How are you doing?"

Sara wiggled her hand in a so-so wave.

After a short interval, the curtain slid back and the doctor entered. He drew up a stool. "Well, young lady, you have a slight concussion. As a precaution, we'll keep you overnight to monitor your progress. Someone will be in soon to move you to a private room. I want you to stay quiet and rest." He glanced at Maddie. "Try not to tire her too much."

When the doctor had gone, Matt ducked outside and joined the group in the ER waiting room.

Shannon was the first one to reach him. "Is she all right, Matt?"

"She's going to be fine. They're keeping her overnight. I suggest you all go home. You can check in on her tomorrow. The doctor wants her to rest but will probably release her in the morning, unless there are complications."

Maddie walked up behind him. "They've taken Sara to a private room." She turned imploring eyes on Matt. "Will she be safe? Perhaps I should stay the night. I don't want to let her out of my sight."

"You need to get some rest. I'm posting a guard outside her door until she leaves the hospital."

"I'd like to stay with her for a while, if that's okay," Maddie said.

"Absolutely."

Seth Davidson, Jeffery Hayden, and Shannon left. Don Tompkins caught Maddie's gaze. "I'll wait here until you're ready to leave, then I'll drive you home."

Matt watched Tompkins take a seat in the waiting room, then followed Maddie to Sara's room. What was Tompkins doing here? Something Matt intended to ask Maddie. The man headed Matt's list of suspects. He didn't like the idea that the security guard was involved in Sara's personal life.

While he waited for the officer to arrive, Matt slipped into Sara's room to check the windows. The turns this case had taken heightened his concern for her safety. Someone wanted her dead. That wasn't going to happen, not if he had to handcuff Sara and lock her in a cell.

He opened the window locks, re-bolted them, and then drew the curtains.

Maddie stroked Sara's hand, smoothed her hair away from her face, then gave Sara's hand a squeeze. "Guess I'm ready to leave." She turned to Matt. "Will you stay until the guard arrives?"

"I won't leave her unguarded for a minute."

Later, when the police guard arrived, Matt pulled him aside. "Don't leave this door for any reason. I'll send a patrol car by to relieve you for breaks. This lady is in serious danger. I'm depending on you to keep her safe tonight."

The fresh-faced young cop gave a solemn nod. "Don't worry, Chief. I've got it covered."

With the guard in place, Matt stopped at Sara's bedside. Eyes closed, she looked pale and vulnerable against the white sheets. As if sensing his presence, her eyelids fluttered, then opened wide. "Oh, it's you, Matt, I thought..."

"Sorry, I didn't mean to startle you. I wanted to check on you before I left. I've posted an officer outside your door tonight so you can rest easy. I'll come back tomorrow morning and take you home. Then I'll want to hear everything that happened."

"Thank you, Matt. For finding me..." Her voice trailed off again. The after-effects of her ordeal had kicked in.

"You're welcome," he said but she'd fallen asleep. Matt pulled the door closed behind him.

Matt stopped in front of the guard. "Remember, nobody goes into that room but hospital personnel. Check their ID. No ID, no entry."

The guard straightened his posture. "Yes, sir."

Joe waited outside to take Matt to the restaurant to get his car. They drove in silence for a while. Stopped at a red light, Joe glanced across at him. "I think what happened tonight was a God-thing. If we hadn't gone out to Cook's place, the kidnapper could have come back and killed that woman. What made you decide to go there tonight?"

Matt leaned against the headrest. "Who knows where hunches come from? All I can tell you is that for some reason, I wanted to check the place out to look for clues that might help me find her."

"How long have you known Sara Bradford?"

"I've known *of* her for more than ten years. She was Mary's best friend. But I didn't really know her. She and her husband moved in different social circles."

As they waited for the light to change, Joe's gaze swept over Matt's face. "Did I imagine it, or did I see something developing between you two?"

The question caught Matt off guard. Was there something happening between him and Sara? True, he'd admitted to Seth he felt an attraction there. "I don't know, Joe. I really don't know."

Sara Bradford's Home

253

Maddie rode with Don in silence from the hospital through the empty late night streets. She didn't feel the need to make conversation. Don seemed to feel the same way. He maneuvered his SUV with practiced efficiency through the streets of the industrial area that surrounded the hospital. He turned left at the stop sign, then merged onto the freeway.

At home, Don pulled under the portico and stopped.

"Would you like to come in for coffee? It'll only take a minute to make."

"That sounds like a winner." Don got out and came around to open her door.

Before Maddie could insert her key, the door swung open. Beatrice stood in the entrance, face pale and drawn, an unspoken question in her eyes.

Maddie drew the Spanish woman into a hug. "Sara's okay. Go on to bed, you need to rest. I'm going to make coffee before I retire."

Switching on the kitchen lights, Maddie led the way inside and started the coffeemaker. She held up the pot. "It's decaf. I hope you don't mind."

"That's what I drink at night." Don pulled out a stool from under the island bar.

Maddie felt his gaze follow her.

"How bad is your eyesight, Maddie? You seem to be able to do almost anything you want to do."

She smiled as she removed a chocolate cream pie from the refrigerator and placed it on the counter. "I have my limitations. I can handle most things reasonably well, except driving and reading. I've learned to compensate for the things my vision can't accommodate. I really don't notice it very much anymore." She chuckled. "Although,

I'm still a great back-seat driver, as Sara and Pete will testify."

While the brew finished its cycle, Maddie cut two wedges of pie onto plates and slid one across to Don. When the coffeemaker's red light came on, she poured the hot liquid into mugs, then took the stool beside Don.

He tested the brew with a tentative sip. "What are you going to do about this situation with Sara? She appears to be in serious trouble. I'd like to help, if I can."

A smile tugged at the corners of her mouth. "To be honest, that's why I invited you in. I'm going to hire a bodyguard for her. She'll hate it, but I'm not giving her an option. I hoped you could advise me where to start, or perhaps, you would be interested in the job. I'll pay whatever the going rate is. I want protection for her right away, someone to watch over her twenty-four seven until Matt finds whoever's responsible. Perhaps two people in twelve-hour shifts. If you're interested, you could stay here and drive Sara wherever she goes."

"I've been thinking along those lines myself. I don't want your money. I'll do it because I like Sara." He swallowed a bite of pie and made an appreciative sound. "I have two weeks of vacation coming and can guard her for that period of time. If the police haven't found the perp by then, I'll find you someone to take my place. I'll start tomorrow evening, after I finish my shift at Global."

"That's great, but I insist you let me pay for your services. I'll have Beatrice prepare a room for you."

He finished the pie, pushed back his plate, and stood to leave. "I'll call you tomorrow."

Maddie followed him to the foyer. When he'd gone, she locked the door and leaned back against it, satisfied. She had gained a measure of security for Sara. Don's presence would keep her safe.

Twin Falls Memorial Hospital

Sara awoke early and scanned the unfamiliar surroundings. It certainly wasn't her bedroom, but the beige and green drapes looked familiar. She sat upright, sending knives of pain cascading from her scalp down her spine. Easing her legs to the floor, she poured a glass of water from the white plastic jug on the nightstand and took a deep swallow. Cool drops of liquid rolled over her tongue, soothing her parched throat.

She inhaled a sharp breath, as instant memories of the cellar flooded her mind, accompanied by the terror the last twenty-four hours had brought. But she was safe now. Relief washed over her and she eased back onto the pillow.

What day was this? Then it hit her. Monday. The meeting with Global's new owners was at nine o'clock. Today.

She glanced at her watch. Six o'clock. And she had to go home, shower and get back to Global.

Her fingers found the nurse call button on the bed railing. Almost immediately, a voice over the intercom asked, "May I help you?"

Sara slid her legs over the bedside once again, searching for her shoes. "I have an important meeting this morning. I must leave right away. Can you get my release papers ready?"

Seconds later, a nurse she remembered from last night rushed in. "Mrs. Bradford, you can't leave without the doctor's release. It's hospital policy."

Sara moved across the room, opened the metal cabinet and found her shoes. "You don't understand. I must leave.

If I don't show up...let's just say it's important, really important. I have to leave as soon as possible."

The nurse left, and soon after, Sara's friend Gaye stood in the middle of the room, her arms crossed, and a stern look in her eyes. "If you insist on leaving, you'll have to sign an AMA form."

One shoe on, Sara looked up. "What's that?"

"It means against medical advice. It also means your insurance company might not pay your hospital bill."

Both shoes now on, Sara shrugged. "I can live with that. Would you please bring the form, right away?"

Gaye came back minutes later with the papers. "Are you always this bull-headed?"

Sara's gaze searched the nurse's face. "Gaye, please believe that under normal circumstances, I'm a pussycat. But Ripley's *Believe it or Not* would not believe my life the past two weeks. I'm truly sorry for any problems I've caused you, but there are really important matters I have to take care of in the next three hours."

Gaye gave a reluctant nod. "Okay, you're forgiven, but I don't want to see you back in here for a very, very long time. Do you want me to unhook the IV or do you plan to take it with you?"

"Unhook me, please." Sara signed the papers while Gaye removed the IV and taped a cotton ball to her arm. Realization hit Sara. She had another problem. Maddie had taken her dirty clothes home. "I know this is getting to be a habit, but I'll have to wear the gown home."

Gaye put her hands on her hips. "I see your plan now...you're a hospital gown thief." She chuckled. "Would it do any good for me to say no?"

Sara grimaced and shook her head. "Not unless you want me to send shockwaves through the community."

The officer at the door proved more difficult. "Ma'am, no way can I let you leave here until I speak to my supervisor. My instructions were that no unapproved person could enter or leave the room. That includes you. I'll handcuff you if I have to."

Sara clutched her gown closer to her body, and muttered, "Just my luck to draw Robocop."

The delay cost Sara thirty precious minutes. At seven o'clock, Matthew Foley shoved through the door, fire in his eyes, hair disheveled as though he'd combed it with his fingers. His clothes lacked their usual pristine appearance as though he'd grabbed them off the floor.

His voice raised a notch higher than usual. "Sara, what's your all fired hurry? You need the doctor's permission before you sail out of here."

"I'm sorry, Matt. I didn't mean to get you out of bed. I feel fine. A release is a formality. And it could take hours. I don't have time to wait for that. Today is the first meeting with the new management at Global. I can't miss this meeting. It's bad enough that my division was bombed without being a no-show at their first meeting. I must get home and dress. Please help me. Please."

Matt ran his fingers through his hair and locked gazes with Gaye. "Okay, I'll drive you home. But I'm going to Global with you."

Sara headed towards the door. "Okay, but—"

Matt removed his coat and helped her into it. "Don't argue with me on this. It isn't open for discussion. I'll wait in your office until the meeting is over."

She expelled a deep breath. "Deal."

~*~

Matt dropped Sara off at Global's entrance and she dashed straight to the conference room. Most of the staff stood in the hallway in small anxious clusters. Emily Dean disengaged herself from one of the groups when Sara entered. "Sara, I've been trying to reach you all morning. Roger postponed the meeting until ten o'clock. He wants to see you in his office. I'll take you to him."

Roger never started a meeting late or rescheduled one. He hated indecision. However, this wasn't his party. The new management must have thrown him off his game.

Butterflies did a dance in her stomach as she followed Emily to Roger's office. Still a little shaky from her ordeal, she braced for another meeting with the man.

Passing a mirror in the hallway, Sara glanced at her reflection. Thankfully, her head wound hadn't required stitches, but it had been tender as she'd shampooed her hair earlier. At least, she wouldn't have to explain bandages or a bald spot to anyone. She had selected her red power suit from the closet. She needed all the help she could get today.

Emily tapped on the door of Roger's office then held it open. "Sara's here, Roger."

The door closed behind Emily with a soft click.

CHAPTER 30

Global Optics

Not once since Roger Reynolds removed her from her position had Sara considered another private meeting with him. Yet here she was, standing before a visibly shaken man. The second person in the room to capture her attention was...Adam Elliot. She did a double take. What was he doing behind Roger's desk?

"You're not going to faint, are you?" Adam asked.

Sara wasn't sure, but she shook her head.

Adam shifted his attention to Roger. "You can leave us now. I'll see you at the meeting."

Roger gave a curt nod and left.

Adam cast a concerned look at her. He walked around the desk and motioned for her to take a seat on the sofa. "I didn't expect to see you here today, but I'm glad you made it. Lindsey and I were very concerned about you when we heard you were missing. Are you sure you're okay?"

Sara made her voice as reassuring as possible. "I'm fine, Adam. It was a scary experience, but thanks to our excellent police force, I survived."

"When we have time, I want to hear all about it," Adam said. "It's going to be a very busy morning. I guess you'd like an explanation."

Barely able to draw a full breath, Sara met his direct gaze. "Yes, very much. You're the last person I expected to see today."

"I'm sorry to have kept you in the dark. It couldn't be helped. My company purchased Global, and for reasons too numerous to go into, I wanted to keep a low profile."

Sara shook her head. "Wow, so your firm is Millennium Ventures." She blinked. "Then why are you letting me go?"

"I'm not. I want to offer you a promotion. It's a new position. How would you feel about taking the helm as Global Optics' first president? I'll step into Rogers's shoes as CEO."

A thrill worked its way through Sara's chest. It took heroic effort to keep her mouth from forming a big silly grin. "Why me? I'm not looking for compliments, but I never expected this."

He leaned back against the sofa. "It's simple, really. You impressed me when we worked together. You literally ran the division while I went off to get my masters degree. I need someone loyal who's up to the job. That's you."

She sat forward on the couch. She couldn't take this job, at least not without an explanation. "Adam, there have been some changes in my life this week. I'm in the process of adopting two children. They'll make additional demands on my time. Travel would be more difficult."

Adam's smile lit the room. "I know about Poppy and Danny. I'm a family man, Sara. My wife and kids come first. I don't want to talk you into something you don't want, but I don't think we have a problem. With teleconference capabilities, you can keep travel to a minimum, if at all." He grinned. "It saves the firm a lot of money in air fare and hotel bills. So, what do you think? I'm ready to make the announcement if you want the job. I'll postpone the news if you need more time to consider the offer."

She let what he said sink in for a moment, focusing on the unbelievable opportunity. She'd worked towards this goal most of her professional career. Before Poppy and

261

Danny entered her life.

The flash of doubt evaporated as fast as it appeared. "Yes. I want the job. If my career interferes with my private life, I'll let you know in plenty of time to find someone to replace me. Thanks, for believing in me."

He slapped his hands down on his knees, stood, and shook her hand. "That's all I ask." He walked across the room and held the door open. "Shall we join the others and get this meeting underway?"

Sara entered the conference room with Adam, Roger, and two partners from Millennium Ventures. Out of the corner of her eye, she spotted Charles Edwards. He drummed his manicured fingers on the mahogany table.

Shock waves of nervous energy flowed around the room filled with management, afraid for their jobs. They'd probably thought of little else the past two weeks. The job offer she'd received confirmed the fact Adam wanted people around him he could trust.

The positive thing the staff didn't yet know was that Adam already knew the strengths of almost everyone in the room. An old adage she'd learned in college came to mind. "Make as many friends as possible, because tomorrow your co-worker may be your boss."

A hush settled over the room. Most everyone in the meeting knew Adam Elliot. What they didn't yet know was the purpose for his presence here.

Adam stood at the front of the table. Sara took a seat along the wall.

He introduced the two partners. "I apologize for starting the meeting late, but there were a few details we needed to work out. As you know by now, my firm finalized the Global purchase two weeks ago. Most of you know me, and I'm aware of the great talent assembled in this room. I can promise you some excitement in the days ahead."

He waited a five count, holding everyone's attention, then continued. "Roger is being transferred to our pharmaceutical division on the east coast. We need someone of his quality to head up that division."

Sara glanced at Roger. He wore a strained smile, his eyes fixed on Adam.

"I will assume the position of CEO. Sara Bradford will become president, a new position in the firm."

Every head in the room swung in her direction

"There may be a few other personnel changes," Adam said, "but none of you need to fear for your jobs. We're a large corporation. We need good people. I run a trim ship. I believe in operating lean and mean. Fewer people, higher salaries. I don't plan to lay off anyone. We will let attrition take its course. As associates leave the company, we won't replace them until we have the personnel level we need. In the interim, if a department needs people, we will try to transfer from other departments that have more people than they need.

"I'll be happy to discuss your concerns. See Emily for an appointment. Just keep doing the great job, you've been doing."

With that, Adam closed the meeting. He shook hands with everyone before he left for the plant tour.

Still dazed, Sara made her way through the crowd, amid congratulations, and headed to her office. She'd just been handed the job of a lifetime.

Adam said he'd tried to contact her for the lunch they'd planned, but couldn't reach her at the office or at home. No wonder. She'd been too busy dodging a killer. For now, she wanted to enjoy the glow of the promotion.

The turmoil of the past weeks vanished until she found

Matt Foley sitting at her desk.

Jane followed her into the office. "So, what happened? Do we move up or move out?" She cast a wide smile at Sara. "I always wanted to work on mahogany row."

Sara plopped into the chair in front of her desk, unable to contain the smile that spread across her face. "We move up. Definitely move up. I still can't believe it. I only found out an hour ago. However, we can't move until Adam tells us which office will be ours."

"I'll start packing," Jane said as she walked out with an exaggerated twist of her hips.

Matt lifted one eyebrow. "Who's moving where?"

"I was given a promotion." She suppressed a squeal. "To president of Global Optics."

Matt laughed. "Congratulations. It appears a bombed division didn't hurt you, although that's an unusual career strategy. Are you ready to go home?"

Sara looked across the desk at him. In the blush of success, she had forgotten her promise to leave after the meeting. A pledge made when she'd thought she no longer had a job. "Matt. I can't leave. I must talk to Nancy before the grapevine tells her about the change. She'll be concerned, and she deserves to hear it from me. Give me a few hours to take care of things here. Then I'll be ready. I want to get home in time to pick up the children from school."

"Pick them up in what? We have your car at the station. Besides, I'm not letting you drive anywhere alone. You are still in real danger, Sara. Don't forget that."

He stood and shoved the chair under the desk. "I'll go home to shower and get breakfast. Call me when you're ready."

"Thanks for everything. I mean that, sincerely. I promise

to call when things are wrapped up here."

He gave a curt nod. "Do that. I'm tired of saving your hide."

Could he really be mad at her? She owed her life to him—not once, but twice—and she had acknowledged that more than once. Perhaps it was only temporary frustration. He'd get over it. She should have paid more attention to her mother's admonition. Never press a man when he's hungry. Something to do with low blood sugar.

Sara found Nancy and brought her up to date. Afterwards, she walked through the warehouse, surprised at how well things were running. It looked as though the explosion never happened. No visible after-effects. A new high-rise lift had replaced the one they'd lost.

The blinds were open when Sara returned to her office. She took a seat at the desk and turned the chair to face the bank of windows. Bright sunlight filtered through the pane, hopefully warming the cool morning air.

Sara rested her head against the chair's soft leather back. Now that the thrill of the new promotion had passed, doubts plagued her about the responsibilities of being Global's first president, not to mention the first woman president.

She would not, could not, let this distract from her commitment to Danny and Poppy. Both were still hurting from their loss and they were much in need of her attention.

The threat of personal harm still hung over her. The danger wasn't imaginary or exaggerated. As much as she'd tried to bury the fear, it was a physical presence that followed her.

A light tap at the door made her swivel around. Charles Edwards stood in the entryway. "Hello, Sara. I wanted to tell you how pleased I am about your promotion. It couldn't happen to anyone who deserved it more."

"That's kind of you, Charles."

He leaned against the doorframe. "Need a lift home? I saw Chief Foley drop you off earlier, and his car isn't in the parking lot."

"He's coming back for me, but thank you."

Charles gave her a mock salute and turned to leave. "Don't mention it. I'm trying to make brownie points with my new boss."

She picked up the phone and called Matt.

CHAPTER 31

Sara Bradford's Home

Sara had had a full day and she and Matt made the trip in silence. He pulled under the portico behind her rental car and killed the engine. His hands rested lightly on the steering wheel and he turned to face her.

She waited. Apparently, he had something on his mind.

"I think I owe you an apology."

"Matt—"

He held up his hand, then rested it back on the wheel. "I need to say this. I put you through a lot of emotional pain, accusing you of Josh's murder, because of circumstantial evidence and statistics."

"That's been resolved, Matt. I don't hold a grudge."

"You need to understand why I acted the way I did. To understand how cops think. Perhaps, if Mary hadn't been sick, and I'd had my head totally in the case, I wouldn't have jumped to the wrong conclusion. But then again, I might have reacted the same way. Law enforcement deals with statistics. Most of the time they are reliable. More times than not, those averages are dead on. As you said, it's over, but I wanted to say I'm sorry."

"Apology accepted. Thank you for bringing my car home, and for the chauffer service."

His gaze lingered on her for a moment, and a shadow of a smile crossed his face. "Don't mention it. I do this all the time. It's part of my job description." He got out, came around the car, and opened her door. "Remember, don't leave without and escort."

267

She entered the foyer, glad to be home and anxious to see the children. They'd been getting ready for school when she got home this morning and she'd had little time to spend with them.

Before she took three steps, a squeal from the second floor landing shattered the quiet.

"Sara, you're home!" Danny straddled the banister, slid to the bottom, then bounded into her arms. Visions of him sliding down the rail and busting his head open, flashed through her mind. The stairs were something they needed to discuss. Soon.

Sara gave him a hug. "Why are you home so early? I'd planned to pick you up at school."

He wiggled loose. "Teachers' half-day off. We got a nice policeman who's gonna live with us."

Processing this new revelation, Sara's gaze landed on two black leather suitcases at the bottom of the stairs. "Oh, we do, do we? And who is this nice policeman?"

"That would be me." Don Tompkins, still in his Global uniform, strode from the kitchen, Maddie followed behind him. Don reached out to tousle Danny's hair.

Sara cast a questioning gaze at her aunt.

"You were in such a rush this morning, I didn't get a chance to tell you. I hired Don as a bodyguard. At least until Matthew finds out who's responsible for the attempts on your life."

"That arrangement okay with you, Sara?" Don asked. "We felt your situation demanded immediate protection."

Sara removed her coat and hung it in the foyer closet. "I don't have a problem with it. In fact, I think it's an excellent idea. Wish I'd thought of it. Where's your car? I didn't see it when I came in." To Maddie she said, "Has Beatrice set up a room for him?"

"Yes. He was just on his way upstairs to settle in. I told him to put his car in the garage."

"Great." Sara turned to Don. "Then I'll see you at dinner."

She took Danny's hand. "Where's Poppy?"

"She's makin' dinner with Miss Beatrice in the kitchen," Danny said. "I hope they hurry. I sure am hungry."

Maddie winked at Sara. "This kid is a bottomless pit. However, he's a great hand in the garden. He's been Pete's shadow all afternoon."

Sara called to Don at the top of the stairs. "Dinner will be at six-thirty. Better be on time or Danny may not leave anything for you."

~*~

They gathered around the table at the bay window for dinner. The meal took on a festive atmosphere when Sara told them the news of her promotion.

After dinner ended, Sara took the children upstairs for a bath, and got them ready for bed.

Once the children were safely tucked in, she joined the other two adults in the library for coffee.

"How are you holding up, Sara?" Don asked.

"To be honest," she confided, "I'm feeling a little overwhelmed. But I can't stay in a cocoon or hide under the bed until Matt catches this guy. I can't live that way. Your being here gives an extra measure of security at home. Be assured, I'll be extremely cautious. I have no desire to meet this guy alone again."

Maddie shivered. "I can't bear the thought that he's still out there somewhere. Perhaps we should leave town for a while, take a cruise or something."

"That would only postpone the issue." Sara shook her head. "Besides, I can't leave work now, plus, the children have school. Don can take me to work. I won't make myself an easy target again. We'll be okay, Maddie. Truly we will."

She felt almost as confident as she sounded.

Climbing the stairs to her room, she plumbed her memory back to the night Penny vanished. Something about the dark figure who loaded the sleeping bag into the van pinged at her sub-conscious. But the elusive shadow danced through her mind without revealing his identity.

In her room Sara undressed, changing into pajamas and a warm robe. She pulled her laptop from the bedside table and opened it. The screen was dark.

With all that had happened, she'd forgotten to plug it into the charger. She hadn't checked her email since last Friday. With the Global buyout, she might have missed something important. She'd need to use Josh's computer in the library.

The bed looked tempting, but not now. She needed to take care of this before retiring.

The library's warmth invited her in. The fragrant aroma of oak and chestnuts wafted from the fireplace, filling her mind with memories of happier times.

Deciding a cup of hot cocoa would be nice while she worked, she went to the bar, nestled in an alcove between the bookshelves. She retrieved a cup and a hot cocoa packet from the bottom shelf, filled the mug with water from the small sink, and placed it in the microwave.

While the water heated, she sat down at the desk to boot the computer. Josh's email account still existed. She should have taken care of that long ago. She signed on to delete any mail that might still be out there.

As she scrolled down the subject lines, one with Matt

Foley's name in it jumped out at her. It was a message sent from Josh's cell phone to himself. The day Josh died.

What in the world?

She opened the memo and began to read.

Chief Foley:

I may be paranoid, but I visited a man this afternoon, Robert Cook. He told me quite a story. Admittedly, he was seriously intoxicated, but I figured it was something you needed to know. He claimed to have witnessed the burial of a child who disappeared some years ago when he worked at a church retreat. I asked why he didn't report it, but he never gave me an answer. The man who buried the body was—

The persistent ding of the microwave in the background tried to distract her, but she couldn't believe the story that unfolded. Her concentration was so intense she failed to hear when the man entered the library until he spoke.

The voice came across the space between them, cold and threatening, the gun in his hand pointed at her heart. "I'd hoped not to have to do this face to face, Sara. I like you, strange as that may seem. But you have left me no choice."

Twin Falls Police Station

Monday afternoon, the desk sergeant rapped on the door frame to Matt's office. He looked up and motioned the officer inside. "What's up?"

"My shift just ended. I brought your messages." He handed Matt two slips of paper, but held another one in his hand. "This is from an attorney, David Johnson. He called earlier. Said he represented a client who left an envelope with him some years ago, addressed to the police in the event of his death. Johnson wants to know if you want to pick it up, or if he should mail it."

Matt shoved his chair back. "Did he name the client?"

The desk sergeant looked at the slip of paper. "Yeah, Robert Cook."

"Call him back. Ask him to wait for me. I'm on my way." Matt grabbed his coat on the way out.

Matt stood outside the attorney's office with Robert Cook's letter. He ripped the envelope open and read the contents. A scene from a B-movie from the '40s ran through his mind—where an extortionist left behind a letter identifying the killer he'd blackmailed, and why.

It never happened in real life.

But, here it was. A letter from the grave, naming Penny Pryor's killer.

All the threads came together. The name wasn't a big surprise. Years in law enforcement gave Matt insight into the mindset of killers. The one fault they shared was an abundance of pride. It took a lot of arrogance for someone to believe he could commit murder and get away with it. Almost three decades after the fact, the scales of justice tipped in the right direction.

Matt drove back to his office and reached for his desk phone. It rang before he lifted the receiver almost making him drop it. The call was from Miles Davis.

"We lucked out, Chief. We couldn't get a warrant to search the financial records of our suspects, but I did an end-around with Colin Connelly. Off the record, of course. One of the suspects had an account at Connelly's bank. The account showed withdrawals a few days before the money was deposited into Cook's account. We only checked back four months, but there's no question in my mind. This is our guy."

"Who's account?" Matt asked, but he already knew the answer. He listened as Davis confirmed it.

"You guys deserve to make this arrest, but I want to tag along. Meet me at the department. I'll get the arrest warrant issued. We'll take care of this one tonight."

CHAPTER 32

Sara Bradford's Home

Sara's gaze flashed from the computer monitor to the face of Charles Edwards, whose steel gaze stared into her own wide eyes. Not sweet, gentlemanly Charles, the man she'd known for so many years, but a menacing stranger, holding a deadly looking weapon with a silencer attached.

For a moment, she was too stunned to speak, then found her voice. "I can't believe you're responsible for all this, Charles."

She couldn't deny the truth. Realization hit her like a rockslide. The posture that distressed her memory for days on end was distinctly his.

He lowered the revolver and tightened the silencer, then moving in front of her, he raised the gun again, this time aimed at her head.

A moment of uncertainty grabbed her as she watched him. Could this be some horrible nightmare she would soon wake up from? No, the man and the gun were all too real. She kept her voice calm. "How did you get in?"

"It was quite easy." His tone sounded almost weary. "When I drove your car to the hospital, after the explosion, I stopped and made copies of your keys—figured they might come in handy. I didn't realize then it would be so difficult to get rid of you. You've left me no choice."

Sara shook her head. "People always have choices, Charles. The ability to reason and make the right decisions is what separates man from beast. What do you have in mind?" She needed to keep him talking. Don had to be nearby.

Charles must have channeled her thoughts. "If you think Tompkins will come to your rescue, forget it. He tried to stop me when I came in. I had to shoot him."

"You killed Don?"

Charles checked the gun's silencer again, giving it a twist. "I'd hoped to make this look like a suicide, but Tompkins' presence ruled that out. I planted your notebook in the Mustang a few years back. This week, when the Herald reported the police found the car, I knew they'd find the calendar. I hoped the authorities would assume you'd taken your life because of guilt for killing your husband. Now I must let the police form their own conclusions. Robbery, perhaps."

How could this seemingly gentle man be responsible for so much violence? "Why kill Penny? What reason could you have to murder a child?"

"Actually, I didn't, I only buried the body. The most difficult thing I've ever done." He hesitated for a moment. "Marnie killed her. It's difficult to believe even now this all began with an unavoidable accident."

Memories clouded his eyes. He seemed to want to tell the story. "I had four-weeks of R and R in Hawaii while stationed in Cambodia. Marnie was to meet me. At the last minute, I decided to surprise her, to fly home so we could travel back to the islands together.

"We stopped off at a bar to celebrate. Marnie drank too much. She insisted on driving. We planned to spend the night at home then catch a flight out the next morning.

"On the way home, Penny chased her dog into the street in front of our van. Marnie couldn't stop. The front bumper struck the back of Penny's head. The impact snapped her neck. I don't believe I could have missed the child if I had

275

been behind the wheel. Marnie braked, but too late.

"I couldn't let her face the scandal that would have followed, it would have meant prison. Marnie's family always thought she married beneath her. They'd have blamed me for letting her drink and drive."

He shook his head as if to dismiss the recollection, and looked at a point above Sara's head. "Curious that there wasn't any blood. I've always wondered about that."

A chill crawled down Sara's spine. He showed no hint of compassion for Penny and her family or for Josh's death. He couldn't be in full command of his faculties.

"Even though it wasn't her fault, Marnie would have gone to prison because her blood alcohol level was over the limit. There were no witnesses. I made a snap decision to remove the body. That wasn't my most shining hour. It's a decision I've regretted over the years. With a good attorney, we might have avoided all this."

"I saw you that night, when you came outside as I placed the body in my van. I watched to see what you would do. When you went back into your house, we drove away. I took Marnie home, then drove to the retreat grounds. You know the rest. I killed Josh and Tompkins to protect Marnie. One more murder won't make any difference."

Sara could almost feel pity for him. "Does Marnie know about all the lives you've destroyed to protect her?"

He shook his head. "She only knows about Penny. That's all. The rest has been my secret. I didn't want her to know. She would never have allowed me to go this far. She'd have turned herself in."

She couldn't let Charles see Josh's email. If his plan succeeded, the memo would give the police all they needed to convict him. She eased her finger to the computer tower and pushed the off button.

One more question Sara had to ask. "Why did you kill Josh?"

Charles raised his shoulders and let them drop. "Because he visited Robert Cook, who witnessed Penny's burial. Cook watched it all from a window in the retreat, and had blackmailed me ever since. I made it a practice to keep tabs on him. He told me from the start if anything happened to him he'd left a letter with his attorney. The police would know what I had done. I didn't know if the old man told the truth or not, but I couldn't risk the chance it was a bluff.

"Josh answered the phone when I called Cook that afternoon four years ago. I figured Cook might feel the need to clear his conscience. A bit paranoid of me, I admit. I drove out to Cook's place and saw your husband changing a tire. A traffic accident seemed harder to trace than a bullet."

A heavy breath left his chest. "All my efforts to protect my wife have been in vain. She has terminal cancer—a month or less to live. All I can protect now is her good name."

Sara leaned forward in the chair. "If Mr. Cook left a letter with his attorney, the police will find out, eventually. If you kill me, you'll have another strike against you."

"You could be right." Charles moved a step closer. "I can only hope the old man lied. If not, there's always the possibility his lawyer might have died or misplaced the letter. Twenty-five years is a long time. Regardless, by the time that happens, Marnie will be dead. I won't care what happens to me."

A slight movement in the doorway caught Sara's eye. Maddie.

Sara willed him to keep his attention on her. She had to keep him focused on her. "You planted the bomb in the forklift? I'm impressed, Charles. I didn't know you were so handy with explosives. It isn't everyday knowledge."

He gave a slight shrug. "A little talent I picked up in Cambodia. Brought a few samples home with me. The only useful thing the Army taught me. Except to kill without remorse."

Fear for Maddie and the children kept Sara calm. "How did you know I would move the lift?"

"Elementary. Roger told me you would stay late to clean out your office. I knew you'd be alone. As a rule, you always checked the warehouse before you left for the day. You wouldn't leave the lift unplugged. However, I didn't expect you would put your handbag on first. You spoiled a lot of hard work."

"You carry plastic explosives around in your car?"

He smiled. "Not exactly. I picked up the bomb from my garage after I heard the body had been found."

Somehow, she had to stop Charles. He was unhinged enough to kill everyone in the house, including the children. Keep him talking without goading him into action. "I can't say I'm sorry I spoiled your plan. You also drove the truck that pushed me into the lake and it was you who hit me at the church." A statement, not a question.

"That was risky for someone who doesn't like to take chances." Her frantic brain searched for some way to signal Maddie to leave and call the police.

Charles shrugged. "You spooked me by the call you made to my home to ask about the sleeping bag. I realized the police were trying to trace it back to the donor. It was the mate to the one I buried Penny in. I could hardly admit

I'd donated it."

Maddie moved at the same time Charles saw her. She snatched the crystal tennis ball from the shelf and hurled the glass orb like the fastball she had been famous for in her college days, just as Charles raised the gun and fired.

Charles Edwards' Home

Arrest warrant tucked inside his jacket pocket, Matt and his two detectives drove to the Edwards home. The pretentious mansion sat in the better part of town. Only one car in the driveway, an older model Chevy that didn't look like it belonged to the Edwards's.

When Matt knocked on the door, a solemn maid answered.

"I'd like to speak to Mr. Edwards," Matt said.

"He's not home. Mrs. Edwards is here, but…" the maid's voice cracked. "She's in hospice."

A pang of awareness tugged at Matt's heart. He was all too familiar with what hospice meant. "I'm sorry. We'll wait outside for Mr. Edwards."

They returned to Matt's SUV, when the radio blared an ADW code. "Assault with a deadly weapon at 220 Woodbine Trail. Two people down. All units in the vicinity proceed immediately."

Matt pounded the steering wheel and started the engine, muttering under his breath. "That's Sara's address."

CHAPTER 33

Sara Bradford's Home

"**N**o. Dear God, no."

Sara sprang from behind the desk, knowing she couldn't reach him before he fired. Sara's scream sounded loud in her own ears as Maddie hurled the glass tennis ball at Charles Edwards. The shot rang out and Sara's gaze watched as Maddie collapsed onto her knees.

"Maddie, Maddie." Sara gasped for air and dropped to the floor beside her aunt, pulling her close. Sobbing, uncontrolled tears streamed down her face.

Maddie returned the hug. "Sara, I'm okay." Her aunt pointed at Charles Edwards's body, prone on the carpet in front of the desk, eyes wide open. "He missed."

"Dead?" Sara asked.

Maddie grabbed hold of an end table and pulled herself upright. "I have no idea. You'd better get the gun."

"I thought..." Sara reached for the gun but realized it wasn't necessary. Charles was dead. She backed away.

Maddie, her face ashen, nodded. "I know, but the shot went wild. It hit somewhere above me." She pointed to a hole above the doorframe.

Confused, Sara stared at her aunt. "But, why did you fall?"

Maddie gave a shaky laugh. "I didn't fall, I collapsed. Nerves." She patted Sara's arm. "Now I need to sit down. My knees hurt."

Sara glanced at the crystal tennis ball by Charles's body, and it struck her that the decision she'd made to keep the souvenir, had saved her and Maddie's lives.

She helped her aunt to the leather chair by the fireplace. "Oh, Maddie, you did it. You stopped him."

"We'll talk about that later. Right now, we have to get help for Don."

~*~

Matt made the twenty-minute drive to the Bradford home in twelve.

The car skidded to a halt behind an ambulance and Matt raced to the front door.

The heavy, double doors at the entrance stood ajar. Just inside the entryway, Pete Martinez stood near the library. He smeared the palms of his hands on his pants. "Hi, Chief. Sara and Miss Maddie are in the kitchen. The medics are loading Mr. Tompkins onto a stretch now. He was shot, but he's still alive."

Matt expelled a deep breath. He'd braced himself for bad news, but Sara and Maddie were safe. The anxiety dissipated and logic took over. "What was Tompkins doing here?"

The gardener swallowed hard and nodded toward the kitchen. "Miss Maddie hired him to bodyguard Sara."

Matt stepped past Pete into the library. The first officer on the scene had set up a sign-in log and Davis had taken over as lead detective.

Matt signed the log, pulled on the blue booties, and entered the room. Charles Edwards's body laid face-up on the polished hardwood floor.

Lisa Martinez entered behind Matt, pulling on sterile gear and working the plastic gloves over her fingers. She knelt beside the body and probed the carotid artery in

Edwards's neck.

Matt threw her a questioning glance.

She nodded.

He turned to the patrol officer nearby. "What happened?"

The young officer straightened his posture. "As I understand it, Chief, the victim held a gun on Mrs. Bradford. The older lady entered the room and threw the crystal tennis ball." He pointed to a glass object next to the body. "It hit him in the right temple."

Hunter and Davis remained with the crime scene, and Matt headed into the kitchen to find Sara and Maddie.

The two women sat at the bay window. A white-faced Maddie leaned against the cushions, immobile.

Sara handed Maddie a china mug. "Drink this. Beatrice made the tea strong and sweet. It's good for shock."

Poppy lay with her head in Sara's lap. Danny huddled in the booth corner, wide-eyed, taking everything in. These kids just couldn't catch a break.

Matt pulled out a chair and sat next to Sara as Beatrice placed a cup of coffee at his elbow. "How did Edwards get inside the house?"

"He had a key made when he brought my car to the hospital after the explosion. He shot Don. Thank God the shot wasn't fatal."

Matt masked his rage at Edwards's devious determination to kill Sara.

Sara stopped in the middle of her story, and cast a glance at him. "Why aren't you surprised the killer turned out to be Charles Edwards? If you tell me you knew it all along, I may shoot you."

"We found out late this evening. Hunter, Davis, and I were at his home to arrest him when the call came in about the disturbance here."

Sara sighed and drew a shaky breath. "Charles confessed everything. Marnie drove the van that killed Penny. She'd been drinking, he tried to protect her. Incredibly, Charles also murdered Josh, and made the attempts on my life."

Strobe lights flashed through the windows, and siren blared, as the ambulance headed to Twin Falls Memorial with Don Tompkins. Two uniformed officers followed Hunter and Davis into the kitchen and stood in the doorway. Davis pulled out a chair next to Matt, and Hunter took a stool at the island bar.

"Who hit him?" Hunter asked.

Matt nodded toward Maddie. She raised her head to look at Hunter. "I did."

The two detectives exchanged a look of surprise, and Davis turned to Maddie. "What happened?"

Maddie took a sip of tea. Her hand trembled as she sat the cup back on the table. "I heard noises and came down the passageway from my room to investigate. I almost tripped over Don on the floor. He was conscious and whispered for me to call the police. I went back to my room and placed the call. When I came back, Don had passed out.

"When I reached the library, I overheard the man, Mr. Edwards, telling Sara how he had killed Joshua and was going to kill her. I was afraid to leave. I thought he would shoot her. I picked up the glass tennis ball on the shelf and threw it. I didn't know what else to do. Because of my vision, my aim isn't as good as it used to be. I planned to knock him unconscious but he must have heard me and turned."

"How did you see well enough to hit him? "Davis asked.

"I can see people at a short distance, although I can't always recognize who they are. I just threw at his head."

Hunter whistled. "That's amazing."

Maddie looked down into her teacup. "I guess that depends on your perspective." She shuddered. "It was awful. It must have killed him instantly. He didn't make a sound."

Matt placed his hand over hers. "That must have been a powerful fastball you threw. Don't blame yourself. You saved Sara, Don and possibly the children's lives, as well as your own."

She nodded. "I'll try to remember that, Matthew. I did a lot of praying before I threw it, knowing if I missed, he would kill both of us. But taking a life is an awesome responsibility, even when it's unintentional and perhaps, justified."

Matt acknowledged the small woman's courage with a squeeze of her hand. He turned to Sara. "Are you all right?"

She laid her hand on Poppy's head and her countenance lightened. "I'm fine."

He'd seen that look on Mary's face in the months before her death. Like his wife, Sara had reached inside herself and shaken off all the terror and pain from the last couple of weeks. Drawing strength from a reservoir of faith only a few possessed. The knowledge, that whatever happened, God was in control.

Sara gave him a weary glance. "How much longer will this take, Matt? Maddie and the children need to rest. She blames herself for Don being shot, and insists on going to the hospital tonight.

"I'll put the kids back to bed and ask Pete and Beatrice to stay with them. Then I'll drive Maddie to the hospital." She lifted the little girl into her arms and motioned for

Danny to follow her.

Matt helped the boy off the cushions and set him on the floor beside her, then turned to Davis. "How much longer will you be?"

"The crew has finished filming the scene and they're bagging the evidence. Shouldn't be more than an hour. We'll have to seal off the library. Any more questions we have for these ladies can wait."

Matt stood and glanced at Sara. "I'll be glad to drive you and Maddie to the hospital."

"I can do it." She pulled Poppy tighter to her chest. "Matt, Josh sent an email to himself the day he died, intending to give it to you. Cook confessed he'd witnessed Charles burying Penny's body at the retreat. The email is on the computer in the library."

Matt glanced over at Davis and nodded.

The detective left the room, headed to pick up the computer.

"Are you going to be all right here tonight?" Matt asked.

She smiled up at him. "We'll be fine, now that we know we're safe again. We just need a little time to recharge our batteries. I've been bombed, almost drowned, kidnapped, and nearly shot in a little over two weeks. Soon, I intend to go to my room, pull the cover over my head, and have a quiet nervous breakdown."

Twin Falls Memorial Hospital

Don Tompkins was out of the OR, when Sara and Maddie arrived at the hospital. The bullet went through his shoulder, requiring a minimum of surgery.

Maddie eased up to Don's bedside and took his hand. "How are you doing?"

285

Only a florescent tube above his bed, lit the room. Don's face looked pale and pasty in the dim lighting. Bandages covered his shoulder, and they had placed his arm in a sling to keep him from moving it.

"Okay, I think," he said, his voice weak and raspy.

Maddie took his hand. "I'll stay with you until you fall asleep."

Sara slipped from the room, closing the door softly behind her.

The immensity of God's mercy never ceased to amaze her.

CHAPTER 34

Twin Falls Police Station

Next morning, Matt sat with his two detectives to finalize the report that would go to the district attorney on the Pryor case.

Outside the office window, low gray clouds blocked the sun. A light flurry of large white flakes drifted to the ground, leaving a fine dust of powder on the lawn.

Hunter rose and moved to the window. "Is that snow?"

Matt swiveled his chair around. "That would be my guess. However, this is Texas and it's October. Could just be global warming."

Hunter chuckled and sat back down.

"You have anything to add to this?" Matt handed them copies of the report and waited for the two men to finish reading. "The DA should be pleased. You guys solved two murders, three attempted murders, an explosion, and a kidnapping in record time."

Davis scanned his copy, then stuck it into the inside pocket of his sport coat. "Looks good to me, Chief. Edwards's confession to Sara clears up most of the details...that and the email Josh Bradford sent the evening he died."

Matt rolled his chair back. He pulled out the bottom desk drawer and propped his feet up. "The FBI returned the results from the VMD samples McCulloch sent. They confirmed two partial prints on the jumper belonged to Edwards. It would have been nice to have received that information a week ago."

287

Hunter pushed out a deep breath. "Yeah, and imagine if Mrs. Bradford had found that email four years ago, it would have saved us a ton of work and a lot of shoe leather."

"You guys have any questions?" Matt tossed his copy of the report into his file basket.

Hunter patted the report in his pocket. "That does it for me, Chief."

"Me too," Davis said. "By the way, we found out where Tompkins' money came from. Seems his father was an electronics wizard. The old man held a number of patents worth a ton of dough. He left it all to Tompkins."

Hunter chuckled. "I should be so lucky. The only thing my old man ever invented was a beer keg that fit in the refrigerator with a nozzle through the door so he didn't have to open it to refill his glass."

"Maybe he should have patented it." Davis said, laughing. "A lot of couch potatoes would buy one during football season."

The two detectives stood and moved to the door. Matt followed them into the hallway.

Officer Stein strode down the corridor. He stopped in front of Davis, giving him a high-five. No words were spoken. None were needed. A salute for a job well done.

That had been happening all day. A light mood filled the station. Deservedly so. They had all helped to close a difficult series of murders and sent a message to the bad guys. It might take time, but eventually justice would prevail.

There was no high quite like it.

County Court House

Two hours later, Matt drove the short distance to Gabriel Morrison's office. Even the weather couldn't dampen his spirits. Snow was such a novelty in this part of the country, even adults acted like kids. He would go home and crank up the fireplace as soon as he finished with Gabe. Perhaps his mood had nothing to do with snow. Could be because the past couple of weeks were behind him. Whatever the reason, he'd take it.

At the courthouse, Matt was the only person on the elevator on the ride up to the DA's office. He exited on the third floor. People in the corridor greeted him with congratulations. He stopped midway down the hall at Gabe's office. The secretary motioned him to go right in.

When the door closed, Matt took the chair proffered.

Morrison finished reading the report. He removed his glasses and plopped the sheaf of papers on the desk. "You should feel proud of yourself. That's pretty remarkable police work."

Matt shrugged, uncomfortable with the praise. "I make it a point to surround myself with smart people who make me look good."

"Don't be modest, Foley. It's an outstanding piece of investigative work. In fact, you must have broken some kind of record solving a case that old, that fast." Gabe rocked back in his chair and gave Matt his full attention. "I'll pass it on to the *Herald*. Just to tick of The Terror. Maybe your boss can get you a pay increase in next year's budget. Look at the money the city saved by not having to hold Edwards over for trial."

"I was just along for the ride," Matt said. "If the city is passing out raises, I'll see they go to the detective squad. They did the work."

"Tell me, why do you work if you don't need to? In your

position, I'd retire and play golf every day for the rest of my life."

Matt grinned. "I don't golf."

"There's got to be more to it than that," Gabe said.

"I like my job. One man can't save the world, but I like to think I make a difference in my little corner. I felt a calling into law enforcement, to protect society from a lot of evil people.

"We create our own monsters. And all too often, a flawed justice system finds loopholes and lets them back on the streets. But occasionally, the rule of law prevails, as with this case. That makes it all worthwhile."

"You're preaching to the choir. I met Marnie Edwards socially a number of times. Even now, I can't think of her as a killer. It's difficult to believe someone of her background could be part of this sordid mess."

"It is hard to believe. But consider the agony she put the Pryor family through for all those years by not admitting her guilt."

Gabe shifted in his chair and nodded. "What have you done about her?"

"That's your call. She's still in hospice, in the last stages of bone cancer. When she heard about Charles, she went into a coma. Soon, she'll stand before a much higher authority than you or me."

CHAPTER 35

County Court House

The week before Christmas, Detective Miles Davis and his partner filed out of the courtroom with the rest of the crowd. They'd finished testifying before a grand jury on a new case and were on their way to lunch. Davis leaned over the rail and looked down on the atrium that stretched from the ground floor to the roof. Dressed in her seasonal finery, the Christmas season showed off the courthouse to its best advantage. The atrium, a postcard of holiday splendor. An enormous tree soared to the third floor where he and Hunter stood.

White lights sparkled, showcasing the large red ornaments and bows that were the tree's only decorations. Familiar holiday music whispered over the intercom, adding a festive atmosphere to the magical spirit of the season.

As they headed downstairs, Davis spotted Maddie Jamison in a small group near the elevators. She held an animated conversation with a much-improved Elsie Kaufman and a man he recognized as Todd Hastings.

Davis caught Maddie's eye and she waved them over. "Gentlemen, I believe you have met my friends, Elsie and her son-in-law, Todd."

Hastings' charming wife was nowhere in sight.

"What brings you folks into the halls of justice?" Davis asked as he gripped Hastings's hand.

Maddie put her arm around Elsie's shoulder. "The judge released Elsie from Serene Acres two days ago, and just freed her from Dora's guardianship. Isn't that wonderful news?"

Maddie's blue eyes sparkled. "I took your advice and contacted Todd. He's been very helpful as you suggested he might be."

Hunter turned to Hastings. "How did Mrs. Hastings take the good news?"

He chuckled and rocked back on his heels. "She took it quite well, for Dora, after she understood I'd made up my mind. I explained she could either live in the home I provided for her, or she would need to find a place of her own."

Elsie turned to Davis. "You two must come to lunch after I get settled back in. You are welcome anytime you're in the neighborhood."

He and Hunter departed after hugs from the ladies and a handshake with Todd Hastings. When the elevator doors closed, Davis shot his partner a sideways glance. "Well, go ahead and say I told you so."

A broad smiled crossed Hunter's face. "Consider it said." He raised his right hand high in the air. Miles Davis hesitated for only a moment before he struck Hunter's hand with a resounding smack.

Twin Falls Police Station

Matt looked at the papers on his desk without really seeing them.

Blain had stopped by earlier in the afternoon to bring him a preview of the *Texas Tattler Magazine*. His father-in-law had used his connections to obtain a galley copy.

Pepper Parker had indeed poured out her vitriol on paper. She hinted Matt and Sara had an affair while Mary was dying of cancer. That Matt covered up Sara's involvement in her husband's death and framed Charles Edwards for the crime.

The *Tattler* had pushed back the release date to February, so the rag's attorneys could test the waters against a potential libel suit.

Matt rubbed his finger across his bottom lip. Smart move. Because the minute the publisher decided to run the story, the magazine would find itself defending a civil lawsuit for slander. Nothing he could do until then.

He pushed his chair back and put on his jacket. Darkness had fallen when he stepped into the brisk evening air. After locking the outer door he moved towards his SUV. Lucy Turner's blue Ford Escort sat in the parking lot, the back towards him. A quick glance told him she was just sitting in the car, no lights, with the engine running.

He strode forward. She might have car trouble. As he neared, the sound of muffled sobs echoed through the window, her head was pressed against her hands on the steering wheel.

He tapped on the glass with his knuckle. "You okay, Lucy?"

She gave an angry swipe at her eyes and glared at him. "No, I'm just fine. Can't you tell? I always have a good cry at the end of my shift."

Unapproachable. Definitely unapproachable. "Can I help? I'm a good listener."

"You could never identify with my problems, Mr. Rich Man."

"Try me. Open the passenger door. It's cold out here."

The lock clicked as he walked around the Escort. He opened the door and slid in beside her. Cigarette smoke and the smell of greasy fast food greeted him. The seat covers were frayed, but the interior was clean.

He waited for her to speak.

Coldly, her gaze met his. Unattractive mascara rivulets ran down her otherwise pretty face. "Is this part of your job description, Chief? Stepping down from your lofty perch to comfort the little people?"

He watched her, perplexed. What was wrong with the woman? She was obviously upset, but why with him? To his knowledge, he'd done nothing to warrant her ire. He removed a handkerchief from his pocket and handed it to her. "I'm not the enemy, Lucy. I'd just like to help if I can."

The handkerchief only smeared the mascara over her cheeks. She blew her nose and handed the cloth back to him. When she spoke, her voice was tight. "You spend your off hours with people like the governor. This job is just a hobby to you. But it's not to me. It's my lifeblood. I'm always one paycheck away from being homeless. Are you sure you want to leave your perfect little world and find out how jacked-up mine is?"

He could see she was struggling not to cry. "I'm sorry if I've offended you..."

"How could you possibly offend me?" She gave a bitter laugh. "You don't even know I'm alive. I'm just one of the minions who populate your fiefdom."

"No one's life is perfect, Lucy, least of all mine. I don't intend to fight the culture war with you. But if you'll tell me what's really bothering you, I'll try to help."

She fumbled in her handbag for a pack of cigarettes and pulled out a long filter tip. After lighting it with a cheap lighter, she inhaled and blew the smoke towards the roof like a kettle releasing pent-up steam. "Okay, I don't want to keep you awake at night, but you asked for it."

With a light tap on the power button, he vented the

window, letting some of the smoke escape.

She brought the cigarette to her lips again. He recognized it as a delay tactic to gather her thoughts. She raised one hand and numbered off her problems. "The tires on this car you're sitting in are bald as a bowling ball." Her voice caught. "I wanted to take the boys to Oklahoma for Christmas but I don't dare make the trip on these tires."

One finger folded down. "The heating/air conditioning unit in my house bit the dust a month ago. I'm using space heaters to keep the house warm. And, yes, I know how dangerous they are. Never mind what it will do to my electric bill."

Another finger fell. "Last, but certainly not least, I have a break in the main sewer line in my front yard. It couldn't happen on the city's easement. No, it had to happen on my property, broken by tree roots. And it's my responsibility, or so they say. If I don't get it repaired in a week, they will fine me for every day until it's fixed. And guess what? My bank account has a whopping sixty-five dollar balance." She snorted a rueful laugh. "Merry Christmas to me."

She gazed at him with insolence. "Satisfied?"

Matt sat in silence for a moment. Sexual harassment suits were common in law enforcement and she could be setting him up. On the other hand, everything she'd told him could be the truth. There was a good chance her partner knew the real story. Partners had few secrets from each other. "Is Cole still here? Does he know about your problems?"

She looked down at her hands and stuffed out the cigarette. "Yeah, we talk. He was finishing up some paperwork when I left."

"Call him. Ask him to come out here."

"Why?"

"Just do it."

A few minutes after she made the call, Cole sauntered out the backdoor and over to the vehicle. "What's up, Luc."

"Don't ask me, ask him." She jerked an angry nod at Matt. "He called this meeting."

Matt opened the door and stood in the gap. "Cole, ride with her and follow me to the bank on the corner."

Lucy's head jerked up sharply. "I didn't tell you my troubles because I wanted your charity. You wouldn't leave me alone until you knew the story of my life."

"Cole, make sure she follows me."

"No problem, Chief."

At the bank, Matt strode to the ATM then went back to the Escort, and pecked on the driver side window once more. When it lowered, he handed her the cash he'd withdrawn. "Tomorrow, go to Doc's Royal Treads, here in town. He gives law enforcement officers a discount. Take your kids to see their grandparents for Christmas. After the holidays, come see me."

She shook her head. "I can't accept money from you..."

"Call it a loan, if your pride will let you accept it. You can pay me back five dollars a week until the debt's paid."

"That will take me more than ten years. What if I quit?"

"Then I'll write it off as a bad debt and send someone to break both your legs."

Cole snorted a laugh.

A half smile almost made it past her guard. "Fair enough. But I don't like being beholden to you."

"That's entirely up to you. There are no strings on my part."

She didn't say thanks and he didn't expect her to. It wasn't her nature. She had a master's degree from the School of Hard Knocks.

On the drive home, he punched Joe Wilson's number. "Hey, Joe. What are you doing this weekend?"

"I know I'm going to regret saying this, but nothing so far. What do you have in mind?"

"Want to play Santa Claus? Before you answer, it doesn't include taking toys to tots."

"Uh...maybe I should ask what I'm signing up for."

"A little handy-man work, painting, a little home repairs, etcetera."

"Who for?"

"Do you know Lucy Turner, one of my detectives?"

"Yeah, I've met her. What happened?"

"It's a long story. Meet me at her house at seven o'clock Saturday morning. I don't have the address with me, but you're a cop you can find it. I'll fill you in when you get there. In the meantime, I'll see if I can't draft some more hands."

"Will do," Joe said. "Hey, you called that girl?"

"What girl?"

"Don't play dumb with me, Foley. You know who I mean."

"Haven't called yet, but I'm just about to."

"You'd better not procrastinate too long. Some lucky guy's gonna snatch the lovely Sara up. Then you'll be out of luck."

"Point taken. How about you, have you called your girl?"

"Better than that. I'm taking Lisa and Paul to Vale for New Years."

Matt Foley's Home

Rowdy danced around Matt's feet, happy to have some company as Matt entered the foyer. He went into the kitchen to see about dinner.

Stella had left him two Ruben sandwiches with home fries in the microwave. He took the food into the den by the hearth and made a fire.

The burning logs filled the house with a woody fragrance that pleased his senses as he polished off the meal. Outside, the wind whistled around the corners of the house, but inside, the fire crackled with warmth as twigs burst into flames, sending a shower of sparks up the chimney.

He sipped a mug of hot cider, and memories returned of the many evenings shared with Mary, here by the fire. He and Stella had decorated the tree last evening and he'd felt Mary's presence as they placed her favorite ornaments on the limbs.

The crippling malaise left by Mary's loss had lessened. Thoughts of her now brought pleasure and reminded him how fortunate he'd been to share his life with her, if only for a few years.

He punched autodial on his phone and listened as the ring sounded.

Sara picked up with a soft, "Hello."

He recognized the music in the background as Kenny Rogers and Wynona Judd's rendition of "Mary Did You Know?"

"Can you cook?" he asked. Her caller ID would identify him.

She laughed. "Well, that's one way to start a conversation. I make a mean PB&J sandwich."

"Uh...that won't do. We're feeding hungry men, not kids. You can make a meal run to a local eatery, can't you?"

"That I can handle. When and where?"

He told her Lucy Turner's story.

"I'm in. And I know a couple of ladies who will volunteer to clean up as you guys finish the projects."

"Great. I'll pick you up Saturday morning at six forty-five."

Lucy Turner's Home

Thanks to a friend of Matt's in the construction business, the major repairs, sewer and heating, had been finished earlier in the week. Off duty cops, firefighters, and church members wielded hammers and paintbrushes. By six Saturday evening, the place was coming together nicely. An hour later Lucy's home sparkled like a new penny.

Sara busied herself with a gigantic red bow while he thanked the hastily assembled Santa's helpers as they left the house, one by one.

Matt set the thermostat on sixty and switched off all the lights, except the pot lights over the kitchen bar. He walked up beside Sara and leaned against the bar. "You about ready to go?"

"Hummm. Just one final nit to fix here," she said. She affixed a card to the bow and smiled. "Now I'm ready."

She wore jeans and a long-sleeved fitted T-shirt. Her head bent over, silky strands of dark hair hid her face. Her sandalwood scent drew him to her like a magnet. He took hold of both her shoulders and turned her towards him, then lifted her chin with his forefinger. He leaned down and placed a slow, soft kiss on her lips. When it ended, he drew her close. "I've wanted to do that for a long time."

"What stopped you?"

"I wasn't sure how it would be received, wasn't sure I was ready."

She looked into his eyes. "Are you sure now?"

He nodded. "I am. How about you?"

"I've been sure for a while," she said.

"There's something you need to know," he said, holding her tightly. "I don't play the field."

"I suspected that. Neither do I."

"How about the Greek god?"

Laughing, she said, "Jeff? He isn't important. Never was, really."

"Dinner tomorrow night?" he asked.

"Absolutely," she said.

He put his arm around her, led her outside, and locked the door behind them.

She hung the bow on the front door and adjusted the card. It read:

Dear Lucy:

I hope you like the improvements. My helpers worked really hard.

Santa

Twin Falls Baptist Church

As the choir sang, Seth Davidson sat in a chair behind the pulpit and looked out over the sanctuary. His heart swelled as his parishioner's filled the seats, and the ushers busied themselves bringing in extra chairs at the back.

The last time the church exceeding its seating capacity was the Sunday after Penny Pryor disappeared. Of course, the church had been smaller then. That Sunday, the people came out of fear. Today, they came from a mixture of sorrow and joy. Sorrow for the deaths in the community, joy that the killer had been found and the victims had

300

received a form of justice. His flock felt safe again.

The Pryor's entered through the double doors and took a seat. The first time they'd been here since Penny vanished twenty-five years ago. Seth sent up a fervent prayer that they would find peace after the tragic loss of their daughter.

Matt Foley sat in the front with Maddie, and Sara's two children.

Sara moved from her seat in the choir to stand at the pulpit for her solo. The pianist began the familiar strains of "How Great Thou Art." What an appropriate choice, Seth thought, for this morning filled with blessings.

Sara's clear, lovely voice filled the sanctuary. The choir joined in on the chorus, and buoyant notes swelled around Seth, lifting up to heaven, and he felt God smile.

THE END

Thank you for taking the time to read this novel.

If you enjoyed *Works of Darkness,* please leave a brief review at Amazon.com. Reviews are tremendously important to an author.

Feel free to contact me at any of the following:

Website: www.vbtenery.com
Blog: www.agatharemembered.blogspot.com
Twitter: www.twitter.com
FB   Author   Page: www.facebook.com/vbtenery
EMail Address: vbhtenery@aol.com

Turn the page for a Sneak Peek at Book 2 in the Matt Foley/Sara Bradford Series. I hope you enjoy the first three chapters of When There Were None:

Then There Were None

V.B. TENERY

CHAPTER 1

Grayson Manor

Light filtered through the cottage windows as Sean McKinnon drained the last sip of the strong brew from his teacup. He took the empty mug to the sink, rinsed it out, and placed it in the dishwasher. He pulled on a jacket, picked up his cap and umbrella from the rack by the door, then strolled up the hill to the big house.

Morning clouds hung heavy in the gray sky and heavy raindrops began to splatter the stone walkway. Sean sucked in a deep breath of cold moist air and smiled, glad to have the family home from their stay in England. The big estate was lonely when they were gone. He increased his pace as the rain pelted faster. He hummed in spite of the weather, looking forward to breakfast in the kitchen with Amanda Castleton. Aye, he'd missed the woman's cooking.

He crossed the large expanse of manicured lawn and bright flowers. It was a bonnie garden. He'd come over with the Graysons more than thirty years ago. Those had been dark times for the family.

The task Mr. Grayson had set for him—planting a proper English garden in this arid Texas land, had proved a mighty one. He'd faced many failures before the land yielded its secrets. He breathed in the sweet fragrance of English roses, pleased that the garden rivaled any to be found in his native country.

He slowed, examining a recently replaced rosebush. Satisfied, he move closer to the manor's back door. As he drew closer, the blast of smoke alarms pierced the silent morning.

Sprinting toward the manor's back entrance, he stumbled on the stone path but managed to keep his balance. He stopped, snatched a deep breath and hurried on.

Black smoke engulfed him as he jerked the kitchen door open and rushed inside. "Mrs. Castleton! Mrs. Castleton!"

Only the deafening blast of the alarms answered.

Smoke billowed from the huge gas range on the right, just inside the doorway. Pulling his jacket over his nose, he pushed farther into the room, switched off the stove's burners, then flipped on the exhaust fan. The acrid smell of scorched food burned his nose and stung his eyes. Through a blur of tears and smoke, he grabbed oven mitts from a rack and carried the charred pans outside.

His mind raced. Something was wrong. Dreadfully wrong. Where was Mrs. Castleton? She would never leave dinner unattended. And where was the rest of the family?

The questions would have to wait. For now, he must switch off the blasted alarms and attend to the smoke.

With the burned food outside, he breathed easier. He re-entered the kitchen and moved around the large island to open the bank of windows on the other side of the room. He rounded the corner and stopped, his feet glued to the floor.

Three bodies lay on the floor behind the counter.

Sean whispered, "Dear Heavenly Father," the sight too horrible to comprehend. He staggered and fell to his knees.

Twin Falls Police Station

Police Chief Matt Foley shrugged into his jacket, walked to the door when his phone rang. He gave his watch a quick glance and picked up the receiver. Still a few extra minutes before his meeting.

Charles Kennedy, the desk sergeant's voice sounded in his ear. "Glad I caught you, Chief."

"What's up, Charlie?"

"Ethan Grayson's gardener called 911 earlier..." Kennedy hesitated, his voice subdued, tense. "Said bodies were scattered everywhere in the big house."

The full implication hit Matt like a sledgehammer. Ethan Grayson was a friend. "Dead? Is he sure? All of them?"

"The cook and her daughter, too. Six bodies. That's what the gardener reported."

"I'm on my way. Detectives Turner and Allen are on call. Have they been notified?"

"They left a little ahead of McCulloch and the crime-scene crew. Mac told me to let you know."

Mass murder didn't happen in Matt's town. It didn't happen to his friends. He closed his eyes as white-hot anguish flowed through his body and lay like lead in his chest. Inhaling a long breath, he let the oxygen calm the turmoil until the pain became manageable. He'd deal with the grief later. "Call the DA and cancel my appointment."

Matt wanted Miles Davis on this case. He was the senior detective in the division and a professional. Lucy Turner had a year in the department. A good detective, but she was also as prickly as a porcupine. The giant chip on her shoulder made her nearly impossible to work with. Her partner, Cole Allen, seemed to be the only one who could handle her. He laughed off her bad temper.

Matt hurried out the private entrance to his office. His black Explorer sat by the curb. He jumped inside, shoved the gearshift into reverse, and spun out of the parking lot.

Reaching for his cell phone, Matt found Miles' mobile number and waited for the connection.

"Morning, Chief," Miles said. Traffic noise in the background meant Miles was on the road.

"You hear about the Graysons?"

"Yeah, Charlie filled me in. Lucy and Cole are up for this one. Right?"

"Yes, but I'm going to make a switch. You'll be lead. Lucy will be your partner."

A groan came through the line. "You know I want this case, Chief. But partnering with Turner is above and beyond the call."

"This isn't a suggestion, Miles, it's an order. I need both of you. You'll be good for Lucy. She could use some of your finesse. But I won't have any squabbling. This case is too important."

"Understood. But she's not gonna be happy."

"That's her problem. Meet me at the crime-scene. I'll fill Lucy in when I get there."

Traffic was light on the familiar streets. Most commuters headed to Dallas and points south had left hours earlier.

A heavy sky hung over the city and a light morning drizzle wet the pavement. Mirrored buildings along Highway 75 reflected the gray weather in their dark windows. June was well into the hurricane season. Things would get worse as the day progressed. Condensation formed on the windshield and he switched on the air conditioning to clear the glass.

When he reached FM320, the road leading to the Grayson estate, an ambulance flew past, headed in the opposite direction, sirens wailing. Maybe someone had survived the carnage.

Grayson Manor

The ornate black gate stood open, and Matt swung onto the private road. The open gate wasn't the norm. Ethan Grayson valued his privacy. An elaborate security system provided a shield from the outside world. Some called Ethan eccentric, but it was the man's prerogative.

Matt pulled in behind the coroner's white ambulance. His own Crime Scene Unit's blue van and two black-and-whites filled the circular driveway. County Sheriff Joe Wilson, a childhood friend and colleague, slid to the curb behind him.

Matt slammed his car door and waited for the sheriff to catch up.

"Lisa gave me the news." Joe extended a large hand for a firm hand shake, in keeping with the rest of his six-three frame, in a firm grip. "Came to see if I could help."

In the distance, a local news crew tried to sneak through the front gate. Matt tapped a young officer on the shoulder. "Turn that van around and post a man at the entrance."

With an affirmative nod, the officer stepped into the driveway and headed to intercept the van.

Matt stomped water from his shoes and joined the sheriff at the entrance. They walked into the mansion together and signed the crime-scene log on the foyer table. After donning booties and gloves the officer provided, they ducked under the yellow tape and stepped inside the manor.

Across the entryway, Lucy Turner chatted with one of the crime-scene techs. Turner was short and a little overweight, but attractive despite her customary scowl. A cascade of auburn hair was pulled back into a ponytail that hung past the collar of her navy pant suit.

Matt strode across the tile to where she stood. "I passed an ambulance down the road. Please tell me one of them survived."

She nodded. "Victoria Grayson still had a pulse when the first officer arrived. Five confirmed dead."

"Where was she found?"

Turner pointed to the wide staircase leading to the second floor. "The shooter grazed her head as she came downstairs. She lost a lot of blood."

A chalk outline and a large red stain on the stairwell marked the spot. "What do we know so far?"

"The security system wasn't breached. Whoever the killer was, someone admitted them or they had the gate entry code. I pulled the security camera data. We should have a picture of the killer or killers entered through the front gate."

"Could they have gone over the wall?"

"Cole checked it out," Turner said. "The rain washed away any footprints there might have been. The fence is electrified and has razor wire. So it would be difficult to breach, but not impossible."

Matt glanced over at the security system by the entrance. "They must have shut down the system before the murders."

"It was off when we arrived. The smoke alarms would have summoned the police and fire department if the system had been on."

Miles Davis walked through the entrance. He was easy to spot with his rugged dark face framed by short-cropped black hair and expertly trimmed beard.

Lucy's steel gaze zeroed in on Davis. "What's he doing here?"

"I told him to come."

Angry red spots flushed her cheeks. "Why? This is my case, Chief."

"I made an executive decision, Lucy. Davis is coming onboard. You'll work with him. He'll be lead on this one."

She froze at his words, mouth twisted with suppressed rage. "Why, because I'm a woman?"

"No, because he's a grade three, and you're grade two."

The tension in her body and the stoic expression that formed on her face revealed her feelings more than any words could.

From behind Lucy, Joe rolled his eyes and stepped away to join the crime-scene unit.

"Good morning, Chief, Lucy," Davis said. "You'll never guess who followed me in." Davis jerked his head toward the entrance. "Our esteemed mayor."

How had Hall heard about the murders so quickly? Unless he kept a police scanner in his office, someone must have tipped him off. The thought left a bitter taste in Matt's mouth.

"Must have smelled blood in the water." Matt had dealt with Terrence Hall when the man served on the city council. The experience had not been pleasant.

Hall, with a fresh-faced clone in tow, tried to march past the cop at the door. Matt crossed the room. The officer would need assistance to keep Hall at bay.

Hall's cold stare settled on Matt. "What happened here?"

"We've just started to collect evidence. You'll need to

sign the crime-scene log." Matt glanced down at his feet, then up at Hall. "You can't cross the yellow tape without footwear."

In his Armani suit, Hall rivaled Davis for best dressed, but where Davis exuded masculinity, Hall came off effete. If Matt knew the mayor, he wouldn't mar his carefully crafted image with the blue booties.

Hall waved the cop with the log away. "So you know nothing?"

Matt debated whether to push the point that he had just arrived. It wasn't worth the effort. "We know five people are dead, one survivor, at least so far. We'll know more after the crime-scene is processed."

"Who survived?"

"Ethan's daughter, Victoria."

"Get on top of this, Foley. Ethan Grayson is an international player. You don't want to end up looking like a local yokel on prime-time television."

The mayor was right in one respect. Keeping this tragedy quiet would be impossible. Ethan was one of the big three in the microchip industry. When news of his death surfaced, the press would flock into town like a swarm of killer bees.

Hall was yanking his chain, but it wouldn't work. Not today. "Ethan Grayson was a friend. You don't have to worry about me giving the case my full attention."

"I'm calling a press conference this afternoon." Hall straightened, a stance Matt recognized as Hall's officious posture. "We will need to update the media, daily. I want you and the DA present."

He should have been prepared for this from Hall. The mayor always went for the limelight. "The family members haven't been notified. The oldest son lives outside the U.S.,

8

so it may take a while."

Hall stepped so close the smell of his breath mint and cologne was intense.

Matt held his breath and moved back. Hall wasn't welcome in his airspace.

"Let me know the minute they're notified." Hall whirled and started for the exit, then turned. "I want a daily written report on the case status. This will put Twin Falls on the map. I don't intend to have my office, and this city, portrayed as a bunch of amateurs."

Shaking his head, Matt watched the mayor leave the premises, then he joined the two detectives.

Davis adjusted his coat sleeves over the cuffs of his shirt. "Politicians should be like groundhogs. Come out for a few minutes once a year, and then go back into their holes."

Matt led Davis and Turner down the hallway. Every light in the foyer burned, and the crime-scene techs were busy stringing cords to set up extra lighting for video. Nearby, a tech gathered three shell casings from outside the door and numbered the spots where they had fallen.

Matt leaned over, and the tech handed him one of the shells. He examined the markings then gave it back. "Any more of these around?"

The tech nodded. "Three more in the kitchen."

Matt glanced at Lucy. "Rifle casings. Any of the guns missing from Ethan's collection?"

"The gun cases were locked and nothing appears to be missing. But we'll check them out anyway."

The marble floor from the hallway continued inside the room, where a green and gold Persian rug covered most of the area. Two impressionist paintings hung on one wall across from the hearth, part of a priceless collection of original Monets. The fact they were still here ruled out robbery as a motive.

Matt swallowed hard as his gaze moved closer. He'd learned to become detached at crime-scenes—a form of survival. If you didn't disengage, you took it home with you. But when it was personal, the mechanism didn't work.

Ethan Grayson's body rested in a large leather chair, next to the fireplace. His head slumped forward on his chest, almost as if he had dozed off, except for a large, dark circle over his heart. Even in death, he had an enviable elegance. Not a tall man, yet his compact frame had held a sense of power. His dark eyes, always alight with humor and intelligence, were now dull and vacant.

In a matching seat across from her husband, pretty Ann Grayson's head rested against the chair back as though she'd turned to face the killer before the fatal shot left a gaping hole in her chest. Her face, ashen now, had delicate features and a wide, sensitive mouth. A passionate face in life, filled with wisdom and strength.

Matt blew out a deep breath. His jaw muscles tightened, unable to stop the question he had taught himself never to ask. *Why, Lord?*

He stood back and let his gaze roam around the room, filing every detail again. He wanted to remember, sear the scene into his mind. *I promise you, Ethan. Somebody will pay for this.*

Joe walked up and placed a hand on Matt's shoulder. "You okay?"

Matt rubbed the back of his neck and nodded. "Looks like the shooter stood in the doorway. Shot Ethan, then Ann, then caught Victoria as she came downstairs. Odd. Why a rifle and not a handgun?"

Joe shook his head. "Maybe the rifle was the only thing available."

"That's possible. But this looks too deliberate to be random. My gut tells me this was well-planned in advance."

Matt moved on into the back of the house toward the kitchen. The pungent smell of smoke still hung in the air.

The acrid odor of burned food grew stronger as he reached the kitchen. A lab tech had marked and numbered the three shell casings outside the entrance for the photographer. The bodies were gone, but chalk outlines indicated where the victims fell.

The same scenario as the library. Shots came from just inside the room. Arrogant and accurate. Only one shot per victim. "Looks as though these three were shot first."

"What makes you say that?" Joe asked.

Matt stepped into the room. "If Peter Grayson had heard the gunshots, he would have gone to check them out."

"And Ethan wouldn't have checked because . . . ?"

Leaning over the island, Matt examined the chalk drawings on the floor. They almost overlapped. "Peter was a hunter, like his father. He was always shooting at targets. Ethan wouldn't have paid any attention to the noise, figuring it was Peter."

Joe readjusted his hat. "Wouldn't there have been screams after the first shot?"

"Most likely, but the sound of shots would carry farther than screams. The kitchen is a good distance from the front of the house, and the walls are thick. Ethan and Ann were used to horseplay between the young people."

Behind him, Lucy scratched notes in her notebook.

Detective Davis caught his attention. "The gardener's in the den. We're ready to talk to him if you want to sit in."

"Yeah," Matt said. "Did Sean identify the bodies?"

Lucy nodded.

Halfway down the corridor, Davis halted abruptly and turned to Matt. "We'll want to notify the next of kin before Hall gives it to them in the news. You have any idea where to start?"

"I'll take care of it. I met Martin Norris, Ethan's assistant, last year. I'll give him a call. He'll know how to contact what's left of the family."

Sean McKinnon sat almost catatonic in an antique French crapaud armchair, his face pale—eyes red from a heroic effort to hold back tears.

Turner's partner, Cole Allen, stepped into the room, carrying a large white Persian cat. "Look what I found."

"That's Longfellow, Mrs. Grayson's cat," Sean said, holding out his arms. "I wondered where he'd gotten off to."

Davis pulled Lucy aside. "You take the questioning."

Her eyes widened in surprise. She gave a curt nod, pulled up a chair next to Sean, and placed her recorder on the end table. "Tell us what happened."

McKinnon recounted his movements that morning. He stopped twice and took deep shuddering breaths. When he finished, he leaned back and closed his eyes.

"When did you last see the family alive, Sean?" Lucy asked, her voice gentle.

She was good with the old gardener, Matt thought. Sean had relaxed a little, breathing more normally. Too bad she didn't use that empathy with her co-workers.

The gardener opened his eyes and turned an unfocused gaze on the detective. "When they arrived early Saturday afternoon. I brought in their luggage then went about my duties. All except for Miss Emily. She dinna come home with the family. She must have arrived after I left.

12

"Why didn't she fly back with her mother?" Lucy asked.

"Amada said she stayed in London for a friend's engagement party. The only one I saw last night before I left, was Amanda." His voice broke. "I stopped by just before six to tell her I would be eating dinner in town."

"Why? I mean, since the family had just arrived home?" Lucy asked.

"Sunday is my day off. My son, Jack, called and asked me to meet him at the Red Dog Bar and Grill to catch a bite and watch the game."

"What time was this?"

Sean rubbed a rough hand over his chin. "I arrived about five-thirty."

"Did you notice anything unusual when you left the estate, any cars outside the gate?"

McKinnon shook his head.

Matt moved into the gardener's line of vision. "Was the family expecting guests last night?"

"Not that I know of. It wouldna be like them to have guests when they'd just returned, not having a full staff. The butler Perkins, Amanda and Miss Emily always traveled with the family. Perkins stayed behind to close up the London house."

He gulped and a lone tear trickled down his cheek. "I'm to pick up Perkins at the airport Wednesday. I canna tell him they're gone."

"Do you know of anyone who might want the family dead, who might be responsible for this...?"

The gardener shook his head slowly.

Matt eased from the room. In the entryway, two black bags rolled past him on gurneys. Certainly not the first body bags he'd ever seen, but somehow they seemed unbefitting, too dehumanizing for Ethan and Ann.

County Coroner, Lisa Martinez and Joe Wilson trailed behind the bodies.

"Any idea what time the murders took place?" Matt asked Lisa.

"From the body temperatures and the progression of rigor mortis, they've been dead about ten to fourteen hours. You do the math."

He stopped at the yellow tape. "You guys wrapping it up?"

"These are the last two victims," Lisa said. "The others have already gone to the morgue. Not sure how much longer McCulloch will be here. Probably until Davis is satisfied everything has been tagged and bagged." She touched Joe's arm. "I'll see you outside."

"Call me if you need anything." Joe patted Matt's shoulder and followed Lisa through the entrance.

The crime-scene began to break up, leaving only Matt, Sean, and the two detectives inside.

The bodies were gone, but the aura of death lingered.

Only Victoria had survived...if she pulled through. And survive she must. She could identify the killer.

CHAPTER 3

Grayson Manor

Davis stood under the portico out of the rain and watched as Lucy gave vent to her anger. She stopped Cole in the vestibule. Gesturing with irate body language, catching his arm, she spoke in a low guttural voice Davis couldn't understand.

"Turner, you want to ride with me?" He'd rather have a tonsillectomy with a dinner fork, but he had to start somewhere. Lucy Turner was a good investigator. He just hated the thought of tiptoeing around her *feelings* while trying to solve a major murder case. Besides, he'd flunked sensitivity training.

He hissed out a deep breath through his teeth. With any luck, the brutal crime-scene back there would convince the woman to do her job without the drama.

Ignoring the rain, she stomped out to Davis' unmarked Ford. He considered letting her stand in the rain to cool off, but he pushed the lock release button on his key fob instead. She jerked the car door open, slid into the seat, slammed it closed, and crossed her arms.

Davis took his seat behind the wheel and turned to face her. "We need to get something straight from the get-go, Turner. I won't put up with you actin' like a four-year-old. I'll have Matt remove you from this case so fast you'll think you broke the sound barrier. I let my daughter get away with tantrums, but you ain't no child. Five people are dead. It's our job to catch the killer. I won't accept anything but a professional attitude and your best work. You got that?"

A red flush started at her neck and spread to her face.

She gazed out the window for a long moment, then unfolded her arms. "Yeah, I got it."

She didn't sound happy, but he'd spoken his mind and he meant every word of it.

Silence hung heavy before she spoke again. With a glance at his ring finger, she said, "If you have kids, you must be married."

Davis shook his head. "One kid, divorced. You have kids?"

"Yeah. Two boys. Where are we going?"

"We're going to the station to look at that gate surveillance tape, see what we find, and send a couple of black-and-whites out to ask if neighbors saw or heard anything yesterday. Then we wait for Lisa to call and tell us when she starts the autopsies. She's pushing this to the head of the line. When the call comes, we go to the morgue."

~*~

Lucy watched Davis as he drove. Dressed in his nine-hundred-dollar suit, he bore a remarkable resemblance to Denzel Washington. Where did Davis get the money to dress in designer suits? His salary couldn't cover his wardrobe expenses. A glance down at her own off-the-rack pantsuit added to her insecurities, which were legion.

Davis was arrogant, but she respected the man for laying down the ground rules. She knew where the lines were. Most of all, she hated that he was right. This wasn't the time to vent. But she was hopeless at hiding her emotions. Thoughts rolled off her tongue before her brain engaged. Anyway, her quarrel wasn't with Davis. Matt Foley had made the decision to remove her as lead.

THEN THERE WERE NONE

The Grayson case was the biggest of her career. Solving it should get a big atta-girl in her personnel file and a pay-grade promotion on the next performance review.

With two kids, a mortgage, car loan, and insurance, money issues were never far from her thoughts. No child support from her low-life ex-husband, but it was better that way. At least Hank didn't know where to find her and the kids. That was a blessing.

A family had been viciously murdered, for no apparent reason. Her head had to be completely in the game. The motive wasn't burglary. None of Grayson's priceless art objects appeared to be missing. This one had been personal.

~*~

Matt made sure the officers secured Grayson Manor, and then he saw Sean McKinnon back to his cottage. "Sean, can you ask Jack to come stay with you? Or can you go stay with him?"

"Jack left this morning on a hunting trip to Wyoming with his friends. That's why he called last night. Wanted to see me before he left."

Beneath Sean's words was an unmistakable concern about his son. Did he think Jack was somehow involved? It wasn't inconceivable. There'd been bad blood between Ethan and Jack. Matt couldn't ignore the fact Sean's son was a viable suspect. "Where in Wyoming, Sean?"

Sean lifted a weary gaze as Matt spoke, and when he answered, his tone signaled he understood the reason for Matt's question. "Jackson Hole."

Back in his car, Matt pulled out his cell phone, punched in the number for Grayson Limited, and asked to speak to

Martin Norris. A few seconds passed before Norris picked up the phone.

"Norris, this is Chief Matt Foley in Twin Falls..." He paused for a moment to collect his thoughts. There was no easy way to say it. "I have bad news for you." As succinctly as possible, he told Norris what happened.

In an English accent, husky with emotion, Norris asked. "The whole family, except Victoria? She'll get the best of care, won't she?"

"If it's something the locals can't handle, they'll airlift her to Dallas."

"Thank you for calling, Chief. I wondered about Ethan. He's never late without ringing ahead. I tried to call him a few times this morning and didn't get an answer. I'll notify the family. And, of course, I need to advise the Grayson Board of Directors, unless you feel I shouldn't."

"You can tell them, but ask that they keep it quiet. The sooner you contact the family, the better. I don't know how long we can keep this from the press."

"Of course, I'll get right on it," Norris said. "Alexander, their oldest son, is in Australia. Lady Ann's brother, Sir Ian is a missionary in Mexico. Lady Ann's father has been in poor health. I'll let her brother decide when to tell him. Ethan had no family. He was an only child, and his parents died years ago."

Matt looked out the car window at the immaculate garden, vivid in the late-morning mist. "Someone will need to let the morgue know which mortuary you want to use."

Norris exhaled an audible breath. "If I can't contact Sir Ian soon, I'll make the decision."

Matt disconnected but didn't put the phone away. He had another call to make—a difficult one. He activated the phone and punched in a familiar number.

18

THEN THERE WERE NONE

~*~

During her lunch break, Sara Bradford left the Global Optics building, seeking a quiet place away from the hectic morning. She'd spent hours soothing the frayed nerves of regional vice-presidents worried about a new competitor that had sprung up near the company's most profitable retail stores. All part of her responsibilities after her promotion to president six months ago.

She pulled in front of the English bakery on the town square. They had a deli in back that served chicken potpie to die for. Most of the lunch crowd had come and gone. She placed her order at the counter and found a table in the corner. After only a few bites of her meal, her iPhone chirped. Matt Foley's name flashed on the screen.

Sara smiled. Her relationship with the Twin Falls Police Chief had not always been good. For four years, he'd considered her the prime suspect in her husband's murder. Over the last year, something special had developed between them. She'd learned to trust him implicitly. He'd literally saved her life, twice from attempts made by a determined killer.

"Sara..." Matt paused, his voice minus its usual vibrancy. "Brace yourself. Emily Castleton and her mother have been murdered...most of the Grayson family as well. Victoria is alive. She's at Twin Falls Memorial. I wanted to let you know since you knew both girls. I'll get to the hospital as soon as I can."

For a moment, Sara's chest squeezed so tight she struggled to breathe. Emily's lovely face flashed through Sara's mind. A natural with kids, Emily's laughing, gentle presence drew children like the pied piper. "Matt, what happened...who?"

"I don't have any answers right now."

Lunch forgotten, Sara placed her hand on her brow and blinked back tears, unable to absorb the tragedy all at once. Jumbled questions crowded her mind. Who would want to kill the Grayson family? Certainly, there could be no logical reason for such insanity. It made no sense.

She grabbed her purse. "I'm leaving now."

Twin Falls Memorial Hospital

Heavy-laden clouds followed Sara's drive over the short distance from the deli to the newly renovated hospital. The facility was state of the art. The administration boasted of its electronic record keeping. A spacious hallway in a blue and mauve theme led to the emergency waiting room.

Sara recognized the pretty blonde near the magazine rack as Caroline Norris, wife of Ethan Grayson's assistant. She and Caroline had become acquainted at a number of local charity functions.

Caroline motioned her over. "Hello, Sara. I guess you heard. Martin asked me to be here for Victoria when she awakes."

She nodded. "I heard Victoria survived. Any news?"

Caroline looked down at her hands and inclined her head towards the OR entrance. "She's still in surgery."

Outside the huge windows, the sky darkened and it began to rain. Gusts of wind increased in velocity, creating the illusion of rain falling sideways. Sudden bursts of lightning filled the room with brief flashes of brilliance, and claps of thunder vibrated the windows.

A hurricane in the Gulf had sent the promised violent weather. The storm's intensity mirrored the struggle in

Sara's soul, a war between white-hot rage and sorrow. Her eyes burned, but she couldn't cry. Tears wouldn't change a world where humanity held life in such low esteem.

She shivered as visions of Victoria Grayson and Emily seared her thoughts, so much alike they could have been sisters. Both just turned twenty, tall and slim, with the perfect complexion English women seemed blessed with. Victoria's hair was dark brown, her eyes hazel, while Emily's hair had light brown hues, and her eyes the most extraordinary shade of violet-blue.

Victoria, the quiet one. Studious and soft-spoken, Emily a born crusader. Tenacious and fought tirelessly to change the living conditions of the children in the church bus ministry. Her death seemed a mockery of all that was good.

~*~

Matt stopped off at the city manager's office to bring his boss, Doug Anderson, up to date. As he left, Davis called, "Lisa just told me she'll start the cuts on the Graysons in twenty minutes if you want to sit in."

It wasn't something he wanted to do, but he felt compelled to go, out of respect for Ethan.

The parking lot behind the morgue was unusually crowded. Maybe Lisa had called in extra help. Somewhere nearby, an engine roared to life and someone racked a hotrod's glass pipes.

Matt pulled into the only available space, and joined Davis and Turner at the entrance. They exchanged nods, entered the building, and walked silently down a long green corridor to two metal doors. The smell of industrial-strength chemicals intensified with each step. Inside a scrub room, they donned paper gowns, masks, and booties before entering the autopsy room.

In the center of the room, four stainless steel tables held four bodies covered with white sheets. Lisa waited for them, dressed in scrubs covered by a surgical gown, a Tyvek apron, Tyvek sleeves, hair cover, and a facemask with attached shield. Footwear included thick white socks and Crocs. She looked like a Martian with comfortable shoes.

Matt braced himself for the onslaught of emotions and disengaged as Lisa first worked on Ethan and Ann. He should probably have passed, but he wanted the results quickly, and wanted to be able to ask questions if needed.

Lisa moved to the third table and folded back the sheet. Hair bristled down Matt's arms as his gaze focused on the face of the young woman on the table. He spoke past the knot in his throat. "Lisa, there's been a mistake. That's Victoria Grayson, not Emily Castleton."

Davis, Turner, and Lisa stared at him.

"Are you sure?" Lisa asked.

"Positive.

BOOKS BY V. B. TENERY

Dead Ringer   published May, 2014

Mercy Lawrence is terrified.

Bermuda airport facial recognition software has identified her as missing runway star, Traci Wallace. Despite Mercy's protests, Traci's husband, ex-CIA agent Thomas Wallace, is convinced Mercy is the mother of his ill six-year-old son. With only his son's welfare in mind, he abducts Mercy and takes her to a private island to care for the boy.

But Mercy soon discovers there are men much more dangerous than a father desperate to save his son. Her doppelganger has made deadly enemies—a relentless team of killers who now want her dead.

When Thomas is lured into a covert mission to rescue a CIA asset and uncover a government mole, Mercy is left isolated and alone—and Thomas finds himself stranded on foreign soil with a compromised mission and a wounded agent. Fighting against a rogue nation's timetable for launching a nuclear strike, he has to escape Saudi Arabia alive and rescue Mercy and his son before assassins finish the job they started.

The Watchman   published Oct, 2014

Gifted with supernatural abilities, he'll protect the innocent and avenge the abused, he is...The Watchman

When Detective Noah Adams meets the abused son of a powerful judge, he knows he must intervene, and fast. The violence is escalating, and even Noah's special gifts may not prevent the unthinkable from happening.

Relentlessly pursuing two cases, Noah receives a chilling

message: Cody's deranged father has taken his son and it's up to Noah to follow the judge's twisted trail to find the boy before it's too late.

Corrupt city officials, a missing socialite, an attempted murder, and a rescue in the middle of a blizzard entangle Noah in the most complicated case of his career. A case that will mean his ultimate redemption or will take him back into the dark history that haunts him.

the Matt Foley/Sara Bradford series:
Works of Darkness   published March, 2014

Some secrets just won't stay buried.

A construction site provides a horrific surprise when a worker uncovers the skeleton of a small child wrapped in a sleeping bag. Police Chief Matt Foley soon links the murder to another cold case, the hit-and-run death of Attorney Josh Bradford.

The long suppressed memory of the young victim's childhood friend, Sara Bradford may hold the key to both crimes. But Matt has mixed emotions about Sara—his prime suspect in her husband's murder.

Matt soon discovers the twenty-five year old mystery has the power to stretch across decades to kill again.

Then There Were None   published September, 2014

Mass murder doesn't happen in Matt Foley's town...it doesn't happen to his friends. Someone is going to pay.

Disturbing crime scenes are nothing new to the Twin Falls Police Chief. But this one is different. The victims are friends. In their Tudor mansion just inside the city limits, a family is dead—husband, wife, two kids, and the family cook.

The killer made one mistake. He left a survivor.

The husband is one of the big three in the microchip industry. The family lived a quiet modest life. It doesn't make sense.

Until...

Boxed set of #1 and #2 ***Double the Suspense***

Published May, 2015

DownFall published May, 2015

Chief of Police Matt Foley has a new bride and the most complex case of his career.

A prominent couple prepares to retire, when an assassin's bullets retires them permanently. And he doesn't stop there.

As the investigation pushes forward, layers of deceit, greed, and bitterness are peeled away, and two families, connected by marriage and murder, face the exposure of their darkest secrets. It's just another difficult case until Matt finds his wife caught in the killer's cross-hairs.

V. B. Tenery's desire to write grew from a love of reading that blossomed at a very young age. Quickly bored with cartoons, she devoured books, impatient for the next visit to the library.

After finishing school she went to work as an administrative assistant in the country's largest optical firm. Writing took a back seat to her career when she became director of service for the firm's national warehouse.

Marriage, a young daughter, and active involvement in church turned her into an occasional weekend writer. During this period she wrote poetry, a series of short stories based on family history, and a number of Christian songs that were performed in her church.

When the company she worked for downsized, she jumped at the opportunity to retire and write full time.

Since then she has written three Christian novels in a suspense series, *WORKS OF DARKNESS, THEN THERE WERE NONE,* and *DOWNFALL.*

She wrote a stand-alone romantic suspense, *DEAD RINGER.*

And she has combined suspense elements with a supernatural theme in *THE WATCHMAN,* her first book in another series.

Website: www.vbtenery.com
Blog: www.agatharemembered.blogspot.com
Twitter: http://twitter.com/teneryherrin
FB Author Page: www.facebook.com/vbtenery

Made in the USA
Columbia, SC
05 November 2017